Forgotten Soldiers

The Tyrus Chronicle - Book 1

By Joshua P. Simon

D1716316

Visit the author at www.joshuapsimon.blogspot.com.

Contact joshuapsimon.author@gmail.com with any comments.

Sign up for Joshua's newsletter at http://joshuapsimon.blogspot.com/.

Cover illustration by Mario Teodosio. (http://marioteodosio.carbonmade.com/)

Cover design by Leah Simon.

Editing by Joshua Essoe (www.joshuaessoe.com)

WORKS IN THE TYRUS CHRONICLE

Forgotten Soldiers
Wayward Soldiers *forthcoming*
Resurrected Soldiers *forthcoming*
Forever Soldiers *forthcoming*

THE EPIC OF ANDRASTA AND RONDEL

The Cult of Sutek, Vol. 1
The City of Pillars, Vol. 2
The Tower of Bashan, Vol. 3

THE BLOOD AND TEARS WORLD (COMPLETED SERIES)

Warleader: A Blood and Tears Prequel Short Story
Rise and Fall: Book One of the Blood and Tears Trilogy
Walk Through Fire: A Blood and Tears Prequel Novella
Steel and Sorrow: Book Two of the Blood and Tears Trilogy
Hero of Slaves: A Blood and Tears Novella
Trial and Glory: Book Three of the Blood and Tears Trilogy

MAPS

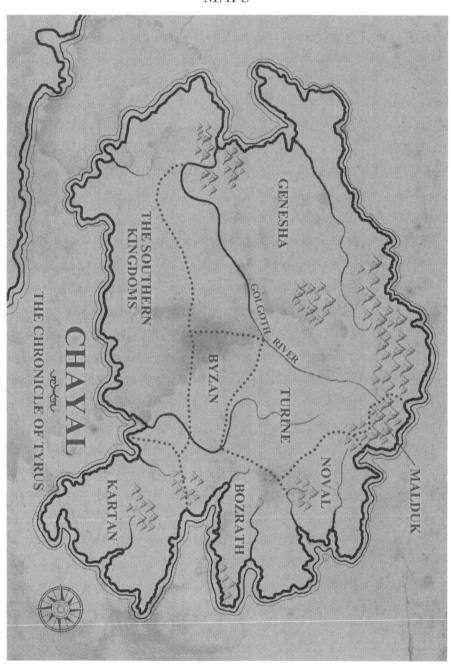

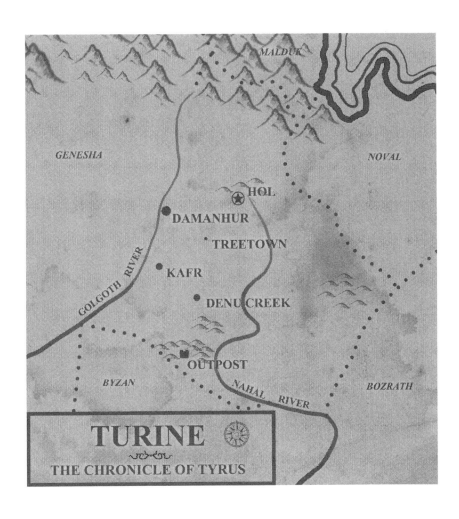

MALDUK

GENESHA

NOVAL

HOL

DAMANHUR

TREETOWN

KAFR

DENU CREEK

GOLGOTH RIVER

OUTPOST

BYZAN

NAHAL RIVER

BOZRATH

TURINE

THE CHRONICLE OF TYRUS

CHAPTER 1

Not even hell could be this bad.

I heard that phrase repeated above all others in the decade I spent in the army. During the early years, those few words sent a cold shiver down a man's back. It often did mine for what they implied.

I heard a private say it while dragging his dead buddy over to a funeral pyre after a battle. I heard it pass through a captain's lips as he watched survivors from a burned out town beg for bread or offer their emaciated bodies up to passing soldiers in exchange for the smallest morsel of food. I heard that same captain say it again, correcting himself, when one of those survivors got their food and refused to divide it with the sickly children pleading for their share.

The captain's whisper still echoed in my mind. "Gods Tyrus, I was wrong. Not even hell could be this bad."

I heard soldiers and mages of all ranks in the infirmary say the phrase, usually between sobs while they stared at a missing limb. I heard physicians and healers mumble the words over and over after their shifts, drowning themselves in a bottle of whiskey, hoping they might forget the horrors of their profession for at least a little while.

Not even hell could be this bad.

In time, the saying slowly changed, taking on a new flavor and becoming something lighter, too light in my opinion.

Dealt a bad hand of cards? Not even hell could be this bad.

Got a bad bowl of stew? Not even hell could be this bad.

1

That same stew gave you the drizzles? Not even hell could be this bad. In-grown toenail? Not even hell could be this bad.

I'm ashamed to admit that even I uttered those words a few times myself over the years in the context they were never intended. It was hard not to when you heard them used so often without real conviction.

Those few words nearly rolled off my tongue once more as I watched unit leaders clamor inside General Balak's command tent. I clamped my lips down before the expression tumbled from my mouth, bitter I had subconsciously treated the phrase with the same irreverent attitude I loathed so much in others.

The back of the tent allowed me a good view of unit leaders acting like unseasoned fools. They fought to gain the position closest to the general in hopes he'd notice them. I shook my head, letting them waste their time. If they hadn't yet figured out that Balak hated men who kissed up to him, they never would.

Only one thing got Balak's attention and that was success. Excel or fail in your mission, he'd remember you. Therefore, the best course of action was to succeed, but with as little fanfare as possible.

Looking back on the early years of my forced enlistment, I wish I had taken that middle of the road approach. Gaining command of my own unit early on had done strange things to me. Traits I had never shown before the army became defining characteristics. The chip I wore on my shoulder grew with each success until I had to draft others to help me bear its weight.

Everyone under my command had taken their share of the load with pleasure. Being part of my unit became a point of pride because we didn't just excel, we outclassed everyone to the point of causing resentment among other units. Admittedly, rubbing our success in their faces didn't do much to ingratiate us to them.

If I could go back in time, I'd probably punch that version of myself in the jaw, but not before telling him to get his head out of his arrogant rear.

Over the years as I matured and others died, forgot, or just plain didn't care anymore, I managed to smooth things out with many of those who once resented us. As a result, my unit didn't stand out as glaringly.

Balak, though, never forgot about us or what we could do.

He expected more out of us.

The general noticed me in the shadows, bushy eyebrows meeting as he glared around the tent. He scowled, making the lines on his face deepen. "Tyrus, close that tent flap and get up here."

"Yes, sir."

My attempt to avoid his notice failed again.

I found a place around the table filled with maps and reports. Two lamps secured to posts above our heads, provided decent enough light. The smell of burning oil made my eyes water.

Many considered the eleven other unit leaders at the table the elite of the army. We answered to no one but Balak, and I guess the king. However, the king never left Hol, the capital of our great country Turine, so that technicality never came into play.

Most unit leaders thought we were special because we circumvented the normal chain of command. Not me. That just meant if Balak was in a bad mood, we received his wrath directly rather than having it filtered down to us.

The tent grew quiet.

The Geneshans had invaded Turine nearly a decade ago in the hopes of expanding its ever growing empire. We weren't as easy to conquer as they thought. All of their other military efforts had ceased in order to focus on defeating us. Battles had been fought on both Turine and Geneshan soil, each side having the upper hand at some point or another.

Momentum had swung to our side once again, and the last thing we wanted was to lose it.

Balak handed out slips of parchment, detailing our orders. Each unit received a series of targets to take down behind enemy lines. Most focused on Geneshan supply caches or communication outposts. Standard military tactics to hinder our enemy.

Some unit leaders asked questions, a few pertinent, the rest an obvious attempt to suck up to the old general. I kept quiet. The orders seemed straightforward enough.

Balak answered questions calmly, carefully enunciating each and every word. After questions, he knocked on the table, punctuating the end.

A small grunt escaped my throat. I knew that behavior well enough to see he was holding something back. I didn't bother raising the concern. It wouldn't prompt him to share anything new.

Balak cleared his throat, and tapped the table once more. "Dismissed."

I mixed in with the others filing out. We'd all be leaving in little over an hour, and I was anxious to get my unit ready.

"Sergeant Tyrus. Stay behind. I'd like a word with you."

I had almost escaped.

I stepped aside. Several of the younger unit leaders looked jealous as they filed past. I had tried to set them straight before, but they still clamored for a private audience with the general. They thought of their role as a stepping-stone into a higher-paying officer's position. I remembered thinking the same in the beginning. It didn't take me long to realize the foolishness in that. Eight years after my appointment without a single promotion or pay increase only validated my current cynicism.

Balak walked around the table, posture perfect, hands behind his back.

"Sergeant, you seemed disinterested."

"No, sir. Not at all," I lied.

"Then why didn't you ask any questions?"

"The orders aren't anything we haven't done before."

I thought it unfitting to add I also wanted to get the heck out of there.

Balak and I had a love-hate relationship. We both knew it, but neither of us admitted it openly. The general loved that my unit never failed a mission. However, I think he also hated having to rely on us so much.

I hated getting stuck with the most dangerous jobs simply because we were good at what we did.

Every day in the army was one away from my family. Each new mission reduced the likelihood I would ever make it back to them. Needless to say, I never got excited about risking my life.

The only thing I loved about General Balak was that he was easy to read and fairly predictable. After learning how to read him, our conversations were not nearly as painful as they had been.

Balak grunted. "This mission isn't as routine as you might think. The Geneshans managed to form another alliance with the Malduks."

I shrugged. "We've beaten the Malduks before."

The Malduks are a nasty people full of determined fighters from the far north. The ever-expanding Geneshan Empire had tried using them in the early years of the war. Because the Malduks consisted of individual tribes rather than a unified nation, the Geneshans had struggled to gain more than a thousand of them in support, not nearly enough to swing the war in their favor.

Balak shook his head. "It's different this time. I'm not sure how, but our reports indicate that the Geneshans brought up eight thousand fighters."

My mouth dropped. That did change things. "I didn't think the Malduks had that many men of fighting age. There must not be anyone left in the mountains but women and children."

"There's more," said Balak.

Of course.

"The Geneshans managed to maneuver a small force around our western front. A few thousand."

I nodded. Since he was being so generous with information I took that as a sign that asking questions just might yield me answers. "Do they know that we know?"

"All information from scouts and mages says no. But busting their communication lines is more important than ever if they're planning something major for tomorrow."

"How are we going to counter their movement, sir?"

"I'm moving the Seventh Regiment to the western front. They should be able to defend it while the rest of the army focuses on the main assault at dawn."

I clicked my tongue.

He cocked an eyebrow. "What is it?"

"We might be underestimating them."

"How so?"

"The Geneshans have always been the most resourceful when their backs are against the wall. Isn't that where they are now? We hold the better position and have better numbers. Yet, they managed a last minute alliance with the Malduks and brought around a regiment to flank us with little warning. We're missing something." I paused. "I know you don't want another Wadlow Hill, General."

He clenched his jaw.

No one on our side wanted another Wadlow Hill. Five years ago we had nearly lost the war despite having a better position and better numbers. Casualties set us back for years. A little luck from weather and my unit's assassination of their top general bought our army the time it needed to make it out with enough strength to regroup.

In the aftermath of the battle, the Geneshans recovered most of their lands and had even begun to gain a foothold into Turine again.

Balak's jaw relaxed and he grunted. I knew that grunt. It meant he wanted my thoughts on what to do next, but was too prideful to ask for it. I walked to the map. He came up beside me, smelling of sweat and worry.

"Would it be possible to add the Eighth and Ninth regiments to the Seventh, sir?"

"And pull away a full third of our forces from the main lines?"

"Well, it's likely the Geneshans have more than what the reports indicate. You know they're good at masking troop movement. Why not throw them off guard and attack? Those three regiments won't break unless the entire Geneshan front swings that way. There's no way they could conceal that."

"But what if it's only the few thousand we know about?"

"Then have the Seventh, Eighth, and Ninth keep pushing through. Have them clear the area then break off back toward the main line while our other forces hold their ground."

I doubted it would come to that. It was probably a hunch, but I just knew the Geneshans were planning something big along the western front.

"I'll give it some thought," Balak said. That was code for "I agree but I won't start issuing orders until after you leave."

I backed away from the table. "Sir, I really need to get to my unit." I raised my hand, which held the parchment he gave me earlier. "Orders and all."

He stared at the map, waving a hand at me.

I took my first step toward the tent flap when he called again. "Tyrus."

"Sir?"

"Those targets are crucial. Even more so if your hunch is correct."

"Yes, sir."

I left the general's tent in a hurry, noting that despite the late hour, the camp bustled with life. Men took advantage of light offered by the moon, stars, and raging campfires to complete their work. Officers barked orders while messengers darted between gaps in the chow line to reach their destination. Everyone seemed to move with purpose, even if their purpose was simply to find a place to eat their steaming bowl of stew. A lot still needed to be done before soldiers tied down for the night.

Hamath, my second, met me a few steps outside of the command tent. He shook his head, red hair flopping over thick sideburns as we walked. A couple inches over six feet, he had me by as many, easily matching my gait. Like most in my unit, he didn't carry a lot of extra weight, but what he did carry was solid.

"The old whoreson kept you back so you could tell him how to run his army again, I see."

I chuckled. "Depends on how you look at it. He never has come out and asked me for advice."

Hamath spat. "Why should he? You tell him everything he needs to know, and after it works, he takes all the credit. He never would have become a general if not for you. He'd probably still be stuck as a captain."

"That's not true. He's good at getting men to fight for a cause. He just needs a little help now and then when it comes to strategy."

"More than a little," Hamath muttered. "I don't see how it doesn't bother you."

I shrugged. "It did in the beginning. But at this point, Balak can have all the glory he wants so long as it means ending the war. Gods, it's been ten years since I've seen Lasha and the kids. Four since I've gotten a letter from them thanks to the army's mandatory silence with outside communication."

Hamath grunted. "Sorry. It's just that you should be the one leading us, not him."

"I've got enough to worry about already. I don't want to think about looking after the tens of thousands Balak has to."

He took a deep breath. "Speaking of worrying, I came over here because we have a bit of a problem."

I stopped and closed my eyes. "What is it now?"

"Your sister caught a new recruit in unit three roughing up one of the camp whores."

I pressed my lips together, shaking my head as I opened my eyes. "Let me guess. She couldn't let things go."

"You know Ava."

I did. "What happened?"

"She confronted the recruit, and they had words. He didn't know not to argue with her. By the time I got there she had his pants around his ankles and some sort of spell squeezing at his crotch. I swear I'm going to have nightmares about that. It was all swollen and turning purple." He shivered. "I got her to stop, and the healers said the boy would recover, but it'll take weeks. Unit three is going to be short-handed until then. I managed to smooth things over as best I could, but their unit leader is calling for your sister's head. Those she's wronged in the past are supporting him. They plan to take it all the way to the Council of High Mages this time."

"Did you tell her any of that?"

"Gods, no. You know she won't listen to anyone but you. As worked up as she was, I was worried she might do the same to me as she did to the recruit. I calmed her down a bit and then let her go."

I sighed. "See what I mean, Hamath? You want me to manage an army when it's a struggle to keep my own unit in line."

"Not your whole unit. Just Ava. And you only have one sister."

"Thankfully." I handed the general's orders to Hamath. "Here, start getting the others ready while I talk to her." I nodded to the full moon. "Make sure everyone's mudded up."

Hamath swore. "I was worried you'd say that."

* * *

I found Ava pacing back and forth at the edge of the forest outside of camp, stomping the ground with such determination it looked like she was trying to put out a fire. The guards on patrol made sure to give her a wide berth.

Without her cloak, moonlight shimmered off her black leathers. She ran a thin hand through short, brown hair, and rubbed the back of her neck—a tell-tale sign that her run-in with the recruit bothered her more than usual. When I saw the faintest hints of sorcery crackling at her long fingertips I knew Hamath did right by letting me talk to her. She was having a hard time controlling herself.

Luckily, I didn't have to worry about any serious injury if she lost her temper. I was one of the rare cases of someone born with a resistance to sorcery. Each of our special units had someone resistant among them. Considering the crap Ava tried to pull on me as kids, it's a good thing I had the gift. Otherwise, I would have ended up missing a limb or worse a long time ago. It was also a good thing for others near me in battle as one of the nice things my resistance afforded me was the ability to draw sorcery out of others injured by some spell.

"Well?" I asked as I came upon her.

She stopped and gave me a bitter look. Tall for a woman, she could almost give me that look at eye level. "Well, what? I'm ready. Lay into me if that's what you're here for."

"I'd like to know what happened first."

"Hamath didn't tell you?"

"I want to hear your side."

She put her hands on her hips. "Some idiot wanted to prove how tough he was by beating on one of the camp followers."

"Whores."

"What?"

"Call them what they are. Unlike the merchants that come and go, the only thing she was peddling was what's between her legs."

She grit her teeth. "Fine. Whores."

"Did you find out what prompted him to lay into her like that?"

"No."

"Don't you think you should have?"

"No."

A long breath passed through my lips. "You know, we've had this conversation far too many times over the years."

"We're going to keep on having it if little men continue to think they can mistreat a lady."

I snorted. "A lady? Look, you know I don't condone hitting women, and I would never put up with someone in my unit doing it, but I'd hardly call a whore a lady. You need to be more concerned with protecting those fighting alongside us, not someone who can't stay off her back. Quit taking matters into your own hands. You should have reported the incident to the soldier's sergeant. Now, his unit is shorthanded for tonight."

She ignored my last point. "Nothing would have happened if I had reported it. You know that."

I said nothing. She was right. I hated it when she was right.

"There were still better ways to handle the situation than how you did. Ways that would have punished the soldier without possibly crippling him for life."

She shrugged. "See if I care. Her face is no less important than his manhood."

"Don't make me out to be the bad guy here. I'm not trying to defend his actions, I'm just mad at how you handled things." I shook my head. "Well, maybe the woman will get out of the trade now that she knows the risks."

"I'm sure she knew the risks, and she chose the trade anyway. What does that tell you?"

"That she doesn't have her head on straight."

She frowned. "Could be. Maybe she just saw the money she'd make and didn't care about getting slapped around. But how many choose that life because they feel that's the only chance they have to survive?"

"Here you go again."

Ava cocked her head to the side. "What if that had been Lasha?"

My eyes narrowed. Hypothetical or not, if anyone other than Ava had suggested such a thing I would have been all over them. "Don't. It wouldn't happen."

"You don't know that. We've been gone almost a decade. Neither one of us knows what things are like back home."

"Stop, Ava. I know my wife. She'd never stoop to that. She's too smart. Too resourceful." I opened and closed my hands. "Besides, Lasha's got friends to look after her and the kids if it came down to it."

Somewhere in the last few exchanges I had closed the distance between us. I realized that because I saw fear creep into Ava's eyes. It was odd. I hadn't hit her since we were kids just being kids, yet I guess part of that older brother and younger sister dynamic remained.

I backed away a step. I hated to see that look in her eyes. She could make me angrier than anyone, but I loved her.

"Sorry," I muttered. "Look, I'm done arguing. We've got orders, so we'll have to continue this later. But I'm going to have to do something.

This is getting elevated to the High Mages. Maybe if I take care of it on my own first, they'll be more lenient."

She rolled her eyes. "Don't do me any favors, big brother. Ao can curse the High Mages as far as I'm concerned. All the gods can," she snapped.

Ao, goddess of sorcery, was the mother of the gods within the Turine pantheon. All other gods and goddesses descended from her and her husband Molak, god of all things nature. They ruled the heavens according to our culture.

However, ask any other nation and you'd find a completely different set of beliefs. Genesha's religion was the most puzzling. One and only one god, Beel. A mean piece of garbage who, according to the Geneshans, cultivated power through human sacrifices.

It seemed that they would have wised up long ago and suppressed Beel's power by just ceasing the sacrifices. I've always been of the opinion that the fewer people meddling in my life, god or otherwise, the better.

I shook my head in response to Ava's curse. "I thought you'd say something like that."

Had she not burned so many bridges, she could have been a High Mage. She had the talent, just not the tutelage. No one wanted to take Ava on as an apprentice knowing they would have to contend with her temper.

"Return to the unit and get mudded up," I added.

"I don't need to do that. I can just cast a spell."

"Call it pre-punishment. Besides, no sorcery unless I say otherwise."

"Fine." She stormed off with fire in her eyes.

Nearby guards on patrol halted as they watched her depart. None wanted to cross her path.

* * *

In the woods, a night sky filled with stars and a full moon could be a blessing by making it easier to find water, shelter, or perhaps even some food. If nothing else, the extra light could go a long way in preventing a twisted ankle.

None of that mattered when leading a unit behind enemy lines. Stealth was crucial. Light reflecting off the steel attached to each person could get a soldier killed.

By the time I got back to my unit, Hamath had most everyone covered in mud. If someone missed a spot, another person eagerly helped conceal it. No one wanted to die because of another's laziness.

I jumped right in with the others and began picking up handfuls of sludge, slathering it on my legs. Before I even finished, hands from the other members of my unit were all over me. What I received from them came on extra thick.

I took it in stride. Let them have their fun.

The smell of the mud finally got to me, making me gag as I smoothed the last of it around my nose and lips. "Gods, Hamath. Did you haul this in from the latrines?"

He chuckled. "At least the mosquitoes have finally left us alone."

Summers in Genesha were brutal. Besides the heat, mosquitoes the size of small birds hounded you.

"Well, I guess that's one positive."

Hamath grinned, white teeth rimmed in black muck. "I may not even wash this off when we're done. Not if it means having a good night's sleep without that constant buzzing at my ears."

I inclined my head. "You're actually thinking of sleep? What about your traditional romp with one of the whores when we get back?"

"I never said I wouldn't pay them a visit first."

"Covered in mud?"

"They're not going to care what I'm covered in so long as my coin is good."

"You gotta remember, Ty," said Ira, jumping into the conversation. "Hamath gave up on women long ago. Been giving his coin to the animals last I heard." He cackled. "He comes walking up covered in all that mud he won't even need his coin. Pigs might give him a free one."

Ira stood next to Dekar as usual. The two brothers were a year apart, but they looked like twins. Same blond hair, green eyes, and pale skin. They even had the same tone of voice. The mud only added to their resemblance.

Dekar flashed the rare smile at his brother's jest. The two looked alike, but their personalities couldn't have been more different. Ira loud and jesting. Dekar quiet and thinking.

12

The rest of the squad broke out into laughter as well, including Hamath, helping ward off the somber mood none of us wanted to face. Whether a first or hundredth mission, everyone got anxious before leaving.

We all had friends who had never returned.

"Tyrus. It's time."

The laughter faded at the sound of Ava's voice. Her eyes opened. Her hand dropped away from her temple. Communication with the other mages had been severed.

Each of the twelve elite units that reported to Balak had their own mage in order to speed communications. It was a luxury none of us took for granted.

The ominous mood we had tried to avoid washed over us.

"All right," I said. "Let's move out."

We took only a few steps when I heard a familiar jingling from the man next to me. I paused, grabbed Gal's arm and pulled him aside as I signaled Hamath to keep the others moving.

Lots of soldiers had their superstitions or religious quirks. However, I'd never met anyone quite as passionate about his accessories as Gal.

"What are you doing?" I asked.

He tried to give me a confused look, but with his mismatched eyes of gray and blue, he just seemed mentally unstable. "What do you mean, Sarge?"

"Don't start. We're not doing this again, Gal. You know you can't bring all that junk with you. You'll make enough noise to alert the Geneshans long before we get there."

"Sarge, it ain't junk. It all has meaning."

He reached around his neck and started pulling free four pendants that hung there. Each were made of bronze or silver. He started explaining their meanings.

I cut him off. "I don't care. You know the rule. We do this every blasted time."

"But Sarge, this time's different. I got a bad feeling that something is going to happen. The last thing I want to do is turn my back on Molak, Xank, Prax, or even Ao at a time like this."

13

Molak and Ao have three children. Prax is the god of war and therefore favored by soldiers. Xank, the second child, is god of death, and therefore cursed by pretty much everyone. Lavi, the last of the three original children, is known as the goddess of love and peace. She is always at odds with her two brothers, even to the point of pitting them against each other, since her domain contradicts everything Xank and Prax stand for. However, their feuds never prevented them from sleeping together since most of the lesser gods—too many to name—descended from those three.

"Gal, you always have a bad feeling. And you've made it through each one just fine. Take off the pendants or I will."

He started muttering prayers of forgiveness to the gods as he did so. I bit my tongue so not to make things worse.

"Don't forget the ones on your wrists and the one at your belt too."

"But—"

I narrowed my eyes in a way that said the discussion was over.

"Fine," he muttered. "But if I die because I didn't have my charms with me, it's going to be on you."

"Just get it done and hurry up."

I walked away at a brisk pace to catch up with the rest of my unit. I shook my head thinking of Gal's last words.

If any of my men died, regardless of the reason, it would be on me.

The joy of command.

CHAPTER 2

We made it out of camp quickly, moving east as we entered a small bog that smelled about as awful as the latrine I accused Hamath of taking mud from. The terrain was far from ideal, but it provided us the most cover while we worked ourselves behind enemy lines. If the mosquitoes in camp resembled small birds, they were the size of eagles in the swamp.

Hamath took point. He had the best eyes in the group, especially at night.

We turned north, then east, and finally northeast. Balak's orders never specified how bad the ground truly was along our assigned path. The worse it got, the more the cynic in me wondered if that omission had been intentional to avoid any complaining from me while in his presence.

In several instances, we waded through thigh-deep, tepid water covered in duckweed, no small task while wearing light armor and the rest of our gear.

That armor saved my rear when I reached out for a protruding stump only to find a coiled snake the color of midnight resting atop it. It struck my gauntlet before I could pull back.

Dekar sliced the snake in half on the recoil quicker than I could bring my sword around. He gave me a look to ask if I was all right. I nodded, trying not to appear shaken. It'd be a cursed thing to survive all I had been through only to die from a snake bite.

Gal cleared his throat. "You know, Sarge, I had a charm that warded off snakes back at camp, but you made me remove it."

"Well, why don't you go back and get it now," I said flippantly.

"Seriously? I can?"

I gave him a look. "No, I'm not serious. We don't have time for that."

He grumbled. "Then why say it?"

"Sarcasm, Gal," said Ira, slapping him on the shoulder. "It's high time you learn it."

Gal scowled, then dropped his head in frustration.

When the water shallowed to ankle-deep, our boots made popping noises in the muck. Not much we could do to avoid the racket and still reach our destination on time. Still, we tried.

Eventually we hit some drier parts, and I forced an increase in pace to make up distance. We arrived when we should have, according to Ava's communications with the other units' mages. Balak wanted us all to coordinate our first attack as closely as possible. After the initial assault, it would be every unit for itself.

I called for a quick rest near several cypress trees with low hanging branches covered in moss. After only the few miles of ground we covered, my legs felt like jelly from struggling through the muck. While we waited for the last of the units to reach their position, everyone reapplied the mud that had washed off their legs in the water.

I looked over to Ava who had her eyes closed.

"Talk to me," I said in a low voice.

"The last unit just checked in."

"Bout time," Ira muttered.

"What do you want me to tell everyone?" she asked.

Even though the other unit leaders and I shared the same rank, they all looked to me when it came to a coordination of efforts. I had seniority by several years. "Send ahead scouts to better assess their targets. Make it quick. Sitting out here like this is asking for trouble."

She nodded and mentally communed the message.

I turned to give Hamath the order, but he had already ducked off toward our objective.

Ira, Dekar, and a few others sat against the cypress, closing their eyes. I wished again for the ability to relax as they did. I could have used a few minutes of it. Since I never had gotten the hang of grabbing sleep when I could get it, first watch naturally fell to me and the others in my unit too anxious to sleep.

My hands fidgeted while I scanned the swamp.

Water lilies sat in the low water behind us while cattails bordered the embankment. I lingered there a moment longer just to ensure nothing human or animal lay in wait. Satisfied, my gaze left the embankment and rested on my sister. Her eyes remained closed, as if in communication with the other units. I knew her too well to believe that. She couldn't stand the other mages and kept contact to a minimum. Their feelings were mutual. No one outside of our unit ever spoke to her. Actually, few in our unit did either unless they had to. Only me, Hamath, and Dekar even liked her.

My sister was that kind of person.

I decided against calling her ruse since I knew she was still aggravated with me from our earlier conversation. Now wasn't the time or place to revisit it.

Ava's eyes popped open. "Hamath's back."

A twig snapped, and Hamath appeared from the darkness half a breath later.

Ira cursed in a hushed whisper. "Prax be blessed, I hope your lazy rear did a better job of staying quiet when you were out there."

Hamath glared in Ira's direction. "Don't get all worked up. I heard Ava announce me. Ain't no one around here anyway. I checked."

He settled next to me.

"Well?" I asked.

"It matches the reports that Balak gave you. Communication post. Ten men stationed there. Three horses." He picked up a couple of sticks, using them to represent the men and animals he saw. He pointed with his finger. "Two of them are hiding here in a covered ditch. Almost missed them at first. Both have crossbows aimed right at where we'd have to come at them. First couple men who hit that opening will be easy targets."

"I'll take care of them," said Ava.

I shook my head. "No sorcery. Tell the other units the same."

"It won't take but a second. If this is because of what happened earlier—"

"You know me better than that," I snapped, aggravated that she'd even suggest such a thing. "When would I ever purposefully risk the lives of others just to get back at you?"

Her tone softened. "You're right. Sorry."

I waved a hand. "I'm over it. I know it might only take you a second to take those two out, probably all eight of them actually. But a second is more than enough time to draw unwanted attention our way. We don't have the resources or the time to deal with someone powerful who might be watching. This is only the first target. You'll get your chance before all is said and done." I cleared my throat. "Tell the other units to wait as long as they can before employing sorcery and under no circumstances are they to do it now."

She closed her eyes.

"What's the plan?" asked Dekar.

"You and Ira split the rest of the men into teams minus me, Hamath, and Ava. Ira has the right. You the left. Ava will stay behind and cover us."

"And us?" asked Hamath.

"We go after the two with the crossbows. It will make it easier for Ira and Dekar."

"I told you we're going to be good as dead once we hit the clearing."

I pointed behind a couple of the larger pebbles he used to mark the post. "We're going to skirt back around this way."

"Nothing but brush, Tyrus. We don't have time to get through that without making all kinds of noise. That's why I didn't suggest it. We just as soon hit the opening and hope those two are bad shots."

"Don't worry, I've got it all worked out."

* * *

Hamath and I got a head start on the others. I told Ira and Dekar not to move until after Ava received word that all other units had checked in. I figured that would buy us a few extra minutes to get into position.

We left the edge of the marsh, moving into grasses chest high with occasional patches of tumbled stone that looked completely out of place given the soft land. The high grasses met a thinly wooded area dressed with a variety of underbrush, mostly consisting of milkweed. We worked our way through it carefully.

"We should get there in another fifty yards. So, what's the plan?" Hamath asked over his shoulder in a voice I could barely make out.

I responded in kind. "We leave our packs and shields here. Ava will know to pick them up on the way in." We didn't need the worry of having them snag on anything. "You go right. I go left. I'll drown out our movements."

He leaned in, inches from my face. "Please tell me you ain't going to use one of your dumb bird calls."

"Why not?"

"Because they're awful."

"They've always worked."

"It only takes one time for them not to."

"I'm hurt." And truthfully, I kind of was. I had used my calls countless times over the years and they had always paid off. "Trust me."

He sighed, shaking his head.

We continued on a bit before splitting up.

Growing up on a farm and hunting for food with my father, I learned a lot about animal calls. My Pa had mastered them all—mountain lion, owl, coyote, whatever. If you could name it, he could do it. He nearly got himself killed a couple of times when someone loosed an arrow into the bushes where he hid, thinking he had been the real thing.

I never figured out half of what the old man knew, but I felt like I was better than most others when it came to mimicking animals.

I hadn't seen or heard anything too exotic in the swamp as far as birds went so I decided on a simple crow while slipping into the underbrush, trying my best to silence the tiny branches rustling against my legs.

The communication post was essentially a tent, a small fire, and eight men in different stages of alertness hunkered down behind several old logs someone had hauled into a semicircle. It wasn't what I would have called a well-fortified position. There weren't any engineers among this bunch. Thankfully, several of the enemy were busy catching a few minutes of sleep while most of those awake ate. I couldn't yet see the two crossbowmen, though I did see the ditch.

I wasn't in the most ideal position for me to give the call, crawling around, ducking and weaving between bushes and rock. Still, I thought it sounded believable.

A sword hissed through its scabbard. "What in the name of the gods is that?"

I froze, rising up just enough to spare a quick glance toward the post. One of the men already awake looked in my direction, though it quickly became obvious he had no idea of my location. I did the call again, this time throwing my voice a bit as my Pa had taught me.

"There it is again," said the man, swiveling his head while trying to locate its origin. "What is that?" He appeared nervous.

I did the call again, this time moving as fast as I dared.

"Sit down, Corporal, and keep quiet," came a voice from one of the men who had been asleep. "We didn't make a bunch of racket during your watch."

"But I ain't ever heard anything like that before."

I kept the call going intermittently during their conversation, changing the pitch and throwing my voice to mix up the location.

"Probably just a couple of squirrels having a romp in the bushes. Now stay quiet."

A few of the men chuckled. I couldn't believe they thought my crow sounded like a squirrel.

By the time the Geneshans settled down, I was in position. So was Hamath. I looked his way through a gap in the brush. I could tell by his posture that he heard the squirrel comment. I knew I wouldn't hear the end of that.

Hamath gestured down and across to the two crossbowmen, making sure I not only saw my target, but could get to him easily enough. I nodded. The man was about ten feet away, weapon butted up against his shoulder while he stared out toward the point the rest of my unit would be forced to attack from. Neither he nor the man next to him seemed to care what could be lurking on either side of them. Lucky for us.

Not long after we got into position, a small pebble sailed into camp, landing in the fire. It sent a tiny burst of ashes into the air, causing a few of the men to curse the "squirrels" they heard moments before.

I knew better. Dekar and Ira were ready.

Hamath and I drew daggers as we burst from our cover. Our signal for the rest of our unit to attack was the sounds of us engaging. We pounced on the crossbowmen.

Our targets swung toward each of us, letting out hollers. Panting, my man hurriedly loosed his bolt. Thankfully, the bolt went wide. Some things boil down to luck, which, at least then, I had. At that distance, there was no such thing as dodging a crossbow bolt.

I heard the rest of my unit reach the campfire as steel sang and men screamed. I ignored them to focus on the task at hand.

I was hoping my target would make another mistake by trying to pull the sword at his waist. He didn't. There was no time in the short distance between us and he knew it.

Instead, he changed the grip on his crossbow and swung it. I ducked under the attack and thrust up with my dagger. He turned enough so the blade caught only his arm.

He screamed as the crossbow came back around. I grabbed the weapon by the shaft, and stabbed. The blade entered his gut. A wet moan passed through his lips. His grip faltered on the crossbow. It hit the ground a second before he did.

I finished him off with another thrust through the chest and then looked to Hamath. He stood over the limp form of his man. We gave each other a quick nod before turning toward the fire. Every one of the Geneshans lay dead.

Over in a matter of seconds, the attack went about as well as one could hope. We hadn't lost anyone, which is always a relief.

Ira called out, anticipating my question. "No injuries, Ty."

"I hope it stays that way," Hamath said, walking over.

"Me too."

I don't think either of us really believed it would.

* * *

"Molak, that hurts," I hissed in the early morning light.

We hid among several empty supply wagons while tending wounds. We had managed to knock out three other targets before arriving at our current location, a small officers' posting.

"Keep your voice down," hushed Ava.

"And quit cursing the Father, Sarge," said Gal, absently rubbing the spot on his chest where his pendants once hung.

No one ever had a problem cursing Xank. As the god of death, people felt he deserved it. However, religious or not, if you cursed the

Father people got pretty uncomfortable. That put me at odds with most everyone since if I cursed any of the gods by name, it almost always ended up being Molak. The way I figured it is if Molak did exist, the old man was more responsible for all the pain and death since he created Xank.

I opted against another religious debate and clenched my jaw as Ava worked on my arm, cauterizing the wound. She wasn't much of a healer, but she could at least stop bleeding, and in a bind, buy time until someone more specialized in that form of sorcery saw to the injury.

However, given my resistance to sorcery, she had to be creative in how she treated me. Her creativity involved heating up a dagger and placing it over the wound. A small grunt passed through my lips as the skin on my arm seared beneath the blade's touch. I tried not to gag on the smell of burnt hair and flesh.

"Done," she announced.

I eyed the rest of the unit. Each of us nursed our own injuries. The information we received from General Balak became less accurate with each target. There had been no mention of one of the enemy's elite soldiers, a D'engiti, guarding the officers.

D'engiti usually stood about seven feet in height, some taller. All muscle and a lot of it. From what we know, the enemy's Master Sorcerers, or High Mages as we called them in Turine, helped create the blasted things through magic and experimentation on their own men.

Thankfully, there weren't a lot of D'engiti as the process was both time consuming and a drain on resources.

I was thankful our side hadn't created such things. Something seemed inherently wrong about the whole process. I doubted our higher ups shared my view though. More than likely, they tried their hands at creating something similar, but failed.

Regardless, we weren't expecting to face one of the monstrosities.

Despite its size, the thing had snuck up on us while we fought the others guarding the post. It killed Jachin, a private who'd recently joined our unit, before Dekar and I brought it down. Dekar nursed quite a few of bumps and bruises after the confrontation.

I rose to my feet, wincing at a pull in my side. Sometime in the fight, I must have bruised a rib.

The rest of my unit looked toward me as a false dawn crept across the sky. The dim gray brought a threatening glow over the pale faces of the dead.

We needed to get moving, and my men knew it.

"What's going on with the other units?" I asked Ava.

She closed her eyes and shook her head. "I can't reach them. They must all be engaged. . . ." her voice trailed off.

Or dead, I thought, finishing what she refused to say. I couldn't blame her. No one wanted to say that out loud.

Small pockets of angry noise grabbed our attention, fighting from somewhere else behind enemy lines. Other units had been discovered. Flashes of purplish lightning and orange flame erupted in those areas, illuminating the dreary morning landscape.

Ira grunted. "Well, we know some of them made it."

"For now," said Dekar.

I was glad that the other units had managed to hold off on using sorcery as long as they had. However, those displays would draw the enemy like flies to honey. It would also put the rest of the Geneshans on edge, looking for others like us among them.

"Let's get back to camp," I said.

"You mean that's it?" asked Ira.

I nodded. "Yep. This was the last post we were supposed to take down. Ava, you've got point with Hamath. Keep us hidden. No sense in refraining from sorcery anymore. The Geneshans are going to be on high alert."

She grunted and bent over, hands going to her head.

"Ava? You all right?"

She held up a hand for silence while the other rubbed her temple. She opened her eyes a moment later wearing a look of disgust. "Plans have changed. Balak just sent orders via the High Mages on a new target. It's high priority."

Hamath swore as did the others. "We never get off easy."

"What's the objective?" I asked.

She gestured to a small rise several miles away decorated in patches of trees. "There's a post near the top."

"You gotta be pulling our legs," said Ira. "We'll be lucky if just one of us gets there alive."

Ava squinted at the rise. "Balak said that capturing it could end the war."

Ira snorted. "He's said that about every mission he's sent us on since the war began."

That warranted a few grunts of agreement.

"So what are we supposed to do once we get there?" I asked.

"There's a small box inside one of the tents," said Ava. "They said we'd know it when we see it."

Hamath started to chuckle.

I cast him a look. "What is it?"

"I just realized what's waiting there for us. I overheard the captains talking about it yesterday." He raised an eyebrow and faced Ava. "That's their Master Sorcerers' command post, isn't it?"

Her lips thinned as she nodded.

My hands balled into fists. "That would have been good to know."

"I was getting there," she said.

"I mean from Hamath too."

He shrugged. "Sorry."

"Did Balak say how we're supposed to take it?" I asked Ava.

"By the time we reach the post, he's supposed to have drawn the Master Sorcerers away with the battle. Apparently, the High Mages are getting involved. If everything goes according to plan, their Master Sorcerers should all be out in the field trying to fend off our assault. We'll just have to deal with the normal men guarding it."

Bugles blared off in the distance. I could tell by the pitch that they came from our side. Balak's timing was impeccable.

I sighed. "They're playing our song. Ava, mask our movements. Let's go."

* * *

Balak could be a jerk, and he sometimes had issues with strategy, but when he decided to take action, he took action.

All hell had broken loose as we left for our target, though I'm not sure hell had the kind of fire and brimstone being thrown around by our mages. We were miles away from the action and I could still smell the sulfur. I wondered why they hadn't done more of that in the ten years before.

We kept our heads down as we snuck closer to the small rise. It was hard not to spare the occasional glance behind us as the sky lit up as if the end of times had arrived.

Geneshan officers shouted orders and troops sprinted by in a frantic commotion, heading toward the storm of sorcery as we snuck through the enemy's camp. All the while, bugles blared and drums thumped.

The beauty of all that panic was it made our job easier. The spell of concealment Ava used was one she had put into practice many times before. It didn't turn us invisible, but it confused anyone who noticed us. A person might assume they saw something else or in some cases forget altogether what they had been doing. It was a great spell, but not without its limitations. Those like me with a resistance to sorcery could usually see through the illusion.

We passed halfway to our goal. The enemy soldier was scrambling out of a latrine to join his squad and came to a grinding halt. He did a double take, pointed, and opened his mouth to warn others. I withdrew a knife quickly and pounced. The edge of my blade slid across his throat. Blood poured down his neck, covering his chest.

I froze for a moment when I looked at him up close, seeing what I hadn't seen seconds before.

The soldier looked no older than fourteen. About the age my daughter, Myra, would be now. That shook me. I ordered Hamath to dispose of the body while Dekar kept a lookout for other Geneshans lagging behind. The immediate danger of our situation was the only thing that prevented me from dwelling on ending the kid's life. I knew his face would haunt me at a more opportune time.

By the time we reached the base of our target, the blood-red sky of dawn had passed. We crested a small rise that led to the larger hill we still needed to climb. It afforded us a better view of the battlefield. A brightening yellow illuminated the teaming masses below.

Armies swarmed atop each other like ants. Large companies attempted to flank and outmaneuver their opponent until clashing once more in a horde of steel and flesh. Despite the sweat on my skin from the morning heat, a small shiver ran up my back. Though it had been many years since I had fought in those tight presses, the smell, the fear, the general uncertainty of where death would come stabbing in from, never left me.

A scent of pine from nearby trees masked the sulfuric odor of the brilliant violet and blue flashes of sorcery. Dark shafts of crimson descended from black clouds that slowly blocked out the sun. Given the distance and the chaos of it all, I had no way to tell who held the advantage. Based on what we could hear, I wasn't sure I wanted to know. Neither side would be the same afterward.

I called for a halt behind a patch of ratty bushes.

Ava already sat with eyes closed in concentration.

Her eyes opened a moment later, and I saw something I had rarely seen before. Fear. She leaned over, trying to hide her emotions. "It's here," she whispered in a quivering voice.

"You want to be more specific?"

"It. The gods-cursed artifact the Geneshans were rumored to have found."

My throat tightened. "Are you certain?"

"Pretty certain. I've never been around it so I don't know its signature like I would some of our weapons. Whatever it is, it's more powerful than anything I've ever felt. That must have been why they said 'we'd know it when we see it.'"

I blinked. That changed things.

All cultures had stories of ancient weapons somewhere deep in their history, lost because of natural disasters, world events, or sheer stupidity. Everyone searched for those weapons, though few found them. In the rare cases that one was found, it almost always fell short of the myth bestowed upon it.

That was what happened to us. In the early years of the war, the king diverted resources to finding the mystical artifacts in Turine's past, hoping they would tip the scales in our favor. All that work, all the lives lost in mudslides and cave-ins, brought us very few benefits. The artifacts did do some pretty useful things like one that always found drinkable water regardless of location. However, none of them actually helped the grunts fighting on the front lines.

Rumors came out a few weeks back that the Geneshans had found their "holy" weapon and this one might be everything it was thought to be. I never believed it. I assumed the Geneshans were feeding us a bunch of false information like we did to them. My assumption changed when I saw the look in Ava's eyes. Whatever she felt, it had her shaken.

I blinked and then kept on blinking. I needed to do something while I gathered my thoughts.

"Tyrus?" Ava's voice had lost some of her fear and found a bit of frustration instead.

I cleared my throat. "Give me a second."

Like everyone else, she looked to me for a way to get out alive. The best option really wasn't an option at all and that was to desert. Those pressed into the army hated the years stolen by war. Those who volunteered eventually felt the same when they realized that once in, they could not voluntarily leave. However, we all respected our fellow soldiers too much to just leave. And as crazy as it sounded, a part of me still believed in the ideals of our king. If he said the Geneshans were evil and needed to be stopped, then who was I to question him? I sure hadn't seen anything to contradict that view.

"All right, what are we facing up there?" I asked her.

"Two dozen. Four D'engiti."

"Four D'engiti?" hissed Ira.

Dekar elbowed him, but it was too late. I had been too caught up in my discussion with Ava about the weapon to realize Ira had drifted over. Heads had all turned, eyeing me closely.

"Well Ava, the D'engiti are yours," I said. The Geneshan creations were tough, but a good mage could tip the scales back in our favor.

She licked her lips. "Sorry, big brother. There's still a Master Sorcerer up there along with two squad level sorcerers."

More muttered curses came from my unit than I may have ever heard in my life. I was among them, wondering how much I truly believed in the ideals of my king with each passing breath.

I wanted to ask Ava to double check her numbers, but knew she probably had already done that at least a half dozen times before telling me.

"You want me to go take a look at things?" asked Hamath.

My second's face had turned grim. Everyone knew what the odds meant. The chances of any of us surviving this assault were slim. That being said, some chances weren't worth taking.

I shook my head. "No. We're going to rely on Ava's report for now. The last thing I want is for some sorcerous trap to snag you and warn them of our approach." I swung my head back to my sister, who had her eyes closed again. "Ava, can you draw something up?"

"Working on it." She opened her eyes after seeing it from a distance with sorcery. "All right. Got it."

We crowded around Ava as she drew a crude outline of the post in some dirt. I constructed a quick plan based on her map with the understanding that things might change once we got closer. Since we still had roughly another two hundred fifty yards to climb, we'd stick together a bit longer.

Hamath took point. Ava stayed a step behind him in case we needed her.

We took our time moving for obvious reasons, but especially since I had Ava cut off the concealment spell. Ava was so good at them that most of our own High Mages had trouble detecting us when she used them. Still, I wasn't about to underestimate the skills of the enemy's mages.

We made good time considering our trepidation and the fact that the sun left us exposed. Adding to our misery, the mud we coated ourselves with had begun to crack and peal in the heat of the early morning.

We came to a halt eighty yards out. Since we hadn't encountered any traps or even a sentry for that matter, I changed my mind and decided to chance sending Hamath up alone. It's not that I didn't trust Ava, it's just hard for sorcery to see everything as clearly as a set of eyes.

Hamath crawled off while we all laid low, weapons drawn.

No one made a sound.

He came back faster than I expected with both good and bad news.

He said little, not wanting to risk more noise than necessary while redrawing a map of the post. The good news was that sentries were just on the outskirts. That meant we'd be able to get closer before engaging and alerting others. Also, several of the soldiers Ava reported were actually messengers who had already slipped away down the other side of the rise.

The bad news was that Ava had been right about the number of D'engiti. Hamath had been unable to spot the sorcerers and assumed they were all inside the tent.

I started numbering off each of the men Hamath marked, starting at the farthest one on the left. Then I assigned targets to the eleven of us.

Since the tent was our primary target, Dekar would lead his team in first to draw away as many of the D'engiti from it as possible. I thought about sending in Ira's team, but decided I needed someone a little more cool-headed for this scenario. Ira had a tendency to let emotions override his thinking. Hamath and Ira would lead the rest of the men to cover me and Ava as we rushed the tent once Dekar had engaged the others.

"I don't like it," whispered Hamath. "I'm going with you."

"No. You stay with the others. Nine against twenty-one, including the D'engiti aren't the best of odds as it is."

"But the sorcerers are the largest threats. Unless you take them quick, those sorcerers are going to destroy us when they're done with you, regardless if we've taken everyone else down."

"You aren't a mage, nor do you have a resistance."

Hamath shrugged. "If this is my time, then so be it." He paused, listening to make sure we weren't being too loud. Considering the sudden sorcerous explosions from the battlefield, I didn't think he had anything to worry about.

He continued. "Look, even if I do nothing more than take a hit and die the second we get in there, it might distract them long enough to buy time for you or Ava to take down the Master Sorcerer."

"He's right," said Ava. "You're resistant to sorcery, but you aren't immune. And I'm not a god. We might be able to survive one direct hit from the Master Sorcerer, but that's it. We need to hit them hard and fast."

I sighed. "All right, Hamath. You're with us. Don't do anything stupid."

Hamath winked. "I won't do anything you wouldn't."

I gave him a look that told him I hadn't missed the jab. Then I turned my attention to Ira. "You're on your own then, so, control yourself."

"Don't worry, Ty. I got it," Ira said, a grin tugging at the corners of his mouth.

My voice hardened, angry at being put in the situation we were in. "I'm serious. If you don't use your head, I'm putting my boot up your rear."

"Only after you remove mine," added Dekar.

Ira's smile faded. Dekar put up with a lot from Ira. He sometimes came across as a pushover. We all knew better. Any threat from Dekar, even a mild one, sobered Ira up quick. Older brothers have a tendency to have that effect on their younger siblings.

Satisfied, I finished outlining our approach, and gave the order to move out.

* * *

Thirty yards from the top of the rise stood a brown, canvas tent. It sat in the middle of a flat patch of land with guards and messengers scattered about. Tall pines enclosed the space. Four hulking figures carried axes and swords. The weapons were so big they would have been comical if not for the creatures wielding them. Unlike the others who openly patrolled the space, the D'engiti stood motionless like stone golems guarding the entrance to some ancient emperor's tomb. If I hadn't known any better, I'd think their lack of movement meant I could catch them on their heels.

I knew better.

They were slower than the average soldier, but not by much. What the D'engiti lacked in speed, they more than made up for in size, reach, and strength. Plus, the abominations were specifically created to take a beating.

We got into position. Dekar and his team to the far left. Ava and Hamath at my sides. Ira and the others waited behind us to our right.

I stared at the tent, estimating the sprint to its entrance would take a good seven or eight seconds. Maybe. A lot can happen in that amount of time. Seven or eight seconds on a battlefield for a soldier who knew what they were doing could mean seven or eight dead enemies. For a soldier who didn't, it could mean getting stabbed seven or eight times.

I silently swore to Molak and every one of the other god that crossed my mind. I had never particularly liked General Balak, but I had never hated him as much as I did then for giving us the mission. While we would deal the enemy a huge blow if we succeeded, I didn't want to die before seeing my family again.

An elbow to the side jarred me from my thoughts. Ava gave me a look that told me I needed to focus.

I inhaled deep and gave the signal, imitating an eastern yellow-backed sparrow.

Hamath groaned ever so slightly as Dekar's team sprinted from cover, making as much noise as possible in order to draw attention their way. We watched them take out several guards to our right while using confiscated crossbows we had picked up earlier from the officers' post. Dekar's team quickly dropped the weapons, pulling free swords to engage the rest of the enemy.

With the Geneshans rushing to Dekar's location, Ava, Hamath, and I broke from cover, legs pumping with everything we had to the large tent at the center of the area. We didn't make it far before being noticed. I raised my shield to deflect a thrown knife flying in from the left.

A crossbow quarrel zipped past my right ear. Apparently Dekar wasn't quite as engaged with the enemy as I had hoped.

I heard Ira bark orders somewhere behind us. His team was more successful at taking pressure away from the three of us as we closed in on the tent.

The flap flew open. In the entrance stood a woman in dark blue robes with wavy blonde hair. Her fingers crackled with sorcery as her eyes darted around at the chaos. She caught us speeding toward her and raised her arm. A knife thrown by Hamath struck her in the shoulder, its force throwing her off balance. The deep purple lightning emanating from her fingers blasted off to the left.

Two steps later, I barreled into her with my shield, knocking her to the ground. I continued pushing inside, Ava right on my heels. Neither of us had time to finish off the woman with a Master Sorcerer nearby. I trusted Hamath to take care of her.

The Master Sorcerer stood in white robes at the back of the tent over a simple table. There was no sign of the other lesser sorcerer. On the table rested a plain wooden box. In that moment, I cared about nothing else. His wide-eyed expression turned to anger. Our ability to get this far caught him off guard. His hands glowed orange. An acidic smell crept into my nose.

I cursed and charged, hoping the tactic might buy Ava the time she needed to take him down.

Bright fire shot across the room. I ducked behind my shield—its etchings softening the attack. Despite it and my own resistance, the force of the blast still catapulted me backward.

I flew across the room and crashed into a table. Its legs shattered beneath my weight. I banged my head on something hard.

The tent spun. I fought to stand, but could not, vomiting instead. I turned my head toward the Master Sorcerer, blinking against the pain of what was likely a concussion. I grabbed something. A cup, I think, and threw it with what little strength I could muster. It missed him by at least six feet. It didn't matter. It was enough to distract him half a second longer.

He realized his error and wheeled on Ava. He was too late.

Thankfully, I managed to stay conscious as my little sister engulfed the whoreson in shadow. The sound of his agony was music to my pounding ears.

* * *

We started our mission with a unit of twelve men. We charged our last target with eleven. When the dust settled we were down to six.

Besides the concussion I earned, the mage also knocked my left shoulder out of socket and further bruised my ribs I had injured earlier. Hamath lost a finger. Ira half an ear. Dekar suffered a broken leg and nose. Of the six of us who survived, none of us had escaped injury.

But we had done it.

Ava had killed the Master Sorcerer and still had enough left in her to help with the D'engiti while I vomited from the head injury and got my feet under me. Dekar had found the other sorcerer with his robes down in the woods. That was about the only thing that went our way.

We had done it all right. I doubted that Adar, Baruch, Hayyim, Yahu, and Gal cared much about our victory though. I stared at their bodies while wavering on my feet. Their blood soaked into the ground beneath my boots. I doubted Jachin, the private I lost earlier in the day would care either. His body would get lost among all the rest and given no special acknowledgement.

I'm sure all six of them were ecstatic about our success.

My gaze rested once more on Gal's body, where it lingered. Before breathing his last, he had managed to bring his hands up to his chest as if hoping his pendants might magically appear and save him. The man's mismatched eyes seemed to stare back at me in a way that said "I told you so."

That bothered me. I knew those charms wouldn't have stopped the sword that took him in the chest, but he had believed they would. Maybe not having his charms had distracted him enough that it led to his death. One more decision I'd question until the end of my days.

"Not even hell could be this bad," I heard Ira mutter, using the expression as originally intended.

A shiver ran down my back, punctuating the remark.

"You all right, Tyrus? You look like you're about to throw up again," said Hamath as he walked up. He had wrapped a makeshift bandage around his left hand. Blood seeped through where his pinky finger had once been. Sweat matted his red hair to his forehead.

"I might. But if I do, it won't be from the head injury."

"Huh?"

"Nothing. We can talk about it later. Did you see anything with that spyglass you found?"

Hamath had climbed up the last thirty yards of the rise and tried to assess the mess of a battlefield from a better vantage.

"I saw a lot. None of it made sense. Lines from both sides are all over the place. Flags are being waved. I can't tell if troops are being redistributed or if one side is surrendering to the other." He paused. "Did Ava have any luck reaching anyone?"

I shook my head. Ava lay on her back, asleep on the thin, yellow grass. Burn marks adorned her arms. Her chest rose slowly with each breath. "She passed out. She needs more rest before she can try to communicate at this distance. Someone will have to contact her first."

"So, we're in the dark?"

"For now."

Ava sat up, open palms going to her temples. "By the gods," she whimpered.

I moved toward her and nearly fell as my vision spun. Hamath caught my arm and helped me over.

"Are you all right?" I asked.

She nodded violently while holding her breath and squeezing her eyes shut. Someone was communicating with her. I knelt at her side and waited. A few moments later, she let out a long breath and took several more while blinking rapidly.

"What was that?" I asked.

She swore. "Some idiot not used to communicating that way. Rather than asking me what he wanted, he bullied his way through my mind to get it. If I wasn't so tired, I could have cut him off, but I didn't have the energy."

"What did he tell you?"

"I'm getting there. How'd you like it if someone was inside your head unwanted?"

I waited.

She took one last deep breath, anger fading as she processed what she had been told. "I can barely believe it."

"Believe what?"

She looked up, face twisting in emotion. Shock. Relief. Confusion.

"The Geneshans laid down arms. All of their major sorcerers are dead or incapacitated. Their generals are already on their way to Balak's tent to sign the king's terms."

I blinked. "What? That fast?"

Ava chuckled. "Yes. We won, big brother. Apparently the Master Sorcerer we killed sent a distress call to the others on the front lines. When he did, it distracted those in the field long enough for our High Mages to gain the upper hand. Also, Balak's precautions along the western front with the seventh, eighth, and ninth regiments stopped the Geneshan counter. They say his strategy was genius."

Hamath snorted and gave me an elbow. "That's cause he didn't think of it."

Ava gave him a confused look. "What?"

"Nothing," I said. Let Balak have the credit. "What else?"

"They're sending a company to come retrieve us and the artifact." She paused. "We're going home."

A few gasps came from the others at the news.

My mouth dropped as I sat back. The image of a beautiful woman with dark hair and chestnut skin grabbed me. She stood in the doorway of our farm crying. A young girl and a little boy tugged at her legs as she faded from sight. The sound of rolling wagon wheels filled my ears.

A tear ran down my cheek.

"You all right, big brother?" asked Ava.

I smiled. "Never better."

I was finally going home to Lasha.

34

CHAPTER 3

The infirmary stank in ways no man should ever know. Blood mingled with bodily fluids it was never meant to touch. It took everything I had not to retch.

The sounds reverberating through the tents only made matters worse. Flies buzzed around wounds. Injured patients wailed at the cutters sawing away on limbs that couldn't be saved. Curses of 'hold still' came from the cutters. They all added a new layer of guilt for me. My injuries seemed trivial in comparison.

One of the mages adept in healing pushed and prodded my skull. He chanted something in a strange tongue, lessening the effects of my concussion. Tears streaked down his face as he worked. His breathing came in gasps. He was one of the few sorcerers strong enough to heal people with a resistance to sorcery. As a side effect, treating me put him through tremendous pain.

My guilt increased.

"There are others who need your help more. Why don't you see to them?" I asked.

"General Balak's orders were to take care of you first."

The weariness in the healer's voice was so strongly pronounced I had to strain to hear him over all the moaning and despair. Mages skilled at healing were a rare thing, so they often suffered from severe exhaustion. After the day's battle, they wouldn't sleep for days. It wasn't unheard of for a healer to die because of the toll their bodies endured while healing others.

And this poor fool got stuck with the task of healing me.

My headache continued to subside. I clenched my jaw in frustration, guilt gnawing at me even more as I watched a cutter walk by, cursing audibly. Blood bathed his leather apron. He held a saw in one hand and a severed foot in the other. He dropped the foot in a wheelbarrow with other severed limbs. Someone would be by soon to cast them into a bonfire.

Bile crept into my throat. I knocked aside the healer's hands and rose to my feet, unsteady at first.

"I'm not finished yet," he said.

"Close enough. I can walk on my own. Go help someone who needs it more."

The healer gave me a faraway look that let me know he was barely there. Heavy bags under his eyes added to a sagging and tired face. I hurried out the tent as he sighed and began to stand.

I had plenty of sympathy for the wounded, but that didn't mean I wanted to linger. The infirmary was the part of military life no one, including me, liked to think about. We faced our mortality every day on the battlefield. None of us needed to be reminded of it afterward.

Those in civilian life weren't much better. Fairy tales described stories of heroics, maybe even a valiant death for those fighting in war. No one ever told the story of the poor cripple who had been in the wrong place at the wrong time and was forced to find a new standard of "normal."

It was night again by the time I started toward Balak's tent. We had been stuck behind enemy lines for nearly half a day before someone picked us up. I lost one other member of my unit during that time. Omar apparently had internal injuries. He collapsed while laughing at one of Ira's attempts at humor. Ava never even had a chance to look him over before he stopped breathing.

I tried to push my thoughts aside. It wasn't easy.

The mood around camp changed drastically the farther from the infirmary I walked. If I hadn't known any better I might have wondered if our army had suffered any casualties at all.

Men from all over Turine congregated around newly tapped barrels of ale. They laughed with half-full cups in hand, happy that there would be no more fighting. It didn't matter who you were or what you looked like before joining the army, once you fought next to a man in battle, you became brothers.

I passed by the hangers-on attached to any army. Merchants near carts peddled indulgences of all types, trying to convince soldiers their coin was best spent with them. Lines twenty men deep stood in front of each cart. Victory loosened the purse of even the stingiest man, and the merchants smiled ever wider because of it.

Despite the activity at the merchant wagons, none of those lines could rival the rowdy ones waiting for the whores outside their tents. Many men wanted to celebrate the victory and release excess energy carried over from battle. Others just wanted the soft embrace of a woman after coming so close to death.

The guard outside of Balak's tent pulled back the flap as I walked up. That was a first. Either the general was in a great mood and couldn't wait to thank me or he needed someone's rear to lay into and mine was his first choice. Thankfully, I didn't see how it could be the latter.

Inside, Balak sipped from a glass of wine, looking pleased with the state of things.

"Tyrus. How're you feeling?"

"Better, sir," I answered as the flap closed behind me. "Congratulations on the victory. I hear your decision along the western front worked out for the best."

He set the glass down and nodded. "It did. The Geneshans were hoping to flank us. They weren't expecting to run into such resistance." He grunted. "The mages are acting like the victory should be theirs though. Lazy fools finally decided to pull their weight around here and now they expect all the accolades I sweated years for."

I chose not to respond. It was no secret that Balak and the High Mages didn't get along. Both resented the other since they each answered to no one but the king himself.

I changed the subject. "I hear terms of peace have already been worked out."

"Yes." His smile returned. "Once they learned your unit had the artifact, they agreed to pretty much anything we demanded so long as we swore not to use the thing. Have you seen it?"

"No, sir. We thought it best not to open the box it was in."

"Nothing wrong with taking a look. Here," he said while going behind the table still adorned with maps.

He pulled out the wooden box we took from the Geneshans. It looked unimpressive. Made of oak, it held no engravings or paints.

He flipped the lid and I moved closer to peer inside.

The artifact was carved from the same wood as the box. It was ugly as sin with the body of a turtle and the head of some sort of insect with long antennae and big, round eyes. I had seen better craftsmanship from the merchants peddling their wares to our army.

"It doesn't look like much, does it?" he asked.

I shook my head. "Is that supposed to be Beel?"

He grunted. "You know, I didn't think to ask. If it is, I understand their religion even less than before."

A strange pulse of sorcery radiated off the artifact. It made the hair on my arms stand up.

"Even with my resistance I can feel the power coming off it. Any reason why the Geneshans never used this thing on us?"

He took a sip of wine. "Because they're scared of it. You weren't here for the peace talks. I think they wish they never found the thing. Apparently, there's some ancient prophecy that says if used, the artifact will end the world."

"And now we have it."

He nodded.

I snorted. "And they're serious?"

His face grew stern. "You should have seen how quickly they agreed to terms. They couldn't stop going on about how the sky would change color, the earth would shake, fire would rain down from the heavens. Plants and animals would change—"

"And us?"

"Lots of death. Lots of sickness. Chaos." He paused and shook his head. "So long as we promised not to use the artifact, I think they would have crawled around on their hands and knees kissing our rear for the next year in order to avoid their prophecies. As it is, they agreed to become a vassal of Turine."

I doubted anyone had predicted the Geneshan Empire ever becoming a vassal. I didn't. Even though we had gained the upper hand in the war for some time, the empire had been too big for Turine to ever hope to conquer outright. At best, most hoped for peace and maybe a bit of land west of the Golgoth River.

Balak closed the lid to the artifact and the pulse of power lessened. "So now what happens to it?"

He lowered his voice. "Well, according to the terms of our agreement with the Geneshans, we'll bury the thing a hundred feet below ground and never think of it again."

Something about his tone didn't sit right with me. "That's not what's going to happen, is it?"

He drained the last of his wine and poured another glass. "No. Orders from the king said I'm to hand the artifact over to the High Mages. They're going to bring it back to Hol to study."

"And you don't agree with that?"

"Of course not. I'm not saying the artifact is going to end the world, but there's obviously something there we should leave well enough alone. But you know how the High Mages think of themselves." He sighed. "If I didn't think it would get me hung for treason, I'd bury the thing myself and never give it up to them." Now, he chuckled. "That would get under their skin."

That admission startled me. Like most, Balak hated the High Mages. They treated everyone poorly, especially soldiers, whom they called an "ugly necessity" even in public. Still, I had never heard him consider going against king's orders to defy them. Whatever he had seen or heard from the Geneshans must have convinced him they weren't lying.

He drained another cup. "Anyway, let's get off this sorcery nonsense. That's not why I wanted to see you."

"Sir?"

"You did good, Sergeant."

"Thank you, sir."

"You've been a big asset to me since the war began. Even with the treaty signed, we still have a lot of clean-up. We need to make sure the Geneshan army disbands their southern forces along our border. I was thinking of promoting you to captain to help with the process. We've got a busy year ahead of us."

A year? I'm not sure if it was because I still felt the effects of the concussion or not, but my stomach lurched and the room spun. I hadn't expected the entire army to pack up and go home, but I also knew that not everyone would be needed to wrap things up. Rumors were already circulating that a very small group of people, important figures in the victory, would be discharged over the coming days. The king felt that patriotism and goodwill would be strengthened by the heroes returning home first. I had hoped that my unit would be among that first group to leave.

"Sergeant? Do I need to call for a healer?"

I shook my head, breathing slowly. "No, sir. I'm all right. It's just . . ." I paused, knowing I needed to be careful how I phrased things. Balak was in a good mood, but his mood soured quicker than milk left out in the sun.

"It's just what?" he asked, the slightest edge coming to his voice.

"My family, sir. I—"

"Yes, your family." He cut me off, spitting the word out like a swear. "Gods be cursed, Tyrus. After all this time, I thought you had hardened up. You're telling me you'd rather go home to a bunch of strangers? At this point that's what they'll be."

Strangers? The word struck me. I had already prepared myself for things being different at first upon my return. A period of getting used to each other again, sure. But to say my family would be strangers? I couldn't believe that.

"Yes, sir. I'd like to go home more than anything else if it's all the same to you."

"Well, it's not," he snapped, glaring at me beneath those caterpillar eyebrows. "You know, with the war over the king might be interested in looking east to Noval. He has the war machine already created. Why not take advantage of it? It could mean big things for people like us."

"That sort of thing doesn't really appeal to me."

He swore, picked up a piece of paper on the table, and threw it at me. It bore the king's seal.

"What's this?" I asked.

"It's what you want. Release papers for your entire unit for playing a significant role in our victory. The king sent them through one of the High Mage's transfer portals shortly after terms with Genesha were signed."

"Then why did you ask me to stay on?"

He shrugged. "I thought I could count on you."

I balled my hands into fists, trying to control my anger. If I hadn't mentioned my family, I wondered if he would have even given me the king's orders. "I guess there's no need for you to count on me anymore now."

He looked at the papers in my hand. "I guess not. You're no longer any use to me, Tyrus. Dismissed."

Balak poured another cup of wine. My mouth hung open at his attitude. Hamath always said Balak took me for granted. I knew he did on some level, but the callousness in the way he treated me after almost a decade of service staggered me. In a matter of minutes, he went from treating me with respect to acting as though I was no better than a dog.

I left when Balak turned back to his reports, hopeful I'd never see the man again.

* * *

My anger waned as I walked back to my unit's section of camp. The general could say what he wanted, but he didn't really know me and he sure didn't know my Lasha. I knew it would take work to rekindle the relationship with my wife and develop a bond with my kids, Myra and Zadok, again. However, it would all work out. Of that I had no doubt.

The remaining members of my unit sat around a crackling fire when I arrived. Though everyone had taken their turn with a healer and looked better for it, the moods were somber, a stark contrast to the rest of the army. Though I knew part of it related to losing more than half our brothers, I could tell that something else was going on.

"What is it?" I asked.

Ira spat a wad of phlegm into the flames, sizzling against a half burnt log. "Third unit came over and broke the news to us."

"What news is that?"

"That despite all we've been through, we're sticking around after all. Balak's orders. Apparently they need us for the transition after the war."

"Did they have orders?"

"Yep. Even showed us the slip of paper," said Hamath, rubbing at the space where his pinky finger had once been.

"Did that paper happen to have our names on it?"

They exchanged looks.

"No," said Ira. "But then again, it didn't have anyone's names on it. Just said all elite units would—"

I pulled out Balak's orders and cleared my throat. "I got this paper here, signed by the king himself. We've been given our releases from the army in light of our effort and dedication in the Geneshan war."

A collective sigh ran through the group.

"What about the other units?" asked Dekar. "Lots of men besides us contributed."

"They did and I'm sure they'll get their release eventually." Though I wasn't so certain about that anymore after hearing Balak's ambitions and his talk of Noval. Honestly, a small part of me wasn't all that interested in what other units would be doing in the months and years to come. "For now, we're going home."

Ira jumped up, hollering with excitement, nearly tripping into the fire. Hamath got up with him, and the two danced like idiots. Dekar just watched with a slight smile, unable to stand because of his recovering leg injury. His concern about the others who would have to stay on seemed to fade as the reality of the situation took hold of him.

Ava alone sat expressionless. She threw a stick into the fire she had been fidgeting with and rose to her feet. She brushed by everyone in a hurry.

"Ava? Where are you—"

Hamath grabbed me by the arm. "Let her be. You know she ain't happy unless she's got a reason to be upset." He shoved a drink into my hand. "C'mon, let's celebrate."

Ava disappeared behind a supply wagon filled with sacks of flour.

I looked back to Hamath. "All right. Just one. Then I'll go talk to her."

* * *

One drink turned into two. Two to three. And so on. I managed to get hold of myself after five. All that drinking did nothing to speed along the healing of a head injury. It also didn't help that I had never been able to hold my liquor well.

I snuck away before Hamath handed me another drink so I could look for Ava. I took it slow getting through camp, unable to tell if the alcohol or the concussion was the cause for my unsteadiness.

Ava leaned against a small fence that enclosed the cavalry horses. She had a leg propped up on the fence while petting one of the creatures.

Since our childhood, Ava gravitated toward horses when she needed time to think, relax, or just to be alone. I never understood it. She hated riding the animals, and the feeling toward her was mutual. She broke an arm once when one of the beasts threw her from its back. Face-to-face however, it seemed neither could get enough of the other.

The horse she petted moved away as I approached, turning its nose up at me for intruding. Unlike my sister, my relationship with the animals was strictly business.

"Took you long enough to come after me," she said without facing me.

I leaned on the fence next to her. "Thought I'd give you some time to think."

"Don't lie to me. I can smell the ale on you, big brother."

I snorted. "All right. You got me. So, I guess you're worried about what's going to happen with you and the High Mages? I was thinking we could go see them together. Just let me do the talking and make sure you look ashamed of yourself. You don't even have to mean it."

"You mean how we used to handle Pa?"

"Why not? No High Mage can intimidate me as much as the old man's stare used to."

She laughed. "That's true. But that's not going to be necessary."

I cocked my head.

"I spoke to them already. Apologized for what happened with the recruit and everything. They actually seemed to think I meant it."

I started. "Seriously? You apologized?"

"It was the only way that I knew they would listen to what I had to say."

"Oh?"

She faced me wearing a nervous expression. Though she was a woman grown, right then she reminded me of the little girl I used to play in the mud with.

"I asked for them to take me on as an apprentice." She paused, thin lips pressed together as she let her words sink in. "They accepted me much quicker than I thought they would. I'm honestly not sure if I even needed to apologize first. I wish I would have known that because I wouldn't have bothered with it. They heard all the details about how we killed the Geneshan Master Sorcerer. Apparently, they couldn't ignore my talents any longer, regardless of my pissy attitude. Their words, not mine. I leave with them tomorrow for Hol."

Hol, Turine's capital, where both the king and the Council of High Mages reside, held a quarter of the nation's population. It had been a dream of ours as kids to visit the place one day. I don't think either of us had ever expected to really make it there.

"What about home? Didn't you hear what I said? We can leave."

"I'm not deaf."

"I don't understand. We've been talking about returning to Denu Creek nearly every day since we were forced into the army."

She shook her head. "No. You talked about going home. I just listened. Personally, I'd rather this war go on for another ten years if it meant I didn't have to go back."

I blinked. "I can't believe I just heard that."

"Seriously? Ignore the alcohol and clear your head, big brother. The memories of our youth aren't exactly fond ones. At least not the ones outside of our family. How many times did I get picked on? How many times did you get into fights trying to protect me? Gods, even after my talent manifested, it didn't get any better. Sure, no one hit me or made fun of me to my face, but I still saw the looks cast my way. I noticed how the girls excluded me from their little get togethers while the boys acted like I was some kind of freak. I don't want to return to that. And despite Ma and Pa saying it would get better when we all got older, it never did."

"But what about Lasha and the kids? Don't you want to know your niece and nephew?"

Ava smiled. "Lasha is going to be too busy making up for lost time with her husband to worry about me. And as far as Myra and Zadok go, they'll both be better off seeing me through your rose-colored eyes than to learn the truth face-to-face."

I shook my head, unable to believe what I was hearing.

However, what she said did make sense.

Life had been hard for her, far more than for me. Part of it had been her personality, but most of it had related to things outside of her control, like sorcery. In a small town like Denu Creek, folks acted as if you were cursed to have a talent for such things. On the other hand, my resistance made some people think I had been blessed by the very gods who cursed Ava as a way to keep my wild sister under control.

"You know they'll make you wear robes," I said, gesturing to her leathers.

Unlike every other mage, Ava refused to wear the traditional garb associated with one of talent. She thought the attire looked ridiculous unless you were an old man pushing a hundred. I agreed, but still liked to give her a hard time about it.

She scowled. "We'll see about that."

"What about me?" I asked, serious once more.

"What about you?"

"Are we going to see each other again?"

She chuckled. "I'm not dead. You can come to Hol any time to visit me. I'd love to show you around. You can even bring the family if you aren't sick of them after a month of being home."

A tight smile came to my lips as I tried to hide my sadness. I could tell by the look on her face that we both knew that wouldn't happen. After a month, I'd be trying to get settled back into a routine at the farm, catching up on all that had happened from our uncle who I had tasked to help Lasha out while we were gone. Once I fell back into that routine, the chances of me leaving for weeks on end would be slim.

"Yeah, that's not a bad idea," I said, lying.

It didn't make me feel any better, but maybe it did for her.

* * *

Ava and I parted a short while later when a High Mage—one of her new tutors, I presumed—interrupted us for something that he considered important. A part of me wanted to slam my fist into his face for not refusing my sister's request to go to Hol. But I refrained. Ava and I weren't children anymore, and I had to let her make her own decisions. I needed to respect her decision, regardless of how much it hurt to do so.

The weight of my conversation with Ava had one positive in that it sobered me up.

Losing her. Losing half my unit. Winning the war. Winning my freedom. With everything that had happened, I felt as emotionally drained as I did physically fatigued. Even still, I knew sleep wouldn't come any time soon so I walked around camp again.

Like a moth to a candle, I drifted toward blazing bonfires off in the distance, careful not to get too close to them. The bonfires were not fueled by wood, but by mounds of flesh. No officer wanted death to linger so close to their army lest all the disease that came with it spread among the survivors.

I stopped fifty yards upwind from the hellish inferno, near a pile of armor and weapons stripped from the corpses. Men stoked the flames licking at the naked bodies.

If there had ever been a sight to damage the allure of war, this was it.

"Gods, you left us for this?"

I turned at the sound of Hamath's voice.

"No. Though it smells better here than downwind of your feet."

He laughed. "Talked to Ava, then?"

I nodded. "She's moving on to Hol. The High Mages are taking her on as an apprentice. Our successful mission really impressed them."

"I'm sorry. Really."

"Thanks."

We didn't say much else for some time, watching body after body smolder and burn.

"Crazy, isn't it?" I asked.

"What is?"

I gestured. "All of this. How many soldiers will be forgotten? One turn of the blade or stab of an arrow separates the living from the dead. They could have been here watching our bodies dumped onto the fire, rather than the other way around."

"Well, I'm glad it isn't like that."

"Yeah, me too. Makes me feel guilty for admitting it though."

"Every soldier feels that way."

"Maybe. It's just sad that a hundred years from now, no one is likely to remember what they died for. Gods, how many people are likely to forget in ten years? One year? Molak be cursed, less than that?"

"I won't forget them. That's for sure," said Hamath.

"Me either."

Hamath turned, slapping me in the arm. "All right, enough of this. We've got all the time in the world to mourn. Let's get back to the others and celebrate. We're going home, and we'll be treated as heroes.

What better way to honor those soldiers who died than enjoying all the accolades for them."

I chuckled as we turned and started walking away. "Heroes? You really don't believe that do you?"

"Trust me."

CHAPTER 4

The next morning I saw Ava off.

I stood in the middle of camp near the officers' tents with Ira, Dekar, and Hamath. They had already wished Ava good luck, and said their farewells. Though Ava could be a hard person to get along with at times, I could tell they'd all miss her. Even Ira. You didn't fight alongside someone for ten years without growing close in some way.

Ava waited for the transfer portal a step ahead of me, nervously shifting from foot to foot.

Further away, High Mages guarded prisoners of war, most of which wore the robes of Geneshan sorcerers. The leader of the High Mages, someone's whose name I couldn't pronounce, carried the wooden box that held the Geneshan artifact under his arm.

The Geneshan sorcerers looked nauseous just being in the box's vicinity. Thinking on my conversation with Balak, it appeared the Geneshans believed the artifact was something to fear.

Loud, rapid popping filled the air. A blue and white flash of radiance followed. It coalesced into an oval of bright light that hung a few inches above the ground.

I've seen dozens of transfer portals over the years and they never ceased to fill me with a sense of awe.

According to Ava, portals were a handy method of travel, though not safe enough to use in battle. After a few disastrous attempts at transferring units close to enemy targets, the mode of transportation had been relegated to delivering messages to Hol to keep the king abreast on the war while he spent his time doing whatever it was kings did.

She faced me, looking nervous. "I guess this is it," she said.

"No guessing about it," I said.

Neither of us knew how to say good-bye. The knowledge that we'd likely never see each other again left us formal and stiff.

"Take care of yourself, Big Brother."

"You too. And be careful."

Apparently, being close wasn't a guarantee of saying what you felt.

My sister followed the High Mages leading the prisoners through the transfer portal.

Ava stood out among the group, but not because she was one of only three women, but because she alone disdained the robes. She wore instead, of course, her black leathers. I wondered how long it would take for them to force a change in her wardrobe. The corners of my mouth turned up as I thought of that confrontation. The High Mages would rue the day they had agreed to apprentice my sister.

Ava paused at the entrance to the portal and spun toward me. I gave her a wave. She smiled, offered a slight nod, and then was gone.

"That was maybe one of the worst good-byes I've ever seen in my life, Ty," Ira said behind me. "Ow!" he added as Dekar cuffed him.

I snorted. "It was pretty bad, wasn't it? Good thing she and I don't need to say much. We know how things stand between us."

And that was true. Granted, that didn't stop me from wishing I had actually said the hundred things running through my mind. Most of all, I wished I had told her how proud I was.

It took some effort not to start bawling like a little girl when the portal closed. I hadn't ever shed a tear in my life except when it came to family. Whether it was the happiness of watching Lasha give birth to our children or the sadness of my parents passing, family tugged at my heart the most. It really affected me to see the person who knew me better than anyone else in the world leave.

* * *

We hung around camp another three days before we were ready to depart.

Those three days took longer to pass than the nearly ten years I had spent in the army. I must have played a thousand hands of cards,

50

lost nearly all my money twice over, and still managed to come out a few coins ahead in the end.

Finally, we set out at dawn on the fourth day.

Most soldiers sent us off with a smile and a wave despite the gods' forsaken hour, believing their turn would come around soon enough. Others more cynical stared with jealous eyes and sneers. The faces of the latter lingered with me the most as I recalled Balak's mention of pursuing Noval after Genesha had been cleaned up.

Though some of the army would be allowed to return home in the coming months, many seemed destined to suffer through another conflict. If successful, I wondered when Balak and the king would finally call it quits, to allow life in Turine to return to normal.

Somehow, I didn't think they ever would. They had tasted success and had become greedy. War just might be the new norm.

Hamath and I stared at the Turine camp from the back of a rolling wagon, feet dangling over the road. Soldiers sat behind us, crammed between barrels of salted pork and oats. Other wagons were loaded similarly.

None of us said a word until long after the army faded from sight. If it wasn't for the occasional grunt when the wagons hit a hole in the old roads, you'd think we were all asleep.

I think we were just taking time to process the return home.

We began talking about things weighing on our mind, each glad they weren't alone in their thoughts. How many more soldiers would never return home? And why did we deserve to leave when so many others were forced to stay behind?

* * *

By evening, the depressive mood shifted to celebratory. We were on our way home.

A clear and starry night hung over us as we finished prepping our camp for the night. We formed a circle with the wagons and tethered the mounts just outside of it to graze on tall grass. Sentries patrolled the perimeter with loaded crossbows.

The war was over and we were happy, but old habits died hard. The likelihood of any bandits brave enough to try their hand at a few dozen veterans was slim, but that didn't mean we wouldn't prepare for such a scenario. You didn't stay alive as long as we all had by taking things for granted.

I took my place in the chow line, behind Hamath. I hadn't realized just how hungry I was until I caught a whiff of the night's stew. My stomach growled.

Hamath turned. "Lasha a good cook?"

"Why you want to know?"

He shrugged. "Just curious. I can count on one hand the number of meals we've had over the last decade that've been prepared by someone outside of the army. Thought it might be something you'd look forward to."

"I guess you're right. The last time was what? Two and half years ago?"

"Yeah. It was when we spent a couple weeks in that city near the battle of Urtok's Ridge. What was it called? After all this time, the places are starting to run together."

"Awarta."

"Yeah, Awarta. I liked it there."

"Really? Don't you remember all the trouble we had with them trying to poison us?"

"I remember. But outside of the poison, the food was good."

I shook my head, chuckling. "I guess."

"Too bad we razed the place when we left," said Hamath. "Balak's never been the sort of person you want to upset."

"That might be one of the only times I ever questioned if what we were doing was the right thing."

"What do you mean? The Geneshans invaded us, remember?"

"Yeah, but to kill the women and children too?" I whispered. "I still hear their screams sometimes when I close my eyes at night, and I wasn't even the one to set the houses to flame."

We shuffled up the line in silence. I noticed the conversations around us had faded and heads were down. Apparently, I had been too loud. The smell of the stew no longer had the appeal of a few moments ago, but I knew better than to step out of line. In the army, you ate anytime you could. Otherwise, you might regret the missed opportunity later.

Conversations eventually started back up again, and I managed to push away my own morose thoughts.

"Lasha's a great cook by the way," I managed to say while watching the steaming black cauldron.

Hamath snorted. "Somehow I knew you'd say that. That woman can do no wrong in your eyes."

I smiled. "You're right about that." I paused. "What about Bilhah?"

Hamath tensed. "Hmm?"

Bilhah was Hamath's lady friend he left behind before the war started. "Is she a good cook?"

"Yeah. Pretty good," he replied quickly.

I grunted, deciding not to push. Over the years Hamath had talked less and less about Bilhah. A part of me wanted to ask why. Another part respected his privacy.

The soldier stuck cooking the meal for the night carefully scooped a heaping ladle full of stew into our wooden bowls. His shirt left more than enough evidence of how many times he had hurried his efforts before—brown and yellow stains decorating the front.

I examined the bowl's contents. A bit of onion, some potato, a piece of carrot, and even a few pieces of meat. Not bad. In fact, better than most of the meals I'd had of late. I grabbed a hard biscuit from the sack next to the stew pot and followed Hamath to a small fire. Ira and Dekar were already there, the former using his fingers to get the last bit of food out of his bowl, the latter taking his time with each spoonful.

Ira looked up at us as we took our place around the fire. "What's the word, Ty?"

I caught a glimpse of his half-missing ear. Though it looked better than it once did, the image was not a pretty one. "Huh?"

"Where are we heading first? I saw you talking to Captain Nehab earlier. Dekar thinks it's going to be Damanhur. I told him to get his head out his rear. It's gotta be Edema."

I raised an eyebrow. "Why Edema?"

"Because it's bigger and along all the major trade routes. It's filled with all sorts of wonders, you know. I was mad we didn't pass through there on the way to Genesha."

I nodded to Dekar. "Why Damanhur?"

He swallowed his food. "Opposite reasons. It's smaller, so the men are less likely to get into trouble and waste all their coin. Plus, trade routes mean nothing to us now. We're returning home. Damanhur is a shorter distance from here too. We go to Edema, we'd add a day to our journey."

"Dekar's got it," I said. "And for all the reasons he listed."

"What?" Ira swore. "Who cares about a day when we could have all that fun?"

I gestured toward Captain Nehab. He sat with his back to a tree, out of earshot, concentrating on eating his stew without dirtying up the thick mustache dominating his face. "The captain does, and Balak put him in charge of seeing us home." I paused. "I think it's the right call."

"Me too," said Dekar.

"You would," said Ira, giving his brother a look.

Dekar frowned. "The last thing I want to worry about is bailing you out of trouble again."

"You act like that happens all the time."

Dekar eyed his brother.

"All right. Fine," said Ira, a sour look on his face. "The problem is that none of you really know how to live. Well, except maybe Hamath."

Hamath choked. "I'm not sure if I should take that as a compliment coming from you."

Dekar chuckled at that.

Ira complained and grumbled a bit more as the rest of us finished our meals.

A few others joined us. It didn't take long for Ira to pull out a couple decks of cards. It took even less time before most of us had doubled our money. Some might accuse us of cheating and most of the time they'd be right. But not then. The truth was that we had known each other for so long that we knew what the other person would play without even seeing the cards in their hand. If that gave us an advantage over other units not as close as ours, then so be it.

CHAPTER 5

Burned out farmhouses and blackened fields greeted us as we traveled. Here and there small shoots of grass, mostly weeds, pushed through the scorched earth. Burning a land with sorcery lengthened the time it needed to recover from a passing army.

The Geneshan Empire had set fire to their own lands in order to slow us down. The tactic began back when the war had shifted in our favor. Though the Geneshan strategy seemed cruel to the peasants, it did make supplying our forces that much more difficult.

It had been more than a year since we last passed through the area. The homesteads stood just as vacant as they had then. Landowners must have started life anew somewhere else rather than chance another army destroying their livelihood all over again.

We crossed a bridge spanning the narrowest part of the Golgoth River. I remember watching its construction after the Geneshan sorcerers blew apart the original structure in hasty retreat. Splinters of wood and broken stone had rained down over a mile in every direction. The heat from such power had boiled all of the fish alive and reduced the water level by half.

The meal the cooks came up with that night had been one for the ages.

Shortly after crossing the Golgoth River, we came across one of the bleakest reminders of war. Worse in my mind than the seared farmsteads.

A sigh passed through my lips.

"What is it?" asked Hamath.

I nodded toward a high mound of dirt a hundred paces from the side of the road. Several others varying in height and width stood near it. I knew from experience that beneath the earth lay the bones and ash of dead soldiers.

Hamath spat. "It's a shame how we ended up mixing the bodies."

"What do you mean?"

"Burying the Geneshans with our own."

"Geneshan bodies bring disease just like ours. We couldn't be prejudiced about getting rid of the things."

"I understand the practical reasons. Just doesn't seem right having them all intermingled like that. I can't see that being a peaceable way for anyone to spend an eternity. Possibly staring at the man who ran you through with nothing you can do to change it." He paused. "Makes you wonder if they're still fighting each other in whatever afterlife they went to."

I kept quiet. Hamath was one of those who vehemently believed in an afterlife. I had too in my youth. He and I had gone around and around on the religious discussion before. I wasn't in the mood to do it again.

It took over a week to cross the Geneshan lands we had conquered. We traveled a few more days after that before coming upon the Turine city of Damanhur. We could have made better time, but Captain Nehab was a cautious man. He kept a slow pace in case of Geneshan holdovers hiding in the countryside who either hadn't heard about the war ending, or simply didn't care.

I was as antsy as anyone else to get home to my family, but I saw the wisdom in his reasoning and was quick to speak up at the night fires when men would get to grumbling about the pace.

Damanhur rose up out of flat terrain, littered with patches of thick, squat oaks. Ira was quick to remind us that the city lacked the grandeur of Edema. Low walls, barely the height of a man, encircled Damanhur. Two round watchtowers, ten feet higher than the wall, stood near the gate, the only two protecting the entire city. Those were just two of a dozen noticeable examples of the poor defensive design the city offered.

I couldn't help but think that if the Geneshans had wanted to attack the place in the early years of the war when they held the advantage, Damanhur would have fallen in minutes. A quick glance about told me I was the only one who even cared. After more than a week on the back of a hard wagon, being jarred constantly, all anyone really wanted was a night of letting loose.

Captain Nehab managed to maintain discipline long enough to tie down the wagons on the city's outskirts and ensure the horses were tended. Men quickly began to sneak off, and he had no choice but to just dismiss everyone. Soldiers peeled away before Nehab finished the command. He tried calling out a curfew, but no one heard it. Most people found it hard to listen with their backs turned and feet propelling them swiftly away from the person speaking.

I never did find out what time he had set for curfew.

* * *

Early in the war, my unit once received a two-day leave. One of my men took off on his own without waiting for the rest of us. I was young and thought nothing of it. The town had looked relatively peaceful, so I figured I'd let the man have a bit of time to himself. All of us needed moments of isolation lest we kill each other before ever reaching Genesha.

A few hours later a corporal had reported my man's body hacked and slashed in an alley behind a local bar. The rest of my unit spent half the night beating information out of the patrons of the tavern until we learned what had happened. Turned out our man had a good night at dice and the loser was bitter about it. He and two friends wanted their money back. Our man refused. His stubbornness got him killed. We found the three responsible before the crack of dawn and made sure they suffered a fate to rival our mate's. It was only the right thing to do.

Balak never came down on us despite the story making its way throughout the army. I think he agreed with the way we handled the problem, and, more importantly, understood we learned our lesson. Especially me. I only wish we could have learned it one day sooner.

After that night no one in my unit traveled in parties of less than three. So while many took off on their own into Damanhur, we four stayed together.

"Well, Tyrus, what's on the agenda for tonight?" asked Hamath.

"I don't know. I hadn't given it much thought. Why don't one of you pick something?" I said, stepping over a puddle.

Damanhur did not boast the sophisticated drainage system one might find in the larger cities of Turine. Therefore, water pooled near the curb, capturing all sorts of bugs, rotten food, and Molak knows what else.

"We always pick where we're going," said Ira. "It'd be nice if you showed a preference for once when we're on leave."

"I did once. And none of you ever let me live it down."

Hamath spat. "We didn't think you'd want to check out the advances in plow design at the local blacksmith."

Ira snorted. "That Ty sure knows how to have fun." Sarcasm dripped from his voice.

"And yet you want me to choose again."

"Thought you might do better this time."

"Doubtful. Farming is still in my blood. Why don't you ever ask Dekar for his opinion?"

Ira laughed louder. "He's worse than you. We'd probably end up at some local merchant's stand looking through books or something."

Dekar shrugged.

I sighed. "Just pick the whorehouse that best suits your interest since I know that's what you and Hamath want anyway. My only stipulation is that it has to have a decent tavern attached so Dekar and I have something to do to pass the time."

"Why Ty," said Ira, exaggerating his words. "that sounds like a marvelous idea." He wore a big smile. "Don't you agree, Hamath?"

"I do agree," Hamath said, mimicking Ira's tone. "I wish I had thought of it myself actually. I guess that's why he's Sergeant and not us."

I rolled my eyes, refusing to encourage them.

Hamath and Ira took the lead as we continued our trek, looking for the ideal place to spend their coin.

Damanhur wasn't as large as some of the cities near the center of Turine, or as grand as Hol or Edema in its majesty. However, it did dwarf my hometown in both size and appearance. Denu Creek boasted over a hundred people if you included those who made their home in the land around it which most people did.

The largest building in Denu Creek was the house on a plantation owned by the Jareb family, an eclectic bunch who had named every one of their first sons Jareb for as far back as anyone could remember. The family boasted many things that others could not. Originality wasn't among them.

The Jareb nearest my age had been a real piece of work growing up. He made life miserable for Ava until her talents manifested. That got him off her back fast. Most everyone in town saw the younger Jareb through the reputation of his father who had a heart of gold. Just to prove the saying 'like father, like son' isn't always what it's cracked up to be.

In Damanhur, the largest building, a circular tower, made the Jareb plantation look like a butcher's shop. It stood at the town's center, seven stories high, and housed the City Watch. Seeing that the artisans were capable of constructing something of substantial size made me wonder even more why the local government hadn't employed those same workers to raise the height of the city's walls.

I guess our army's relative success over the last couple of years made them feel safe enough.

Inns three and four stories high took up residence near the tower. I imagined it was pretty convenient to have the watch next door whenever rowdy customers refused to pay their bills or start trouble.

Ira and Hamath passed the inns without a second look. None of the places they sought would be located so close to the watch.

Though every city, town, and hamlet boasted whorehouses of their own, most residents liked to pretend they didn't exist. These were the same citizens who hated to admit that the bulk of their community's taxes came from those same appalling establishments, without which they wouldn't have the funds necessary to keep the town running.

I had seen a similar attitude before in a town bordering Denu Creek.

Ifrane had been experiencing a major population influx, growing at an unheard of rate in the area I'm from. Most linked the surge in growth to the quality of women brought in from foreign lands to populate their bathhouses. The exotic nature of such women made the town attractive to many young men from the surrounding areas.

Things were looking up for Ifrane until a priest of Quan showed up.

Quan was a minor god in Turine's pantheon, one that's known for his hard line on pleasure. The details of what the followers of Quan believed were long and often contradictory. From my understanding, if something brought you pleasure, it probably displeased Quan.

The priest somehow managed to make that miserable life of restraint appealing, and converted a slew of people to his faith. As a result, the town passed an ordinance that made prostitution illegal. Within a year, Ifrane existed only in people's memories. Those who converted to Quan grew alienated with him after seeing the lack of benefits from their commitment. People moved away in droves. Denu Creek's population grew a fifth in size because of the exodus.

A smile formed on my face as I recalled the day that priest tried spreading his philosophy in our town.

The mayor didn't even have to get involved. A dozen of the town's more prosperous business owners turned him away half a mile outside the city's limits. No one wanted to be the next Ifrane.

"Hey, Tyrus," whispered Dekar.

I blinked. We had been walking through the city, but I was too lost in myself to even realize where we were. I needed to be more careful. That sort of thing could get a stranger in trouble. "Hmm?"

"You notice anything funny about the people on the streets, or am I just imagining things?"

"What do you mean?"

"None of them seem too happy about us being here. I swear that old woman we just passed gave me the Panesh."

The Panesh was a curse used by the cult of Raza out of Vanak. It's pretty heavy stuff according to the cult's followers and therefore used sparingly, only against those they truly hate. Not only do they believe the curse caused anyone who received it the worst kind of harm, but their misfortunes followed them into the next life.

Boils, sores, and loss of bodily functions are rumored to be just a few of the curse's tamer symptoms.

I looked back over my shoulder at the woman in question. The bent figure had stopped under an eave lit by torchlight. On her toes she probably stood five feet, but the glare she cast made her seem much larger. I gave her a wink just to see what she would do. She raised thumb, middle finger, and pinky on her left hand, then turned and shuffled off.

"Well, you were right about the old woman," I said to Dekar. "She gave the Panesh to me too."

"I guess we'll both be damned together then."

I chuckled. "It's good to know I'll have company."

"That it is."

I eyed another passerby, an old man walking with a cane in one hand, a brown package in the other. His look matched that of the old woman. They almost looked related. If his hands hadn't been full I bet he also would have thrown the Panesh our way. "I think you might be on to something, Dekar."

"Why though?" he asked. "I'd expect those looks if we were still in Genesha, but not in Turine."

"You got me."

"It's likely they just haven't seen anyone as ugly as you walk their streets before," said Ira up ahead, chuckling. "Wondering if they're experiencing a sudden infestation of ogres."

Dekar glared daggers at his brother's back. He was ready to say something when Hamath stopped at the intersection.

"Here we go, fellas."

"Bout time," said Ira. "Who ever thought of making their whorehouses so hard to find?"

I came up behind them and peered down the side street. It bustled with life we hadn't seen down the main road. "Seems the locals know where to find it."

"Probably hiding all the women for themselves," mumbled Ira.

Dekar grunted. "Or it could be the two people leading us had no idea where they were going." He pointed toward a couple of men from the army as they exited one of the establishments and entered another.

Ira opened his mouth to respond but Hamath cuffed him on the arm. "C'mon. The important thing is we're here now."

As much of a hurry as those two had seemed to be in, I thought they would have entered the first place they came upon. Nope. They were adamant in choosing the right place to spend their money.

We walked up and down the street twice, admiring the women at each business' entrance. The women wore low cut gowns with skirts up high, exposing all but the bottom half of their breasts and the top few inches of leg. They called out every seduction imaginable to entice us to spend our coin with them.

We stuck our heads into a few of those places, but Hamath and Ira refused to rush their decision.

Eventually, Hamath and Ira selected a house called The Rose which Ira agreed with. They grabbed two of the five women congregating near the entrance. Ira chose a long-legged woman with short blonde hair and fair skin. Hamath selected the most exotic of the group, a short, brown-skinned woman with charcoal hair. Her features reminded me of Lasha. Though I didn't ask, I expected that like my wife, she was from one of the kingdoms in the far south.

Hamath and Ira hurried upstairs without looking back. The other three women did their best to persuade me and Dekar to choose one of them for ourselves, but neither of us were interested in doing more than looking. We were both anomalies in that not only did we have wives waiting for us, but we also wanted to remain faithful to them. The girls weren't buying it and pushed all the harder. We finally slipped by them when some interested locals flashed their coin.

Dekar led the way to the bar, past a couple dozen tables and chairs half-filled with local patrons. We took seats on a couple of stools closest to the stairs. I bought the first round of ale.

Several hours and many drinks later, Dekar and I sat in our same spots, hunched over and nursing our mugs.

"You ever thought of taking one upstairs before?" I asked, nodding toward a redhead sitting off in the corner, one leg propped up on a chair in what I guessed was her way of inviting the next customer. She gave me a wink. I looked away before she did anything more.

"Of course," said Dekar without ever turning toward the woman. "Who doesn't?"

"What stops you from doing it?"

He shrugged. "Lots of things." He took a sip of his ale.

"I'm listening."

"Well, love for one. Ira might think I'm nuts for having settled down so young, but I love Adwa. Thankfully, since we got married so young she'll still be able to rear children when I get back. It'll be nice to start a family."

I agreed on the point of love. "What else?"

"Guilt is another. Sure Adwa would have no way of knowing if I took that redhead upstairs. Ira wouldn't tell her. He's tried to tell me that it's likely she'll think I've done something like that anyway so why not just do it and have the fun to go along with the grief." He shrugged. "Maybe she does think that. But that doesn't make it right. Whether she ever finds out or not doesn't matter. I'd know I did her wrong and that's enough of a reason for me not to do it. I know you're not religious, but I said my vows before Lavi and I aim to keep them."

A burst of laughter erupted from behind. I glanced over my shoulder to its origin. Nothing of significance. Just a few friends swapping jokes. One of the men caught me looking and scowled. I smiled to let him know I had no issues with him. He looked away, whispered something to one of his friends, then got up and left. Potential confrontation averted, I turned back around and took a sip.

"What about you?" he asked.

"Mostly the same reasons as you. You're right though, I don't care about the gods. I don't care about Lavi, even though I said my vows before her. But I believe in what the vows stood for. I love Lasha too much to hurt her like that." I paused. "There is something else though."

"What's that?"

"I don't want to be like Hamath."

He started in surprise. "I don't follow."

"Ira likes his women, but really Ira's no different than any other solider. Gods, any other man for that matter. Hamath though . . . he's almost obsessed."

Dekar grunted. "I hadn't thought of that, but you're right. He wasn't always that way. He barely ever visited a whore during those first couple years."

"True, but the more he did, the more he had to go back. Half the time I wonder if it's satisfying an addiction more than seeking enjoyment."

Dekar grunted. "Well, as long as he's been up there, that's quite the addiction."

"Your brother's been up there just as long."

"Yeah, but knowing Ira, the poor fool had his fun for maybe a good five minutes and then fell asleep."

I laughed and finished the rest of my ale.

Another drink later, head feeling lighter, I looked over to Dekar. "Should we go check on them?"

He eyed his mug. "I'll go." He downed the rest of its contents. "You might as well finish what you got."

I stared at the frothy liquid "I wonder if it's worth it to. Head's going to be killing me come morning as it is."

He stood. "It probably will either way. You never could hold your alcohol. Be careful standing up." Dekar slapped me on the shoulder and went upstairs.

I made quick work of the remaining ale, slapped money down on the bar, and rose to my feet. The room spun a bit, but a deep breath slowed it considerably.

Then it hit me. At some point, and I couldn't say when, the background noise had faded to nothing and the room had gone quiet in the sort of way that happens only when something ugly is about to go down. Blasted alcohol.

A sudden fear pushed aside most of my drunkenness.

My left arm grabbed the bar, which I used to steady myself as I spun around, right hand moving to the hilt of my sword. The entire room had cleared out. Six men approached, passing between the empty tables in the common area. Four carried clubs of various shapes and sizes. Two others held old swords.

Not a good sign of things to come.

They slowed when I faced them, coming to a stop four strides away. It would be tricky trying to draw my sword in such a tight space while inebriated. Still, I openly left my hand on the hilt. They didn't need to know my concerns.

"Is there someone you're looking for," I asked, putting as much grit into my voice as I could manage given the ale sloshing around in my gut. I learned a long time ago that a confident man can bluff his way out of a lot of situations he might find himself in. Unfortunately, I never had put that theory to the test when facing six-to-one odds.

"You," said the man in front. I took him for the leader in part because he spoke first, but also because he carried himself like a man in charge. I guessed him to be a few inches over six feet, which meant he had me by at least three. What he had over me in height he lacked in weight. A decade of marching, digging, chopping, and fighting kept me in better shape than most.

"Me? I don't know you." I made an exaggerated effort to scan the faces of the others behind him. "Or your friends."

"Well, we know you, or at least your type."

"I doubt that. Because if you did, you'd turn back around and hit the streets."

The man laughed. "You're pretty cocky for a drunk."

"Especially for one without any friends," said another in the back.

Everyone but me found that funny. I kept wondering what was taking Dekar so long to get downstairs.

"My friends should be back any moment," I said, hoping that was the case.

A series of loud crashes intermingled with the screams of women came from upstairs. Sounds of wood splintering preceded glass shattering. Three heavy thuds outside followed.

The leader of the six chuckled. "Not anymore. That would be your friends taking a trip out of the third story windows."

I chose not to respond so as not to betray my emotions. Inwardly, I cursed every god I could think of on the inside. When I finished with that, I began cursing myself for drinking so much.

Even sober, taking down all six would have been a heck of a challenge, but with luck, possible. Drunk? No way.

My jaw clenched. I knew better than to let my guard down so completely. Since I was back in Turine, I had allowed myself to get comfortable because I was back on Turine soil.

The leader started to take a step forward when footsteps pounded the stairs to my right. Dekar came running down, sword drawn. Hamath followed, half-dressed. Ira brought up the rear, still wiping the sleep from his eyes. They all breathed heavily, looking as though they had been in a fight.

Hamath spat. "Told you there were likely more."

I took advantage of the distraction and drew my sword. Armed and with three friends at my side, I liked the odds much better.

"Count 'em out, Ty." said Ira. "Idiots woke me up."

A strategy we often employed in certain situations was numbering each of the individuals standing against us, always starting from the left. A person, usually me, assigned who should take which numbered men. The tactic gave everyone a good starting point on the fly.

"Wait." I looked at the leader of the six, who appeared less sure of himself. Something the man said earlier nagged at me. I took a chance to see if he'd talk. "You said you knew my type. What does that mean?"

"We heard the war is over."

"So?"

"So, that means soldiers who haven't been around for years are going to come home and try to take our jobs."

"We aren't settling here. We're just passing through."

"Maybe so, but there'll be others who think they can just pick up the lives they once had before like nothing has changed. Well, a lot has changed and we don't want people like you screwing up what we've got. We've heard all the stories about the war."

The men behind him grunted and nodded in agreement.

I wasn't sure what that meant, but decided not to take the conversation in that direction. I chose to come at him from a different angle, hoping he might see things from our perspective.

"You know, most of us didn't volunteer for the army. The king pressed us into service. And now that the war is over all we want is to get back home."

"And disrupt everyone's lives by pushing yourself back into them."

"That's not fair."

"I don't care what's fair. Just like I don't care if you volunteered or not. Makes no difference to me how you joined," said the man shrugging.

"You pieces of garbage," Hamath muttered.

"Count 'em out, Ty," said Ira, louder than before.

I swore. "Dekar, one and two. Hamath, four. Ira, five and six. I got three."

"You sure about three?" asked Dekar. "I can take three and two, and give you one."

"I'm fine," I said. Three, meant I'd be taking the leader. Sober, Dekar wouldn't have asked me if I was sure about him. He didn't know how focused I had become in spite of the alcohol.

The group had the same reaction as most did when I counted. Pure confusion followed by sudden realization that things were about to get ugly. The leader picked things up first. He raised his sword with both hands, yelled, and charged right at me.

He closed the distance between us faster than I had expected him to. He swung wildly, but with plenty force. Chaos erupted all around me. A chair sailed across my vision. Somewhere, the distinct sound of a table breaking resonated. Groans, moans, and whimpers followed as bones crunched.

I parried several of my opponent's blows while turning him away from the others and giving me more room to maneuver.

Clear of the fallen stools at my feet, I made my move. Rather than parry his next clumsy strike, I side-stepped it. My sword came up against his unprotected lower arms, cutting into the flesh and stopping at bone. He let out a wail and lost his sword. Blood spurted from his forearms. He fell to his knees, tendons severed and hands unable to put pressure on the pulsing wounds. I shook my head, angry that the idiot had forced me to act. The man collapsed to the floor, losing consciousness from loss of blood. He'd be dead within moments.

I swore, killing my own countrymen had not been on the list of things I expected after being discharged.

The room had grown quiet with the exception of heavy breathing and a gurgling whimper. A sword silenced the whimper. I looked up as Ira withdrew his blade.

"Everyone all right?" I asked.

"I'm good," said Ira.

"Fine," said Dekar.

"Idiot got lucky and sliced my arm, but I'll live," said Hamath, tying a makeshift bandage around his upper arm.

"Based on some of the looks we got coming in, we're probably not the only ones who were attacked," said Dekar as he helped Hamath with the bandage.

"Probably not," I admitted, staring down at the man who had charged me. Blood spilled from his arms, pooling on the floor. "A city this big has got to have more than these idiots in it."

Ira said a few choice words. "So much for a night of fun."

As if on cue, angry shouts erupted from the streets. I recognized several of the voices.

"Molak be cursed," I whispered. "Let's go."

We rushed outside. Steel upon steel rang out.

Pandemonium had hit the streets.

Over a hundred of Damanhur's citizens had armed themselves with anything they could find, blunt or sharp. Not the whole city by any means, but a mob nonetheless.

It appeared the soldiers not caught literally with their pants down by the locals had already come together, coalescing as a unit at the entrance of a narrow alley. Many held overturned tabletops like shields to push against the frothing mass.

Smart man, whoever had made that decision.

Pitchforks stabbed like spears, branding irons swung like swords, and cast-iron skillets clubbed like maces. The Damanhur citizens attacked with such ferocity, many of their own fell injured by the carelessness of the person next to them.

"Well, we're not flanking that with only four of us," said Hamath.

"We could just head back to the wagons while no one's paying attention," offered Ira.

He spoke with such calmness it made me realize how empty the rest of the street had become.

Dekar cuffed him.

"I was only joking," muttered Ira.

"We need to draw them away from the alley," I said.

"And what would be the point of that?" asked Hamath.

"To have them chase us. It's far easier for four people to evade a mob than several dozen."

"That's crazy," said Ira. "Besides, there ain't no way we could get enough of them to come after us so everyone else can escape."

"Not necessarily," said Dekar, calling out from back inside the bar. He had slipped inside a moment before. Glass shattered over and over.

"What in the name of Xank are you doing in there?" asked Ira.

Dekar appeared in the doorway, carrying three lit oil lamps. "Creating a diversion. And getting them good and mad so they'll come after us."

He threw one of the lamps down, busting it open. The lit flame ignited the spilled oil, then crawled along the floor. Streams of fire spread across the common area, especially by the bar. Within seconds the entire lower floor was in flames.

"Weren't there people still upstairs?" I asked, taking a step back from the heat.

Prostitutes came running out a side entrance on the right of the building, fleeing down an alley.

"Not anymore," Ira snorted.

"Uh, Tyrus?"

I turned to Hamath. "Yeah?"

"I believe Dekar's idea worked."

I followed his gaze to the mob still at the alley mouth. People in the back had noticed the rising flames and were making it known to the rest of the group. Within a matter of moments, over a hundred angry faces stared in our direction.

"We should probably start running," I said.

"Yep," Hamath said.

The crowd came screaming toward us.

We set off in a sprint, but not before Dekar took the last two oil lamps and threw them through a window of the adjacent building. I spared a glance back long enough to see the window dressing ignite.

A smile crawled across my face as some of the mob regained enough of their senses to stop their pursuit in an effort to put out the fires. Those not blessed with common sense came at us more angered than before.

I lasted a full block before I vomited a couple mugs of ale. The rest came up half a block later. Though I stank worse than ever, the trade-off was worth it as we began to distance ourselves from the mob.

A thought struck me and I called out. "Hamath, slow down a bit."

He looked back, "Come again?"

"Slow down. They're getting tired. We don't want to lose them yet," I huffed.

"Why not?"

"Because they're just going to go back and find the others."

He grunted. "So, what's the plan?"

"You peel off and get back to the wagons. Make sure Captain Nehab wasn't targeted. If he was, then meet us by that lake we passed on the way to the city. If he's all right, help him get the wagons hitched and out of the city to that same lake. Direct others who make it out of the city over to that point. We'll try to buy you some more time."

"All right."

He took the first right and disappeared. Ira moved up and took his spot. I tried to focus on the pace he kept rather than the burning in my legs. It was disheartening that just after a short time on the road, I already felt out of shape.

Dragging or not, we all had to keep moving. Ira made sure of that as we weaved in and out of alleys and side streets that cut through several more commonly traveled roads. Twice we had run-ins with small groups of citizens trying to box off our escape. Twice we survived, leaving dead and dying in our wake.

The swarming mob had begun to catch up to us for a third time, pushing our path farther west of the city center. Ira led us down another trash-filled, grime-covered, death-smelling, alley. The alley banked right, hiding the fact that it ended in a dead end with the brick walls of buildings all around us.

Ira swore.

"Turn around. Hurry," I huffed.

We wheeled quickly, Dekar leading as we retraced our steps. We only made it back as far as the bend before Dekar pulled up. A small horde of citizens pushed their way into the mouth of the narrow pass, stopping as they realized they had us.

"Xank be damned," said Ira behind me.

I counted fifteen men, which were at least ten too many, and fifteen more than I preferred. They held their position hunched over and huffing for air. Thankfully, they were in far worse shape than we were and that was after a night of drinking. I wasn't going to let that advantage slip by.

My eyes scanned the dark alley, seeing for the first time a ledge above our heads jutting out from the building to the right. It was only about two feet wide and looked to be of no use other than adding an architectural touch to the structure. It would have to do. Another eight feet above the ledge, closer to the alley's entrance, rested a small balcony that hung off a third story window.

"Tyrus?" asked Dekar.

"Up the ledge, then to the balcony. Quick," I hissed.

"That ledge has gotta be nine feet, Ty. I ain't no frog," said Ira.

"Better become one," I muttered. Having recovered enough from their jaunt through the city, Damanhur's citizens started coming forward.

Someone from the mob shouted. "Why don't you boys come along now? We can end this nonsense and take you to the watch for questioning."

"Under what charges?" I hollered.

"Arson. Assault. Murder."

"All done in self-defense," I said. "What about the charges against you for attacking us?"

The man said nothing more. I took that to mean that our conversation was over.

I whispered. "Dekar give your brother a boost and then get up afterward. I'll buy some time."

Sword in hand, I strode toward fifteen men like a legend of old, ready to take them all down in a single blow. At least that's how I hoped I appeared. The lingering effects of the alcohol gave me a false bravado, even if the spots of vomit on my shirt worked against the image.

Grunting sounded behind me as the brothers worked on getting up to the ledge. The mob saw their efforts, called out, and picked up their pace. I ran ahead six steps to a stack of old crates, stopping where the alley narrowed. I figured that the four men running abreast would narrow down to two or three once blades started swinging. Odds were still in their favor, but I could at least hold out for a little while against that number. Hopefully, Dekar or Ira would figure out a way to get me to safety in the meantime.

At the last minute, I kicked over the crates. The three men in the lead stumbled over the debris and themselves while crashing in a heap. Most of the men behind them got tangled up in the mess, slowing their attack further. I killed the two closest to me as they struggled to right themselves.

A young man, probably twenty at best, broke free first with the bright idea of leaping over the others in order to reach me. It was a dumb move. I rammed my sword into his chest before he landed. Wide eyes hinted that in his last moments he likely agreed with my assessment of his decision.

The next two attacked together, immediately putting me on the defensive. I blocked the first wild cut, and then ducked under the next, sword clanging against brick to my left. After a few more quick sweeps of their blades, I managed to slip my sword into the armpit of one. Someone took his place before I could take advantage and dispose of my other opponent. The newcomer carried a pitchfork.

Given the weapon's reach, I found myself giving ground, swearing the whole way.

I deflected a stab of the pitchfork and tried to move in close where the weapon would be useless. It worked, for a moment anyway. I sliced the man's unprotected arm. He staggered. However, the man beside him used the opening I gave him to drive his sword through a weak spot in my boiled leather, piercing the flesh below my collarbone. I pulled away before it went deep, but that didn't stop the thing from hurting.

"Back up, Tyrus!"

I jumped backward without thinking, reacting to the sound of Dekar's voice.

Stone rained down on the men in the alley, felling many as heads and limbs were struck. Dust took to the air, blinding most others. I waved the cloud from my face and seized on the moment. I pounced at the closest swordsman with a stab through the gut, then finished off the man with the pitchfork.

"C'mon, Ty. Hurry up."

I looked up. Ira and Dekar waited for me next to a hole in the wall. I wondered how they managed to knock so much stone loose, but that would be a question for another day. I sheathed my weapon, took two quick steps, and jumped, grabbing onto the ledge. Ira reached down and helped me up while holding onto Dekar with his other hand. I managed to get up just before those in the alley recovered.

"The balcony," I gestured.

We climbed up to the balcony and eventually to the roof as the men below pelted us with the rock Dekar had toppled on them. We took a few welts and earned several bruises, but made it up alive.

Taking the high ground we continued our trek through the city, jumping from roof to roof, no easy task in any circumstance.

We lost our pursuers after a couple of blocks.

Eventually, we made it to Damanhur's outer walls.

* * *

Many of our group had lucked out.

Unfortunately, some others had not.

Our attackers had overlooked the captain and our wagons. Hamath made it back in time to warn Nehab. By the time they rode out of the city, the first few returning soldiers left with them.

The captain pulled the wagons off the road into an apple orchard near the lake a few miles outside of the city. Hamath stayed by the road to direct survivors.

Men had escaped Damanhur any way they could. Most jumped over the city's obscenely low wall as we had.

Dekar, Ira, and I were among the last group to arrive—bruised, tired, and exhausted.

When all was said and done, we lost twelve men. Ten more were seriously injured. I tried to take solace in the fact that Dekar, Ira, Hamath, and I had killed well over a dozen citizens of Damanhur alone. Based on the reports of others, we gave a lot worse than we got.

The unevenness in casualties was a small consolation though.

The night was supposed to be one of fun and merriment, a chance to relax after years in service and over a week of monotonous travel. I had even expected to receive some appreciation for our service in the war. It ended up being more of what many of us had hoped to never see again. We wanted a celebration and got a massacre.

Some in our meager group, now roughly forty men, wanted to reform and go on the offensive.

"How dare they do this to us!" someone shouted. "Don't they realize what we did for them?"

Others expressed similar sentiments. With blood racing, I even found myself siding with the mob of angry veterans, but thankfully, cooler heads prevailed.

Nehab attempted to calm us all down before we did something stupid. "Everyone shut up! I know you're mad. By the gods, I'm mad too. We lost good men tonight, and I don't want to lose anymore. I've got a wife waiting for me. Some of you have that and more. Do you want to die here and now on Turine soil by your own countrymen when home is closer than it has been in years? I sure don't."

"So they're going to get away with what they did to us?" someone asked.

"Considering how many everyone said they killed, I'd hardly say we're letting them get away with anything," said Nehab. "But no, I'm not just dropping what happened tonight if that's what you mean. I'll get word to Balak and let him know what's going on. He'll pass it on to the king. Let him take care of it. We need to worry about getting home. Ain't that right, Sergeant?"

I blinked from my angry daze as I realized Nehab was addressing me. "Yes, sir."

"Good. Hamath set up a perimeter and watch. Everyone else get to sleep. We're leaving at first light tomorrow."

People started to shuffle off. I was ready to do the same until Nehab called out. "Sergeant, a moment."

I walked to him. "Yes, sir."

"You all right?"

I rubbed the shallow wound at my collarbone. "I will be. Pretty ugly back there. But I'm fine now."

"I understand." He walked me toward the injured. "I need you to take a look at someone. It's Lieutenant Teyman."

"I'm not any sort of a healer."

"I know. But he had a run-in with a minor mage and we can't get his wound cleaned out."

"I see."

A benefit of my resistance to sorcery was that it not only protected me from spells cast by mages, but it also allowed me to draw away sorcery as well.

Lieutenant Teyman lay on his back with hands around a black wound on his side that oozed a green pus that stank like a dead possum rotting in a ditch. The private trying to clean the wound kept gagging into his arm as he wiped away the infection. Teyman didn't cry out, but the pain was evident on his wrinkled face each time the private touched his skin.

Nehab cleared his throat. "Private, step back a moment and let Tyrus take a look."

I kneeled at Teyman's side. Too busy trying to manage the pain, he didn't even notice.

I placed my hand over the wound. As I made contact, I felt a slight vibration. I never had to do much for my resistance to work.

Teyman began to relax as the green ooze disappeared and the wound went from black to red. Thankfully, the smell dissipated as well.

I moved away quickly so the private could dress the wound.

Teyman opened his eyes and whispered. "Thanks."

I went to sleep that night imagining I heard the Damanhur citizens cheering our departure in the way everyone thought they would cheer our arrival. Returning heroes? Not to them. I recalled the words of the idiot I fought in the bar. They probably blamed us for what happened even though they were the ones responsible.

Attacked by our own countrymen.
I never expected to deal with that.

CHAPTER 6

We hit the road early the next morning. Nehab wanted to put as much distance between us and Damanhur as possible, worried the mob might experience another burst of motivation in the light of day. Thankfully, the worst battles we fought were against our own bewilderment, exhaustion, and moroseness.

We set up camp that night just past dusk. Everyone looked like death and moved like it too. If a man wasn't still nursing a bad hangover, he was tending to the injuries he had picked up during his escape. Most soldiers, including myself, did both.

I cleaned up the scrapes I earned after choking down, and keeping down, the stew of the evening. Others did the same. The mood around the campfires had changed drastically.

Conversations that had dripped with optimism and anticipation were filled with dread, uncertainty, and even fear. Many wondered if their hometowns would match that of Damanhur. I didn't really share their worry. I knew the people of Denu Creek too well. The community was too close-knit for them to act that way.

I left our fire and maneuvered through camp toward Captain Nehab. He sat with bent knees, back against a large rock. He stroked his thick mustache while looking over a map of Turine.

He glanced up as I approached.

"Sergeant."

"Captain."

"Have a seat."

I took a spot next to him.

"You have any idea what caused that mess back there?" he asked. "I've heard so many varying stories that I can't make sense of what's real and what's not."

I told him what little information I managed to gather from the man at the bar.

He muttered a few curses. "Heck of a way to show their thanks, isn't it? Without the army's efforts, we'd be paying tribute to the Geneshans right now and dealing with that madman of an emperor they have." He grunted. "Who knows? We might have even been forced into learning the language. That's what happened to the other nations they conquered before they came after us."

"If you're looking for me to make sense of it, sir, I'm afraid I can't help you. I don't understand it either."

He sighed. "I know. I need to get that message back to General Balak about what happened so he can give the next groups passing through ample warning. Just wanted to run through everything with you first."

"You think this was a one-time deal or is every town going to be Damanhur all over?"

"Your guess is as good as mine, Sergeant. That being said, I'm not taking any chances. We have enough supplies to avoid any cities for a while. Plus, we won't reach anyone's home for at least a week. No reason not to just stay to ourselves."

I nodded. "Makes sense."

He sighed. "It's getting late, Sergeant. Go get some rest. I've still got a letter to write."

"Yes, sir."

I went back to my unit's fire.

After a quick search through my things, I pulled out a bundle of letters tied with a piece of old twine. I removed the twine, unfolded the top letter, and began reading. I had long ago memorized all the letters Lasha had sent me over the years, but I still liked to read them in her own hand from time to time. Something about it allowed me to hear her voice in my head. It was like she sat next to me, leaning on my shoulder.

My beloved Tyrus,

There isn't a day that goes by that I don't wish I was at your side and you at mine. Even under present circumstances, I'd brave whatever the enemy offered if it meant I could see you again. To say I miss you dearly is an understatement. I say this not to bring you down, but instead to give you reassurance that I love you even more today than I did when you rode away in that wagon five years ago.

We will be together soon. I can feel it.

And when you return, be prepared for the best night of your life.

I leaned back and sighed. Gods, that was five years ago. "So much for a woman's intuition," I muttered under my breath.

Shaking my head, I returned to the letter.

Anyway, enough with the romantic stuff. I know you were never as fond of it as I am. Let me tell you what Zadok got into just the other day . . .

Oddly enough, the romantic stuff I was never fond of is what I went back to the most. The assurance of Lasha's passion and love brought me joy on even the darkest of days. After the upheaval at Damanhur, I needed a little more joy than usual so I skipped to the next letter and focused on the romantic stuff there as well.

After the last letter, I retied the bundle and leaned back once more. Heavy in thought, my mind eventually drifted from Lasha and the kids to Ava. I wondered what my sister was up to. Based on my last conversation with Balak, I hoped she was at least keeping an eye on the High Mages from doing something stupid with the Geneshan artifact.

Regardless, her presence in Damanhur would have been a big help to us. Still, a part of me felt that she had made the right decision.

As a mage, she had always felt like an outsider in Dènu Creek.

I sighed. Maybe in Hol she'd find her place in the world.

CHAPTER 7

Just three days later, the well maintained roads we had been traveling turned into old, beat up paths.

We came across a priest of Molak with warm brown eyes and a smile that shown bright under the overcast sky. Due to his wrinkled forehead and graying hair, I guessed him somewhere around his mid-fifties. Tattered at the hem, his red robes had faded to a light pink. Many of the symbols usually adorning the front and back were faint outlines that I only saw by squinting.

Under normal circumstances, Captain Nehab would be the one in charge of addressing the wayside traveler. However, the captain was still anxious about Damanhur and had taken a small squad of five men to scout our back trail. I didn't expect him to return for hours. Command fell to me.

"This isn't exactly the safest road to travel, old-timer," I called out as we slowed our approach.

The priest's smile faltered at my lack of the proper address to someone of his station. If Hamath had been nearby, he probably would have jabbed me with an elbow for the casual attitude I used with the priest. Nehab had taken him though.

The priest recovered quickly. His smile returned. "Yet you travel the same road."

"We have many to watch each other's backs. You don't."

"I need only Molak to look after me."

I grunted as I gestured for the driver of the wagon to stop beside him. "Is that so?"

He nodded.

"Might I ask where Molak was when the bandits attacked you?"

He frowned. "How do you know bandits attacked me?"

"Well, I don't see any supplies nearby." I pointed. "Not even the pouch at your waist where Molak's servants usually keep their ceremonial dust for blessings. Plus, it looks like you're favoring your right side like something or someone hit you."

"You have me there." He began to chuckle, which, in spite of his chosen profession, put him on my good side. "Perhaps Molak was tending to more important matters."

"Perhaps. Where you heading?"

"Nowhere in particular. Wherever life takes me."

"Well, life is taking us that way," I said gesturing down the road. "There's room in the back of the wagon and a warm meal if you're interested in riding with us at least through tonight. My captain will have to decide how much further we extend hospitality."

"Considering my current situation, I'd be a fool to say no."

It was my turn to grin as I threw back a thumb. "Hop on then. My name's Tyrus."

He bowed. "You can call me, Kehat."

* * *

By the end of the day I had begun to regret my goodwill toward Kehat.

I had known many of the men worshipped Molak. What I hadn't realized was how starved they were to renew that faith.

During the war, men would say a prayer or mutter a curse to the gods as needed. However, few really devoted themselves to their chosen deity as there was little time for all the pomp and circumstance needed to do it properly. Balak allowed priests to come and go so long as they didn't get in the way of men doing their jobs. Therefore, few men spent much time talking to priests.

I guessed after Damanhur, some of the men felt like their half-hearted efforts in worshipping the father of the gods had caused Molak to abandon them at a time when all was supposed to be well. They figured that by taking advantage of this golden opportunity with Kehat, Molak might get off his rear and throw them a hand out.

I doubted Molak would do anything. He sure seemed stingy with the blessings during the last decade when hundreds of thousands of men lost their lives on the Turine side alone. It seemed that Molak would have been a bit understanding of his followers' inability to properly worship since they were busy trying to block the swords coming at their throats.

Regardless, Kehat had the men chanting prayers and singing hymns as we set up camp. Even quiet Dekar joined in. We were so far away from any major form of civilization, I decided to let the men go at it and get it out their systems. From the looks of things, they all needed it.

I, on the other hand, did my best to block out the dozens of songs I remembered from my youth, lest I accidently slip into a chorus myself. That was no easy thing. Several times I caught my lips silently repeating the refrain of a specific prayer on their own accord.

Comfortable the work was getting done, and filled to the brim with the carryings on, I placed Dekar in charge, and went to the outskirts of camp to get away. Thinking about Lasha and the kids helped clear my mind.

Some say that religion was infectious. They may have been right, but it was a disease I had no wish to catch.

* * *

Captain Nehab returned just after camp was set. I knew this only because the singing came to an abrupt halt. I heeled and toed it back to camp to greet him but he was already walking toward me.

"Sorry, sir. Didn't mean to be disrespectful. I was farther out than I thought."

"No problem, Sergeant. We can stay out here. Hamath told me about your aversion to all things religious. I don't have quite as strong of feelings as you, but I'm no disciple either. How have you been killing time?"

"Just thinking. Mostly about my sister now. Wondering how she's doing with her studies under the High Mages of Hol. She never got along with them before. Put one in the infirmary about four years ago when he tried to belittle her in front of several others because she was only classed as a squad mage under my unit."

He chuckled. "I remember that. Your sister has a unique personality."

I grinned. "That she does. Hopefully, it's not getting her in trouble. Especially since I know she wanted to be a part of looking over that Geneshan artifact."

He grunted. "Well, I hope looking is all the Council of High Mages is doing. Balak told me what the Geneshans think the artifact is capable of. I've dealt with enough misery and chaos in the war. I don't need that stuff following me home."

"I hear you, sir."

The singing started back up, and I shook my head. "So, how'd it go today?"

We started walking.

"Well enough. No one seems to be following us, which is what we suspected. We came across a small town off the main road. Heaven's Way. Ever heard of it?"

"No, sir."

"Me either. For something with heaven in the name, it sure was a dump. Maybe eighty people or so. I kept the men back and entered on my own after removing all signs of the army about me. Just to get a feel of things."

"And?"

"Not great, but not awful either. They hadn't heard of Damanhur yet, thankfully. But I'm sure they will soon enough. Regardless, the sentiment seems mixed. Most of the general populace doesn't hold the army in high regard. Lots of stories circulating about the war. Some false, some true, some exaggerations of the truth. Those who seemed to be more supportive of the war or at least indifferent to it were around, but outnumbered in their opinion."

"Why?"

He shrugged. "Hard to say, and I couldn't press without being suspicious."

"So, what are your orders?"

"Keep doing what we've been doing. Avoid people as best as we can until it's time to start dropping people off at their homes."

"And what do we do if things are just as bad at those places?"

He sucked his teeth. "I really don't know. That will be up to the individual to decide. Stay, or move on to a place where they'll be welcomed."

"The thought of returning home is the only thing that has kept most of them alive all these years. To not be welcomed there, well . . ."

He sighed. "Yeah. I know."

The singing got really loud just then. We both turned our heads.

"Sorry, sir. I may not be religious, but the priest looked pretty bad off."

He patted me on the shoulder. "No worries, Sergeant. I would have done the same. And if nothing else it seems the men needed him just as much as the priest needed a meal and a ride. We'll let him stay with us for a bit. When we part, we'll give him some supplies to take with him."

I nodded.

"And, Tyrus."

"Yes, sir?"

"Let's not mention what I said about that town to the others just yet. No reason to bring them down again."

"Of course."

"Good. Then I'll leave you to your thoughts. After a day of hard riding, I can put up with some off key singing if it means a full stomach."

CHAPTER 8

Over the next week, Kehat went his own way and we continued to shun any large communities we passed. That practice changed as we reached several smaller towns that were the final destination for several in our group.

To ensure the safety of those we dropped off, Nehab sent half a dozen men into town as an escort. He didn't want to send in anymore, so that the locals weren't threatened by us. The six men selected as escorts were never the same, rotating men out here and there so everyone at least got a brief taste of civilization.

Reports from those who returned to the group were mixed. Some were surprised to see soldiers returning, and asked questions about the war in a more curious than accusatory manner. However, many locals cast sour looks, even crossing the streets to avoid contact. Still, no one tried to raise arms against us like in Damanhur so we at least had that going in our favor.

Since the hostilities seemed minimal, every soldier we dropped off chose to remain in their home town, just as I expected they would.

Several men who returned after one particular trip into a passing town tried to look at the positive, explaining the looks and behavior of the people as just being cautious of strangers. The pessimists of our group felt it proved that many in the world no longer wanted us.

I hadn't decided which side of the argument I fell.

After another night of debating the same thing, Dekar changed subjects. "Hamath, don't you live somewhere around here?"

He threw a stick he had been fidgeting with into the fire. "Yep. We should make it there in a few days."

"You don't sound excited," Dekar said.

Hamath shrugged. "Not especially."

"What about Bilhah?" I asked. "You aren't happy to see her again?"

He snorted. "She got married years ago."

I blinked. "What? You never told me that. When did you find that out?"

"It was in that last batch of letters we all received before the army quit delivering messages."

Shortly after Wadlow Hill, Balak had called for all outside communications to cease. Things were bleak then, and he was worried about our dwindling resources. He didn't want to deplete them further by ferrying personal messages back and forth across country.

"Why haven't you said anything before now?"

He threw another stick in the fire. "Because I knew how much it meant for you to talk about your family. I didn't want to make you feel guilty about it just because I no longer had anyone waiting for me."

"That's a heck of a thing she did to you," said Ira.

Hamath shrugged again. "She waited more than five years. That's more than I thought she would considering we were only betrothed."

"You gonna kill the guy she married?" asked Ira.

"Xank, no."

"A beating at least? He took your woman," Ira pushed.

Hamath shook his head. "She always wanted kids, and she was tired of waiting. I can't fault her for that. Lavi be cursed, I was never sure if I even wanted kids."

"Still, I know I couldn't let someone get away with that. I'd have to at least—"

Dekar cut his brother off in a low voice. "Let it go."

Ira clamped his jaw shut while the rest of us stared at the dancing flames. I spared a quick glance at Dekar and saw the worry lining his face, most likely thinking of the wife waiting for him.

We were all more apt to dwell on the possibility that there wouldn't be much good waiting for us on our return. It was one thing not to have a job, or friends. But to lose your family, your woman . . .

My chest clenched for any man who had to go through that.

* * *

We set out late the next morning. Despite the desire to get home, Nehab demanded we all take a few extra hours of rest. No one argued. We had been pushing hard and it showed.

I sat at the back of the trailing wagon, legs over the side, listening to the clattering wheels as we rolled along. Staring at the beaten road, my mind wandered in a hundred directions—thinking of my stint in the army, the men I lost under my command, and what Ava was learning in Hol. I wondered what those idiot High Mages were doing with the Geneshan artifact. Maybe they had wised up and buried the thing as our enemies had said to do. That would be the day.

Most of my thoughts went back to Denu Creek. How much would it have changed in the last ten years? Would I recognize any of it? Would anyone recognize me?

The conversation from the night before got me thinking about how Lasha would greet my arrival. She wouldn't have found someone else. I doubted that would happen even if she thought me dead. We had talked about that scenario the night before I left home. I had been adamant she find another man to marry.

"Fine, Tyrus. I'll try. I'll try to find someone who makes my legs weak with just the slightest of looks, who makes my heart race with the barest of whispers. I'll try to find someone who treats me better than I have any right ever to be treated and loves his kids like no man I've ever met, including my own father. However, I have a feeling that no one will ever live up to the standard you've set. But, if it will ease that worrisome mind of yours, I promise to do my best if you don't make it back."

That was all a moot point. I wasn't dead, and she knew that. Before Balak cut off communications with the outside world, he allowed all soldiers to write one more letter home stating that another letter would only come to announce our death. Until then, our family had no reason to believe we were dead.

No, what I worried about was how we'd act together after so much time apart. I knew her letters said she loved me, but saying something and acting the same way were two different things. Would the fire between us burn immediately, just as it had before? Or would it need to be rekindled, stoked over time, until it ended up greater than it had ever been? I guessed it didn't really matter how things fell into place as long as they eventually did. And with everything I knew about my wife, I had to believe they would.

The kids though . . .

The wagon rolled over a rough patch of dry road, sending dust into the air. A violent coughing attack seized me, jarring me from thoughts I probably shouldn't have been dwelling on anyway. I reached for my canteen, took a swig, and swallowed. The water was warm, but satisfying. I blinked away the tears in my eyes from coughing and nodded at Captain Nehab as he approached.

"Captain, what are you doing back here?"

"Looking to have a word with you in private, Sergeant. You mind hopping off and walking a bit?"

"No, sir. I could probably use the time to stretch my legs out anyway."

That wasn't entirely true. I still had quite a bit more time on the wagon before I'd have to trade spots with someone walking. We rotated spots in order to be fair. However, since several still nursed injuries, those who had healed up took longer shifts walking than others.

We drifted to the rear of the wagons until well out of earshot.

"You know our next stopping point, Sergeant?"

"No, sir."

"Treetown. Ever heard of it?"

"Can't say that I have. Pretty dumb name though."

"I'm from there."

I winced. "Sorry, sir."

"Don't be. It is a dumb name. The town is very small. Named after this giant white birch growing in the town square. I always thought 'White Birch' or something like that would have been better."

"Definitely an improvement."

Nehab chuckled which made me feel better.

"This must be hard on you to be so close and not be able to stop."

"That's what I want to talk to you about, Sergeant. I'm not going on with everyone."

"But sir, didn't Balak—"

"Yes, my orders are to see that everyone gets home safely. But I can't do it. You and I are rare. We've been in this thing since the very beginning. I've got a family waiting for me just like you. Can you honestly tell me you could pass the place you've thought about every day since joining the army and not stay?"

I shook my head. "Probably not."

"Neither can I. Look, I hate to do this to you, but you're the most senior officer left among us. You, Dekar, and Ira have the farthest to travel among everyone else. So, it only makes sense to transfer command over to you once we reach Treetown. Can you do that for me?"

I thought about it for a moment. "Sure."

"Thank you," said Nehab. The relief in his voice was overwhelming. "I know I don't have to tell you this, but I'm saying it anyway. After Treetown, continue to stay away from the cities and towns you come across. I'd hate to hear you ran into trouble again."

"I'd hate to run into it."

"Good. Let's catch back up to the others."

The captain made the announcement to everyone at dinner that the next day would be his last day with us. He transferred command to me. No one objected. I wondered if anyone cared. Maybe they knew me well enough to know I'd do right by them, or maybe they didn't have an opinion on who they took their orders from so long as someone gave them.

I laughed to myself. What was I thinking? Every soldier had an opinion on who they take orders from. I'd worry about the ones who didn't.

* * *

Around midday we left the road, turning off onto a dirt path overrun with high grass that we all would have missed had the captain not been with us. He took point and led us into a wooded area about fifty yards off the road.

Hamath nudged me. "Are you sure about this?"

"What do you mean?"

"Us going to Treetown. Seems contradictory to what Nehab has been saying about avoiding places as a group."

I shared Hamath's concerns, but Nehab had a good head on his shoulders so I was willing to give him the benefit of the doubt. "Well, he said Treetown is so isolated that most people have a tendency to forget about the place. It's a good chance they don't share the opinion we keep running into."

Looking around at the trees closing in on top of us, I understood the captain's surety of his town's remoteness.

"But if they do?"

"Well, you heard the captain last night when he was describing the place. They aren't going to have enough people to attack a group our size even if they don't want us there."

He grunted. "Let's hope they haven't had a recent population surge then."

A half mile later, we came out on the other side of the woods. Seventy yards from the forest's edge stood the smallest settlement I had ever seen. Farmland stood to either side of eight round hovels congregating in a circle around a massive white birch. Seeing the tree lord over the little community made me wonder if one of the lesser gods occupied the thing. It had that sort of aura about it.

A few residents noticed our arrival and gathered on the edge of town. They held tools of trade like weapons where everyone could see—shovels, hoes, and pickaxes. That didn't bode well, even if I could understand their concern upon seeing several dozen soldiers rolling into their tiny town. I could almost sense Hamath ready to utter an "I told you so."

"Halt!" Nehab called. He dismounted the wagon as it rolled to a stop, unbuckled the sword at his side and made a show of dropping it in the dirt. "Stay here until I say otherwise," he added over his shoulder.

He walked alone, hands out at his sides. Additional people from the town materialized next to the original group. More people lived there than I had thought.

A woman screamed out and burst through the group. She sprinted toward the captain, brown dress flowing behind her. Nehab abandoned his calm approach and took off toward her. They met in a loving embrace with the captain raising her off the ground.

A lump formed in my throat as I thought about Lasha again.

The townspeople relaxed as recognition set in. They hurried out to the couple, white teeth showing in wide smiles. Nehab shook hands and hugged several others all while keeping one arm firmly wrapped around his wife's waist.

After a minute, he waved us over.

"Well, one less thing to worry about at least," I said.

Hamath responded with a grunt.

* * *

Treetown ended up being the opposite of Damanhur in more than just appearance. People shook our hands, thanked us for our service, and even made small talk about the weather. The only time I ever saw a smile leave their faces was when Nehab gave a very brief summary of the events in Damanhur. They offered condolences and said prayers for the dead. It was the reception we had hoped for from the beginning.

An elderly man, tall, wiry, and bent over a cane made a suggestion all could get on board with. A celebration.

I've never seen people move so fast in all my life. In less than an hour, meat dripped on open spits, bread baked in nearby ovens, and corn roasted over open fires. The comforting smells made it hard to keep from drooling. Everyone alternated between eating and talking. Someone rolled out a couple kegs of ale shortly thereafter and things really got going. With each mug of the warm, satisfying drink voices grew louder until all it seemed I could hear was laughter.

The mood had become so infectious that Dekar managed to talk Hamath into a match of Crests, a strategy game that I was barely serviceable at. Dekar had never lost, even winning a tournament the army put together two winters ago when we couldn't do much else but sit around on account of a blizzard. Since then, he nearly had to pay people to play him.

The elderly man pulled out a fiddle while a woman I assumed was his wife began singing songs I hadn't heard since my parents were alive. None of that religious garbage either. These were about the sun, the rain, family and friends—finding joy in the simple things of life.

I sat beneath the white birch with eyes closed, listening to the upbeat tempo and recalling fond memories of my youth. A small sigh escaped my lips, wishing Ava had come along to see this.

"Everything all right, Tyrus?"

I opened my eyes at the captain's voice, watching him as he approached. "Yes, sir. I was just thinking how much this place reminded me of home. Well, a better version of home actually."

"I hope it's even better than how you remember it when you get there."

"Me too, captain."

"You can cut the 'captain' and 'sir' out now. I'm officially a commoner again. Nehab works fine by me."

I nodded and gestured to a line of people, townsfolk and soldiers alike, dancing. "I'm glad you invited us to stay for the night. Not even that priest of Molak mustered this much genuine happiness from them."

He smiled. "I thought they might need it." He pointed and chuckled. "The way some of them are acting, it makes me realize how little I know them."

I followed his hand. Ira danced in a circle with a group of kids ranging between the ages of two and seven. After a few moments he purposefully took an exaggerated tumble and they piled on top of him laughing.

I grinned. "Yeah, most people wouldn't expect it but Ira's always had a soft spot for kids. Don't tell him I told you, but he used to sneak food all the time to give to the younger ones attached to the army. Most of my unit knew about it, but none of us ever said anything to him. We figured if he wanted to keep it to himself, then so be it."

I looked up as the leaves rustled in the wind. "By the way, you were right about the name of this place. Treetown just doesn't do it justice."

Nehab rubbed his hand across the white bark, eyes traveling up and down the thick trunk. "The gods know I've tried to sway everyone's mind, but people here just don't seem to like change."

"Considering this is the best place we've come upon in a long time, the people here might be on to something. Who would want to change this?"

Nehab smiled at his wife as she walked toward us. Her grin was just as wide. "Not me, Tyrus. Not me."

By the gods, I missed my wife.

CHAPTER 9

With the group now my responsibility, I no longer brought up the rear as had become my habit, but rather rode in one of the lead wagons. I kept the pace steady, just as Nehab had, still concerned about the health of those who had suffered injuries.

The countryside looked less ravaged by war the farther away from Genesha we journeyed. Fighting hadn't touched these areas in years, most places not at all.

Lush trees danced in the summer breeze. For once, the wind carried scents that in no way reminded me of life in the army. No animal excrement from overcrowded pens, no urine from flooded out latrines, no sickness hovering over the infirmary. Finally those were nothing more than sour memories. Clean air, fresh grass, and lavender filled my nose instead.

Three days and one stop after leaving Treetown, we reached the top of a low hill. Over the pecan trees standing behind an old wooden fence, we saw the outline of a distant town. Smoke from one of the buildings rose over the trees.

Hamath let out a sigh. "There she is. Home sweet home." He snorted, scratching at his red side burns. "I wonder if old Aviad is the one still stoking that forge." A distant tone took to his voice. "I remember hanging around his place for hours as a kid."

"You wanted to be a smith?" I asked.

"Nah, I had no interest. I still picked up a few things anyway. It was hard not to." He chuckled. "My ma always wanted me to be a tanner.

Gods, could you imagine that smell?" He shrugged. "No, I hung around the forge so much because I liked listening to Aviad pound away with that hammer of his. You know, I think that helped me become a better scout. I got to where I could figure out how and where each blow struck without ever opening my eyes. It got to be a game for us."

"I'm sure if that's him, he'll be glad to see you then," I offered.

Hamath stood in his seat. "Stop here."

"Huh?"

"Just do it."

Confused, I gave the command to the driver. He pulled on the reins and our wagon creaked to a halt. Those behind us followed.

Hamath stepped down. He reached under his seat and pulled at his pack. He got it free and slung it over his shoulder.

"What's going on, Ty? We got trouble?" Ira called out as he and Dekar walked up.

"No. We've come upon Hamath's town."

"Then why are we stopping?"

I nodded to Hamath. "Ask him."

Hamath fiddled with the sword at his waist. "I thought it was obvious. I'm heading off."

"Why get off here when we still got another couple miles before we reach town?" asked Ira.

"Because you don't need to follow me. Supplies are fine. Plus, it's still early in the day. Stopping is only going to set everyone back. I can walk the rest of the way."

"How kind of you to consider our well-being." Ira's voice was lined with sarcasm.

I got down from the wagon. "If you don't want us to come along, Hamath, just say it."

He looked up, speaking in a deadpan voice. "I don't want you to come along."

"Why not?" asked Dekar.

"It's nothing personal," said Hamath, meeting each of our eyes. "I promise. I just—"

"All right," I said, cutting him off. "You have your reasons. I don't know how I'll feel when I get home so who am I to judge what's going on inside your head."

His lips pressed together, and he gave me a nod. I returned it. We stared at each other for a few moments, wondering how to say goodbye.

Gods, it was more awkward than I thought possible. How could I tell my best friend, a man I had fought beside and killed with for years, "see you later?" He had saved my life and in turn I had saved his more times than I could count. Didn't seem like there was a right way to do it.

"When you feel like you've had enough here and need a break, why don't you come my way?" I finally mustered up. "Lasha can cook you up a mean steak."

He forced a smile. "Yeah, sure. I'll be there the first chance I get."

I don't think either of us believed that would happen. Despite how close we had always been, weeks of travel separated his town and mine, which for someone of our class, might as well have been months.

We embraced like brothers and parted. He waved over his shoulder and cut away from the road. He jumped the old wooden fence and disappeared into the grove of pecan trees, heading toward town.

CHAPTER 10

Over the next couple weeks our numbers rapidly dwindled. I watched a lot of awkward good-byes, some even worse than mine. Each parting made me think of Hamath and Ava. I started feeling down about all the relationships I was losing.

But then thoughts of Lasha and the kids would drive those feelings away. At our current pace, I'd be home by the end of the month.

I decided that wasn't soon enough and began pushing harder. Most of our injuries had healed and those that hadn't probably wouldn't for some time. They'd suffer no matter what pace we kept so I saw no reason to delay things further.

A decent-sized town announced itself with an actual sign displaying its name.

Kafr stood on flat land between miles of pasture. Both cattle and sheep with heads down, munched away on bright-green grass. Considering we were down to seventeen men, none of us walking, I thought it time to sell off our remaining wagons with the exception of the one we'd take to the end. Knowing the type of towns we'd come to after Kafr, I didn't think we'd find a better place to do so.

We rolled into Kafr shortly after midday with the sun at its highest. The town seemed deserted, which didn't surprise me. Most anyone who lived in the area was likely working the fields. At night, I imagined things would be different.

Dekar tapped my arm and pointed. "Feed store is over there."

I followed his gesture. "I should probably get the supplies. Anyone else is likely to waste the money. I want either you or Ira to come with me. The other can handle selling the wagons we no longer need."

"I'll come," he said. "You know how Ira likes to negotiate. The man has tried so many scams of his own, he can always sniff one out."

"All right. Hop off here and pass the word."

Dekar jumped down as I guided the lead wagon aside, tying the horses to a nearby post.

I took a moment to shake the stiffness from my limbs while I watched the others ride by. Ira made an obscene gesture at me in jest. I shook my head, climbed up the steps to the feed store, and pulled on the door. A bell jingled on the handle as I went inside.

My eyes took a minute to adjust to the dim light. When they did, I saw a middle-aged man standing behind a counter, bald on top, bushy hair on the sides. He scowled while looking me over. The disgust he wore took me off guard. He pulled out a rag and began polishing the counter.

"Good day," I said while walking over.

He didn't respond.

I stayed calm. Maybe he was hard of hearing. Granted, that didn't explain his scowl. I decided on a different approach, cutting through the small talk and getting right down to business. "I'm looking to make a purchase."

"Inventory is running low," he muttered without looking up. "Probably out of what you're looking for."

I stepped away from the counter and looked around the store. Sacks of flour rested next to piles of potatoes, carrots, and other root vegetables. A barrel of apples stood beside another of limes. Strips of dried beef and lamb hung on hooks. And those were the items fit for human consumption. Grain for the horses was in a different part of the store with various tools a farmer, butcher, rancher, tanner, or so on might need. Should I be so inclined to take up knitting, I could even buy a pile of yarn.

"I'm pretty sure you've got what we're looking for."

The man looked up. "None of this is for sale."

"Huh?"

"It's all been paid for in advance. Most of it just came in actually. No one's going to come by to pick it up until this evening though."

A small bell chimed, and Dekar entered, rubbing his eyes just like I had. The old man's scowl somehow deepened. He backed away a step.

Blinking, Dekar walked over.

"All right," I said, facing the man once more. "What is for sale in the way of food and grain? Even if it's not all we need, it will help us along until we get to the next town."

He folded his arms across his chest. "Come to think about it, I don't think we have anything for sale. You and your friend might do best just heading out to that next town. I'm sure you'll have more luck there."

Having quickly figured out the situation, Dekar said "Just say it like it is. Plenty's for sale, just not to us. Am I right?"

The owner nodded.

"Why in the name of Molak not?" I said. "Our coin is just as good as anyone else's. I never heard of any business man prejudiced about how he makes his money."

The owner puffed himself up. "I can run my store anyway I want. Now that you know the way it is, I suggest you get on out of here."

"Tyrus?" asked Dekar.

I stared at the man and he stared right back. Despite not carrying any noticeable weapons, his gaze didn't falter.

"Let's get out of here," I said.

"You sure?" asked Dekar.

"Yeah. We got enough food to last us until the next town. We can try our luck there. I don't want another Damanhur."

The man flinched at the name like he had heard of what had happened. I guess it was possible. Bad news travels fast and we had chosen to travel the safest path, not the fastest.

I cursed to myself. If they had heard about Damanhur from someone besides us, he might be thinking we started the whole thing. I opened my mouth in an effort to make our case one last time, when the store's door flew open, slamming against the wall.

"Sergeant, you better get out here right away. We've got trouble."

"What is it? Where's Ira?"

"Outside with the others. He's the one who told me to grab you."

Dekar cursed and followed the soldier out. I went after them, using some colorful language of my own. Ira rarely called for help.

My hand immediately shielded my eyes from the harsh sun as I rushed out of the store. Squinting, I followed Dekar further into town. I heard cattle shuffling around in their pens as we neared the edge.

Behind an old barbershop rested the animal pens I heard earlier. The men I sent off with Ira to sell the wagons and mounts stood with weapons in their hands. Anger and fear lined their faces. I spotted Ira at the front of the group. Sword at his side, he said nothing. Never a good sign. For all Ira's talk, when things got grim, he got focused and quiet.

I walked up, Dekar beside me.

Across from our group, over thirty men from the town, mostly ranchers, stood with various weapons of their own. A few had swords or machetes. Most improvised with woodcutter's axes or pitchforks. A handful wore patches of armor. Several others held makeshift shields. They were a rag-tag group, obviously unaccustomed to fighting. However, the townsfolk had numbers on us. Again. We'd take them, but not without losses of our own.

"What's going on, Ira?" I whispered.

"Idiots trying to steal from us," he answered back in a voice just as low.

Men continued to run in and join the group across from us. Inexplicably, none seemed in a hurry to do much more than stand around and try to intimidate us. That strategy suited me just fine as it gave me time to catch up with Ira. It also let me know that we had a chance of getting out of here while avoiding any violence.

"How so?"

"I made a deal with the owners. Fair for both sides I thought. I even had the men get the horses in pens for them. Then when the idiots came to pay us, they only gave us half of the agreed amount. Said they changed their minds. I threw the money at their feet and called for the men to get the animals back out. When I did, people ran out with weapons drawn."

"I'm surprised you haven't killed anyone yet," said Dekar.

"Don't think I didn't want to. Just trying to do what you would do, brother."

"You did good," I said. "Which one is the leader?"

"The one carrying the scythe. At least he's the one who told us we couldn't get the animals back. Everyone seems to be waiting on him to do something."

I grunted. "He looks the most nervous of everyone."

"He's had time to think," said Dekar. "Probably second guessing whether this was all worth it."

"Let's hope." I sighed and undid my sword belt, letting it drop to the ground. "Best to try this the easy way first."

"Be careful," said Dekar.

I walked out into the space separating the two groups, stopping halfway. "I'm here to talk to who's in charge. I took my sword off as a sign of peace. Bring whatever you want with you for all I care. I don't intend to kill anyone."

All eyes went to the man Ira tagged as the leader. He didn't move at first, but realized quickly he needed to in order to save face. He brought the scythe he carried with him. Apparently, he didn't need to save that much face. The curved blade looked comfortable in his hand, like a man who had used one all his life. He probably had and that worried me a bit.

He stopped about five feet away, scythe leaning outward between us like some barrier he dared me to pass.

"Good day."

He didn't respond. Whatever the man at the feed store had was catching.

"I hear there's a problem in regards to payment for our animals and wagons."

"No problem from our perspective."

"Of course. Even still, we've decided the deal just isn't worth it to us. If you and your friends would kindly step aside, we'll get our wagons hitched again and get out of your way. What do you say?"

The man looked over his shoulder. Several of the men behind him shook their heads. "I can't do that."

"So theft is something accepted here then?"

"We're not stealing anything."

"Sure you are." I gestured behind me. "My friend made a fair deal."

"It wasn't fair."

"All right. He makes a deal. Fair or not, it was one that you agreed to. Then you have a change of heart. He returns the money. And now you want to keep our animals anyway. If that isn't stealing than I don't know what is."

"The animals stay. You can have the wagons."

"And how would you have me take my wagons away without horses to pull them?"

He shrugged. "Not my concern."

My eyes narrowed. "What is your problem with us? We did nothing to you or this town."

"We heard about what happened in Damanhur. Better we get to you before you get to us."

That made no sense. Even if the truth was that we razed Damanhur to the ground, why would he want to provoke us into doing something similar in Kafr. Scared and threatened, the people had forgotten to think.

I grit my teeth, trying to bite back the words pronouncing his foolishness. I didn't think that sharing my thoughts right then would help matters much.

"What exactly did you hear?"

"That your men were all over the place, raping and pillaging with your first taste of freedom. Reports say Damanhur lost seventy men just trying to protect what was theirs on account of your numbers being so much larger."

"You got it backward. Damanhur attacked us. We lost twelve of our own men defending ourselves. And I promise there was no raping and pillaging."

"Just like there was no raping and pillaging going on in Genesha?"

That took me back. "What?"

"We've all heard the things that went on."

"I never raped anyone."

He nodded over my shoulder to those behind me. "What about them? Could you say the same for them?"

I said nothing, knowing that I couldn't speak for everyone. It was the ugly part of war few talked about. Officers tried to keep that stuff in check, but we couldn't be everywhere and we couldn't see everything.

"I thought so. So, you didn't do any raping. Good for you. I guess that's saying something."

"Watch yourself," I said, voice low as I tried to stay calm.

He ignored me, spinning his scythe. Gaining confidence as he spoke, his voice rose so the others could hear. "How many villages did you burn? How many innocent people who had nothing to do with the war died? People like us. How many families died because of disease and starvation? How many Geneshan children did you press into work gangs?"

I'd always been the sort who could let most things people said against me slide, but the man's accusations struck me like a fist to the jaw. It wasn't the man so much as the truth behind his words.

The man's scythe was in my hand. Its blade pressed against the owner's throat. I couldn't say when, but at some point I had reacted, pulling him inches from my face. I stared into his panicked eyes, smelling fresh urine run down his leg.

"Who do you think you are to judge me?" I yelled. "You think I wanted to be a soldier? I lost ten years of my life because of the army. All because they told me I had to join. It was my duty. Turine needed me. And without people like me, we'd all be speaking Geneshan now!" I paused, seething. "I was taken from the only home I ever knew, from my wife and my kids. I did my part to protect not only them, but also ungrateful people like you who didn't have the guts to fight yourselves. Are there things I did that I'm not proud of? Yes. And I'd do it again, because I know the alternative. I saw what the Geneshans had done to the nations they conquered. I saw piles of children's' bones as tall as a man from kids the Geneshans used as sacrifices to Beel. Yes, people died. Yes, people suffered. It's awful, and it's as much a part of war as the battlefield. Without what we did, you wouldn't have any of the freedoms you enjoy now."

"Hundreds of thousands dead? Thousands more who suffered? I don't want freedom if that's the cost of keeping it," whispered the man's quivering voice.

"Easy to say that since your freedom was never taken from you," I hissed. "How dare you make assumptions about me? About these men. How dare you judge us when you never had to experience what we did?" I pressed the blade against the man's throat until a small drop of blood trickled down his neck. "You weren't there. You never had to make the hard decisions we had to make, the ones every soldier has to make. You never had to watch the man you laughed with the night before cry for his mother as he died. You never had to watch a man who trusted you, a man under your command, helplessly hold his guts in. You never had to look in that man's eyes and lie, telling him everything would be all right. And until you do, you have no right to judge any of us."

"What do you want?" one of the other men from town called.

I looked up trying to find the owner of the voice. Nervous expressions stared back at me. Fear dominated the looks in their eyes where before there was anger. Despite that fear, they still held weapons ready while eyeing the scythe in my hand. They'd pounce on us if I killed their leader.

I swallowed, the spit hanging up as it slid down my throat. I took a breath, lowering my voice. "I only want what we came for. You pay us the price agreed upon for the horses and wagons and allow us to buy supplies at the feed store. Then we're gone."

"If we do that, do we have your word, no harm will come to anyone?" said the same voice from earlier. It belonged to a man with a round face and a rounder belly. A line of sweat down the middle of his shirt split his stomach in half like a cut melon.

"You have my word. We did not start the events that happened in Damanhur."

"We can make that deal. You mind letting him go?" he asked, gesturing to their leader.

I lowered the scythe, but pinned the man's arm as I spun him around. I had been around too long to let my guard down at a kind voice. "I'd like to, but you've given me no reason to trust you. He stays with me until our business is done. You cross us, he dies. And after that you'll be next. I'll kill every last one of you myself if anyone tries to stop me from getting home. Am I clear?"

The man hesitated for a moment. My gut tightened.

Finally, he nodded and began giving orders to the other villagers.

* * *

We got out of town as fast as we could. Weapons stayed out until the place was a tiny speck in the distance behind us. I didn't think those ranchers would be dumb enough to come after us, but then again, I never thought they'd have been dumb enough to try anything to begin with.

We didn't make camp until well after dusk and when we did, I made sure we were well off the road. I doubled the watch and even set up a few trip lines. If there had been time and enough men, I might've even dug a trench with stakes.

The mood in camp wasn't quite as bad as it was after Damanhur. The knowledge that we were all so close to home helped. It was easier to believe that Kafr was so inhospitable because none of us were from there.

I hoped that was true.

* * *

After dinner, card games broke out. Ira came over with a stick of tobacco and offered me a bite. I hated the stuff usually, but for some reason felt like having a piece. Anything to help take my mind off Kafr.

I took a bite and immediately regretted it. It tasted worse than it smelled, like coffee grounds and boiled leather. Ira told me that meant it was a good brand. I worked the stuff around my mouth until I had it positioned in my cheek. Off my tongue, it became tolerable.

Ira sat beside me. "Doing all right?"

I spat. "About as good as one can expect."

"I hear you. Crazy stuff back there."

"Yeah. Hoped we had left all that stupidity behind."

Ira chuckled. "You know stupidity doesn't work like that. That stuff spreads like crotch rot. I wouldn't be surprised if half of Turine has heard about Damanhur by now."

"I've wondered the same. Hopefully, Balak got Nehab's message. Maybe he can get the king to put a stop to this nonsense before it gets worse. Make it easier on the others who come home after us."

He spat. "Maybe. Though you heard that man with the scythe. Most of what they were worked up about had nothing to do with Damanhur. That had just been the tipping point. He brought up stuff that had been going on since the war began."

"Yeah."

"You know they gave me and Dekar that speech about duty when the army recruited us. Unlike you and Ava, we were dumb enough to actually join on our own."

"Really?" Somehow after ten years, I hadn't known that.

He nodded. "Bunch of morons we were." He snorted. "The bones of those kids you mentioned . . . that was in El Ghriba, right?"

I nodded.

"Yeah, that got to a lot of people. Cemented my resolve in what we were fighting for, you know. We had to stop the Geneshans. Who else was going to stop them if we didn't? They had already conquered four nations." He paused "I know you were pressed into the army, but did you ever really feel a sense of duty to what we were doing?"

"Sure. Sometimes. Like you said, it was hard not to after stuff like El Ghriba."

"What about now?"

I blew out a slow breath. "On occasion, but less and less as the days wear on. You?"

He spat. "Nope. Not anymore."

"What did it?"

"One of those villages that man talked about us burning. Hadera. We were making our final sweep after they allowed us to evacuate it before we razed the place. I found a baby crying in a basket under one of the beds. Xank knows what parent would have left their kid like that. Of course, the parents might have been dead for all I know. Anyway, I grabbed the baby out the basket and walked back to camp. Balak saw me and called me over."

Ira changed his voice to Balak's, stiff and deep. "Son, what are you doing with that baby?"

"I found him, sir. Left behind in Hadera," he answered back in his own voice.

"And?" he said once again while imitating Balak's voice.

"Thought I'd give him to one of the whores. I know it ain't the best life for a kid, but at least it's something."

"And are you going to become that baby's surrogate father too?"

"Honestly sir, I haven't thought about it much. Probably wouldn't hurt for him to have someone around while I can do it."

"That's what I thought. Give me the baby."

"Sir?"

"I'll take care of things."

"How?"

"Give it to me, son, or find yourself in the stockades!"

Ira laughed. "Well what was I going to do, Ty? I didn't want the stockades so I gave him the baby." He spat, then worked the tobacco around his jaw. "He took care of him all right. I saw one of his aids burying the child during third watch near the latrines that night. I dug him back up to know for certain and saw his lips were all blue and there was some bruising around the mouth. Likely smothered. I realized then just how awful a person Balak was and what sort of person the king was for promoting him to general. It also said what sort of people we all were for following them both."

We sat in silence, watching the flames dance for some time. I always had issues with Balak, but never did I think he was that cruel. Something dawned on me. "That aid. That was Jahleel, wasn't it?"

He spat. "Yep."

I remembered Jahleel dying around that time. Strangled with a belt. Body dumped in the latrines. No one knew who had done it though Balak did his best to find out. I put two and two together.

It was my turn to spit.

Gods, why had I taken a bite of tobacco? "Well, I guess I know how he died then. And the reason for it."

Ira shrugged. "Yep."

"Why didn't you ever tell me?"

"You had enough on your plate managing us and the never-ending missions Balak threw our way. You didn't need something like that clouding up your thoughts. Besides, if someone had ever figured out what I did, and you knew about it but didn't address it, you'd be in just as deep as me. Probably deeper."

Ira nodded toward his brother. "Dek thinks that most of your threat earlier in Kafr about killing everyone was a bluff. He said it wasn't like you to go around killing civilians. But it wasn't a bluff, was it? You would have cut that man open in a heartbeat."

I shifted uncomfortably. "What makes you say that?"

"Because I've only seen you that angry one other time and that was when we all first joined and them two mages were picking on Ava. You were madder then actually, which only makes sense because of her being family. But this was close. And you nearly killed both of them mages then. Probably would have if me and Ham hadn't pulled you off."

"Good thing you did. Balak would have had me hanged. The lashings were bad enough." I winced as phantom pains drifted over my back and shoulders. "He said it was unfair that I beat them so badly since I had a resistance to sorcery. I told Balak that those idiots should have carried swords."

Ira snorted. "Yeah, they should have. So like I asked, you weren't bluffing earlier, were you?"

"No. I wasn't. I don't bluff when someone threatens my family."

Ira was probably right by keeping that story of killing Jahleel from me. My unit had taken the place of my family during the war and I wouldn't have turned my back on Ira for something like that. Regardless of what would have rained down on me.

I glanced over my shoulder at the men talking, playing cards, a few others already settling down for the night. I knew they weren't perfect, but I'd die for them just as I knew they would for me.

When it comes to family, that's the way it should be.

CHAPTER 11

Eventually it was down to me, Dekar, and Ira. Thankfully, Kafr was the last confrontation we had to deal with during the remainder of our travels. That made the journey more palatable and still allowed us to hang onto our hope of what was to come when we reached our homes. That's not to say the people we came across started throwing flowers at our feet or anything like that. They just never tried to kill us.

Small victories.

Ira and I sat up front while Dekar snoozed in the back of the wagon.

"Gods, Ty. You're shaking the wagon more than the road."

"Huh?"

Ira nodded to my hands that I had been rubbing subconsciously while tapping a leg and rocking in my seat.

"Sorry," I said, trying to force myself to relax. "I'm getting anxious. We should be in Denu Creek within the hour."

He shook his head. "Well, we ain't there yet so calm yourself. I swear you're acting like a kid on his name day."

I chuckled, but stopped at a sudden urge. I stood.

Ira swore. "What in the name of Xank are you doing now?"

"Gotta piss."

"Well, let me pull over then. It won't take but a minute," he said pulling the reins.

"No! Just keep going. We can't stop now. We're too close," I said, undoing my britches.

Dekar woke up. "What are you two going on about? That was the best sleep I had in days."

"Ty's being ridiculous," said Ira. "Man can wait a decade to see his family, but not a few extra minutes to make sure he doesn't get piss on his leg."

"Seriously?" asked Dekar, looking away from my stream.

I shook off and started tying my britches up. "Let's see how you feel tomorrow when you're this close to seeing your Adwa again. Then we can talk." I sat. "You got time to get a bit more sleep if you want."

"Too late now. I'm up, and I'm hungry." Dekar started rummaging around in the back. "I guess we won't be stopping to eat. Might as well do it now. Here." He handed up some jerky for me and Ira.

I was pretty hungry, but my stomach was also in too big of a knot to eat much. I took a bite of the dried beef, and let it sit in my mouth, slowly sucking out the spices before chewing and swallowing. The ritual gave me something to do other than think about seeing Lasha and the kids again.

How would they react? What would they say? Molak be damned, I still hadn't figured out what I would say.

The food only calmed me for a few minutes. After the third bite, I started blabbering about Denu Creek, my home, Lasha, Myra, and Zadok. Stories I knew Ira and Dekar had heard dozens of times before spilled out before I even realized it.

I couldn't help myself.

Ira started to drive the horses harder with each story. We actually had to slow down as we reached the outskirts of town.

Ten years is a long time for anyone to be gone from home. In that amount of time, a baby can become a boy or a boy a man. Even still, I had not expected Denu Creek to be so different. The place had more than doubled in size—inns, taverns, specialty stores, and even a small theater next to the local auction house lined Main Street which actually lived up to its name.

Ten years ago it was the only street. Now there were a couple of side roads branching off. It used to take a man less than five minutes to walk from one side of town to the other. It would take at least twice that long now.

"I don't even recognize it anymore."

Ira grunted. "Makes you wonder what our home is like, doesn't it?"

Home for Dekar and Ira was a small town to the south named Tamra.

"It does," Dekar whispered.

We entered Main Street in the evening. It wouldn't be fully dark for hours, yet business owners prepared for night anyway, lighting oil lamps that hung on the posts of awnings over their doorways. Wagons owned by locals began to fill the street while men and women who looked like they had just come in from a hard day of work walked the wooden sidewalks. Many of them headed straight for the taverns.

"Dekar, how old would you reckon most of this is?" I asked.

He grunted. "You can tell a few buildings are fairly recent by how green the wood looks."

I pointed to a barber shop, something the Denu Creek I remember never had. "What about something like that?"

"Older. Same as the inn on the other side of it. Probably seven or eight years old."

"That's what I was thinking too."

"Why?"

"Just trying to figure out why Lasha never mentioned any of this in the letters she sent to me. She'd write a paragraph about the weather, but not even one sentence about all of this."

He shrugged. "I don't know. I guess that's something you'll have to ask her."

"Yeah. It just seems so unlike her."

Ira gave me a nudge and nodded when I looked his way. "You know any of them people?"

I followed his gaze to a group of men standing near the old, single-room jail. It was nice to see there hadn't been a need to build a bigger one despite the increase in population. I couldn't read lips, but I didn't have to. The eyes of the men at the old jail betrayed enough. They made no attempt to hide their displeasure at seeing us.

"No," I answered.

"What about them?" Dekar asked from behind.

I looked to the other side of the street where a handful of ladies stood outside a tailor shop. They looked just as sour about our presence as the men near the jail. However, most had the courtesy not to act so obvious about it. All except one that is. She spat as we passed.

"Well, that's nice," said Dekar.

"Could be coincidence," I said, not liking the general feeling I had so far. I didn't recognize those women either. Or anyone else walking about on the dirt streets for that matter.

"Right," said Ira. "She had this big wad of phlegm she needed out, and it just so happens she dislodged it right as we passed. Very ladylike."

I noted the sarcasm and gave him a look. He said nothing more as all three of us were too busy focusing on other passersby. I thought I saw a couple familiar faces, but wasn't sure since heads turned away quickly from us. It wasn't until we reached the other side of town that someone I knew for sure caught my eye.

I waved at the slender man standing in the doorway of the tanner shop. "Nason! It's . . ." My voice trailed off as Nason darted inside, looking nervous.

"Friend of yours?" asked Ira.

"Yeah. We used to be pretty close."

"Emphasis on used to be."

"He probably didn't know who I was. I've changed a lot in the years I've been gone. Besides, we all could use a bath after the time on the road."

"A man can at least raise a hand in courtesy when someone calls his name."

"I hate to say it, but at least on the surface, things don't appear much different here than they did in most other places," said Dekar.

"I'm sure things will be better once I come back with Lasha and they see who I am. Then they'll realize I live here and I'm not someone trying to dirty up their town."

"I hope you're right," said Dekar as we left Main Street behind us.

* * *

The tract of land I called home sat a few miles outside of town. That distance had been an aggravation before the war when I'd have to travel it during bad weather to stock up on supplies. Now, it was a blessing as the more distance we put between us and the town, the more our mood lightened. My hope and excitement grew once more as we passed homesteads that reminded me of mine. The township of Denu Creek might have gone through extensive changes in my years away, but the land around it hadn't changed one bit.

The road curved around a small hill bordered by tall oaks. I always hated that curve, especially at night. The cynic in me thought the place ideal for an ambush by thieves. Even though I had Ira and Dekar with me and was a far more capable fighter, my hand still drifted to the hilt of a dagger strapped at my thigh.

Just like every time before, no one jumped out from those oaks, and we rode along without incident.

My plot of earth sat at the bottom of a small dip in the rolling land. It was odd to see it after so long. For the most part it too remained unchanged. Between growing seasons, someone had cleared the fields in preparation for the next planting. The fence looked as though it could use some work, but that wasn't anything I couldn't fix over a couple of days with Zadok.

That thought struck me like a mace to the head. When I left for the army, Zadok was barely two years old. Now, he'd be helping me in the fields, and soon I'd be showing him how to shave. Myra would be fourteen. In a couple of years she'd be starting a family of her own.

Gods, I had missed so much.

I silently cursed everyone who had a hand in taking me away from those years—starting with the Geneshans and ending with myself.

No, I couldn't exactly have avoided the war. Once they learned of my resistance to sorcery, there was no way they were letting me stay on a farm. Although, maybe I could have faked my death or something and returned home sooner.

That never would have worked. The army would have found me eventually, and things would have been worse than before. Unless I forced my family to leave Turine that is.

But that would have brought on a whole new set of problems.

I looked at Ira and Dekar, then thought of Hamath and Ava and everyone else in my unit. Desertion was never an idea I had seriously considered. I just couldn't imagine abandoning my friends like that. Even for Lasha and the kids.

The wagon came to a halt. Ira had pulled over, stopping at the entrance to the long path leading to my house.

My house.

"I actually made it back," I whispered.

Every soldier wants to get home and tells themselves they will. But deep down, I'm not sure how many truly believe it.

A hand slapped my back. Dekar appeared to my right smiling. "You did. We all did. Now go see that family of yours."

"Unless you enjoy our company so much you want to stay on a bit more?" Ira smiled.

I hopped down from the wagon and pulled out my things. "Don't get me wrong, I love you, but not that much." I threw my pack over one shoulder. "Hey, do you both want to come in and say hello? Meet the family? Grab a quick bite to eat?"

Dekar shook his head. "Nah, this is your time. We don't need to be intruding." He looked up at the evening sun. "Besides, if we push on for a few more hours before making camp, we should be able to reach Tamra sometime in the late morning. And frankly, I'd rather be kissing Adwa, than taking up room in your place."

It's funny how close we'd become when before the war the three of us would never have met despite living in towns a day's ride from each other.

I smiled. "All right. Maybe in a few weeks, we can get together."

"Sounds good," said Dekar as he climbed into the seat next to Ira.

Unlike parting with Hamath, I knew I'd stay in touch with the brothers. A day's ride was not the same as several weeks.

Ira flicked the reins to get the wagon moving again, then waved. I returned the gesture and headed toward the house. The sound of clomping hoofs and rolling wagon wheels trailed off as they drifted down the road.

Despite the gear and weapons I carried, it took everything I had not to break out into a run. What stopped me from doing so was not the weight of my belongings, but fear. The fear grew as my gaze shifted from my house, to the nearby barn, and then to the empty fields. It was hard to explain, but despite the familiarity, everything felt different. It wasn't what I expected, and now I worried that my reunion with my wife would be the same.

I knew the war hadn't been kind to me. I carried new scars. I had worn a beard when I left, but that had caught fire. The thing never grew back right and so I left it off. I doubted the kids would recognize me one way or the other. But I didn't know how Lasha would react. The last thing I wanted was for her to bar the door when she saw some beat-up soldier she didn't recognize run up onto her porch. So, I forced myself to walk slowly, doing my best to appear as friendly as a fully armed soldier could be.

The walk from the road to the house was longer than I remembered, but I think that had to do with the anxiety clenching at my chest.

The closer I got, I saw that like the fence, the house also needed a bit of work. I changed priorities mentally, planning to work on the house first with Zadok. Autumn would be around the corner and the last thing I wanted to deal with was a drafty house during the cold months. I'd worry about the fence later.

Thinking about the state of the fence and house had me wondering about my Uncle Uriah. I had him move in with us before I left so he could take care of the farm in my stead. We'd never been close, but he was a good man, although an older one. I hoped nothing had happened to him. His absence would have definitely made it harder on Lasha and the kids.

I was within ten feet of the porch when the door swung open. A big bear of a man filled the entranceway. I froze in surprise. He held a giant broadsword in his hand. The thing looked like it hadn't seen much use, but I didn't doubt a man of his size could do some serious damage with a few well-aimed strikes.

In all my thoughts of how this day would turn out, this had never been one of the scenarios to cross my mind. My eyes moved from his sword to his face. No one I recognized. Too young, and the thin beard he wore looked ridiculous.

"That's far enough," he told me, voice purposefully altered in a way that made it seem as though he tried to hide his unease. "State your business."

By that point I had recovered from my own initial surprise. "My business? I should ask you the same. I know I've been gone for some time, but I never thought I'd see the day when a man has a sword drawn on him on his own property. I'm not sure who you are or why you're standing in the doorway to my house like that but—."

"Ezer, what's going on?" asked a soft voice from inside.

My heart raced. "Lasha? It's Tyrus. I—" I said stepping forward.

"Stop right there!" Ezer shouted. He pointed his sword at me. A woman appeared just behind him. She looked to be about the same age as Ezer and bore no resemblance to my Lasha.

I stopped, blinking. "What in the name of Molak is going on? Where is my family? Lasha? Myra? Zadok?" I called out their names.

Ezer pushed his wife back inside. "I have no idea what you're talking about, mister. I ain't ever heard of any of them people. We just moved into town a month ago and bought this property from the bank."

I felt nauseous. "What do you mean you bought it from the bank? I had no mortgage. It's been in my family since my grandfather was alive. I own it outright."

He shrugged. "Maybe you did at one time. But now I do. You got an issue with that, then you take it up with the mayor. This place had been abandoned for a while. Those people you're looking for are probably long gone."

I shook my head, rubbing my brow with an open hand in confusion. "No, this isn't right. None of this makes sense."

I couldn't accept it and dropped my bag.

Ezer grit his teeth. "Mister, you come closer and I'll kill you. I heard about what you soldiers did in the war. I won't let you do that to my wife."

Red flashed in front of my eyes. I charged forward. Ezer reared back for a massive swing. The move left his torso wide open. Had I actually drawn my sword, I could have opened him up. Lucky for him I hadn't.

I ducked under the sweeping blade as it thudded into a post on the porch, one that still bore the carved initials of my grandfather's name. My fist connected with Ezer's torso. A gust of air left his lungs. I didn't let up, not on someone that big. I connected two more times to the stomach before finishing him off with a blow to the jaw. He fell hard to the wooden planks. I stepped over his unconscious body and entered my home.

With my heart racing, I breathed deeply. That did little to improve my demeanor. Gone was the smell of Lasha's bath soap. The smell of freshly picked roses on a side table replaced it.

Lasha hated roses.

"You try to touch me and I'll kill you. I swear it," said the woman sobbing in the back left corner of the kitchen. She held a cleaver.

I ignored her as I went quickly through each of the three rooms, looking for some sign of my family. Defeated, I stormed out, stepping over Ezer who was starting to come around. I threw his sword out into the yard before picking up my sack. I headed toward the barn to ease my worry I had that maybe my family was being held captive there.

Just like the house, I found no trace of them.

I glanced over one last time to the porch as Ezer's woman helped him to his feet. He leaned on one of the posts with one hand while holding his stomach with the other. A part of me felt bad for hurting him since it seemed he had been telling me the truth. However, another part of me didn't care who I hurt. I needed answers and Ezer didn't appear to have them.

Adjusting the bag on my back, I started back toward town. I'd find someone there with answers to what was going on or I'd tear each one of those new buildings down trying.

CHAPTER 12

During my walk back to town I tried to find a word that might describe what I was going through. Confused? Baffled? Worried? Angry? None of them worked. They were all too limiting. Too small. None encapsulated everything I was experiencing.

Hundreds of thoughts ran through my head, but I couldn't focus on any of them. I knew that birds probably chirped and breezes rustled leaves in the trees, yet I heard nothing and felt less. The smell of familiar fields no longer tickled the inside of my nose. My legs moved on their own accord.

I made it back to the curve in the road near the small hill and tall oaks before my head cleared. I stopped in the middle of the road, unsettled. I was alone for the first time in years, caught in a place I had hoped would bring me joy. It hadn't brought me anything yet but more pain.

Denu Creek felt as foreign to me as Genesha once did.

A growing sense of unease crawled up my spine. Now was not the time to grow careless—regardless of how my life had just been turned upside down. I needed to think.

Taking a deep breath, I decided quickly that my gut reaction to return to town was still the best strategy. I needed to find someone, perhaps Nason, who could tell me what happened, why Lasha had abandoned our home, and most importantly where she and the kids had gone.

The chilly reception I had received going through town worried me. Getting the information I sought might be harder than just asking a few simple questions of the first person I came across. Creativity in my approach might be just as crucial to my success as caution.

I cursed myself for coming home with blinders on. I should have been better prepared for something like this, regardless of how remote the possibility had seemed.

I'm not sure how long I stood in the road beating myself up, but eventually I came out of it when a memory of Lasha's smiling face came to mind. It seemed like she stood in front of me. I swore I even heard the pattering of tiny feet running through the house as the kids played. I closed my eyes, and my hands in determination. I'd get the answers I needed.

My eyes opened as the footsteps grew louder. That had not been part of my imagination. Someone was running on the dirt road up the other side of the hill. I picked up my bag and ran off into the nearby oaks. I hid behind the tree closest to the road with sword drawn. I heard only one set of footsteps, but my heart raced as though there were ten. Who'd be coming this way, at this time of day, and in such a hurry?

Had the town sent someone after me to find out my identity?

A smile tugged at the corners of my mouth as the irony of my situation struck me. I was set to ambush someone from the spot that I spent half my life worrying I'd be ambushed from.

The footsteps closed. I nearly jumped in front of their path until something about their sound gave me pause.

A boy zipped past me. I let him go since he wasn't a threat. Turning my ear back to the road, I listened for others following in his wake but heard nothing. My muscles relaxed.

I flicked my eyes back to the boy who had stopped just up ahead. He bent over and huffed for air. Sure of no immediate danger, I examined him from the shadows. He looked like he was maybe twelve. He was certainly poor. He wore no shoes despite the cool weather, feet black with dirt. Both his trousers and shirt had holes in them. He straightened and looked toward the farm I once called home. I made note of the black, curly hair on his head and the darker tone of his skin.

A note of familiarity struck me. Could it be him?

"It's not there," I heard him whisper, voice sullen. His hands balled into fists. He spoke again through clenched teeth. "She was right. I swore it would be there."

He cursed, using a word I didn't think a boy his age had any business using. He kicked at the dirt, then stooped over, and began picking up rocks off the road. He hurled them down the hill toward the house, grunting and cursing with each of his throws.

After the emotional wave I just experienced, the last thing I wanted was to go through that disappointment again. Despite the hope burgeoning inside me, I approached the situation cautiously.

I slid out from behind the oak and onto the road, staying in the shadows of the low hanging branches.

He finished throwing rocks and stared silently at my old farm. I sheathed my sword. "What's not there, boy?"

He jumped and spun around, taking a step back in fear. Tears streaked down the dark skin of his crusted cheeks. He wiped them away in embarrassment.

I considered what could have upset the boy. I doubted anyone from town sent him after our wagon.

I asked again. "What's not there?"

"A wagon."

That startled me. Maybe I was wrong and someone had sent him after us. "Did someone send you out this way?"

He swallowed, looking nervous. "No, sir. Did you happen to see the wagon?" He paused. "Were you in it?"

I tried to soften my tone. "That depends. Why were you looking for a wagon?"

"I thought there might be someone on it I once knew. Please just tell me if you were on it or if you saw it pass at least."

My stomach knotted and my mouth went dry. I croaked. "Who were you looking for exactly?"

The boy seemed hesitant. He composed himself. He flicked his head back in a way that made my heart drop and my palms sweat. In that small gesture I suddenly saw how much he favored his mother.

"My pa."

I stepped out from the shadows. "Zadok?"

"How did you know . . ." His mouth dropped as he eyed my military garb.

Zadok had his second name day the week before I left home. I doubted he would be able to recall what I looked or sounded like at that young of an age. Yet, something gave him the reassurance he needed.

"Pa!"

Zadok closed the distance between us and dove into my arms. By the time I picked him up, tears streamed down my face. We both squeezed each other with an intensity that said neither of us wanted to let the other go again.

The loss of my home no longer mattered while I held my son.

Zadok eased his grip and rested his head on my shoulder. "Myra said you wouldn't be here. But I had to find out for myself when I heard people talking about the wagon with soldiers. I never believed you were dead. I knew that letter was wrong."

"Dead?" That jarred me from my joyful stupor. I set Zadok on the ground and squatted next to him. He kept his hand on my shoulder.

Up close, I could see the shadow of the little boy I left behind. Though his skin was not nearly as dark as his mother's, it was far darker than mine. For the most part, he had much of Lasha's foreign features—thick curly hair, deep brown eyes, full lips. The only parts of me I could see in him were my nose and jaw line. I think the combination worked well. Cleaned up, he'd be a sharp-looking kid.

"What letter said that?" I asked.

"The letter the army sent us. It was about four years ago. It said that Turine had taken heavy losses at Wadlow Hill and it was too difficult to figure out the names of everyone that died there."

I frowned. That had been true enough, but I hadn't heard of any letter about Wadlow Hill that went out to the citizens of Turine.

Zadok continued. "It said that if a follow-up letter wasn't sent within a year, we should assume you died serving your country."

My head spun in confusion. "No, that's not right. The letter you should have gotten said that the cost of sending messages had grown too high and that unless a letter specifying an individual's death was received, families were to assume their husband, father, son, or whomever was alive."

He wrinkled his brow. "We never got a letter like that."

"You must have. I read a copy of that letter."

"I promise, Pa. I read the other letter myself when I got old enough. Ma used to look at it when she thought we weren't around. Then she'd go off somewhere and cry."

The thought of Lasha so pained at my death had me shedding fresh tears for her sake. She didn't deserve that. I wiped my face and forced a smile for Zadok's sake. "Take me to her. I've got a lot of work to do to set that right."

Zadok didn't return my smile. He stared at the dirt. "Ma died last year."

"What?" My legs gave out and I fell back. Numbness threatened to take over. I stared at Zadok.

"I'm sorry, Pa." His shoulders shook as he sobbed. "I tried to help her, but I'm too small. I couldn't stop him."

My body stiffened. The numbness gone, my voice went cold. "Stop who?"

"The man that killed her. He was drunk and just kept hitting her. I tried to hit him back but he hit me too. When I woke up Myra was shaking me awake, crying. Ma was on the floor dead."

My fists clenched tight. Every muscle in my body flexed as hundreds of questions ran through my head. I wanted to ask them all. Where did all this happen? Who was the man? What happened to him? Why was a little boy trying to defend his mother? Was no one else around? Where was Uncle Uriah? I asked none of them.

Struggling to calm myself in that moment was one of the hardest things I'd ever had to do. I wanted someone's blood. Badly. My chest ached with the knowledge I'd never have the reunion with my wife I had been dreaming about. However, it ached more for the boy who obviously blamed himself, at least in part, for his mother's death. The responsibilities of a father that I had been forced to neglect for years overrode the sorrow burdening me as a husband.

Zadok stood head down and hunched forward. I reached out and pulled him to me. He sat on my lap and tucked himself into a ball, weeping.

I rocked him in the middle of the road for some time, thankful no one was there to disturb us. I did my best to console him by telling him it wasn't his fault and that there was nothing he could have done to stop the man.

He finally began to calm down when I promised him that I wasn't ever leaving again.

* * *

Zadok eventually recovered enough to fill me in on some of what I had missed during the last decade. He did so as he led the way to his sister. Both had taken work on Jareb's plantation.

Due to his age, it was difficult for him to convey everything and when certain things had occurred. Most of what he recounted had originally come from Myra, Lasha, or Uncle Uriah.

Each new detail hit me like a spear to the gut. By the time he finished, I realized my son and daughter had more strength in them than many of the men I had fought beside.

The woes started shortly after I left. Because of a drought followed by a locust infestation, crops came in much lower than expected that first year. Money was scarce. Still, Lasha and Uncle Uriah had managed to keep food on the table.

Two hard years went by before they saw improvement. Uncle Uriah had begun to grow bitter because of their hardships, especially since it seemed nearby farms were recovering faster. He got impatient and made a couple of bad business deals behind Lasha's back. He put the farm up as collateral in order to purchase extra land and new equipment, hoping to recoup their losses at a quicker rate.

I wanted to wring Uncle Uriah's neck for doing something so stupid. But then again, I'm the one who asked him to stay with Lasha to begin with. I'm sure he thought he was making the right call.

Uriah's gamble failed. After a couple more years, the bank repossessed the farm. It had gone through two separate owners since then, a third if you counted the couple I met earlier. Some in town considered the place cursed. I filed that bit of information away. If Ezer and his woman couldn't make things work, I might try to buy the place back at a discount and bring it up to what it had once been. I knew how to get the most out of that land.

I asked Zadok about Uncle Uriah.

"He died a year before we got that letter I told you about."

"That long ago?" I shook my head in disbelief. Lasha never said a word about his death or any of the other stuff everyone endured in her letters.

"Yeah, losing the farm really brought him down," said Zadok. He walked a few steps ahead. "He started drinking away what little money Ma earned cleaning people's homes. One day he and Ma got into it. Both said a lot of bad things to each other. Uncle said some stuff about you too, blaming you for our troubles. Ma slapped him for that. That ended the argument. Uncle Uriah left." He kicked the dirt. "They found his body the next day. He hung himself out in the apple orchard."

"Molak be cursed." I blew out a slow breath. "I'm sorry. I should have been here."

"It's not your fault, Pa. Ma never blamed you. She said that you were doing the right thing, something I should be proud of no matter what the rumors said. We knew you weren't killing kids and stuff. Right?"

I recalled the young soldier near Myra's age I had killed in our final mission. I thought of the dozens of others, some older, some younger, who had tried to kill me. I looked away and chose to ignore his question. "How does Myra feel about everything?"

"Oh, she hates you."

Gods, that wasn't exactly what I meant.

Zadok continued. "Even though she thinks you're dead." He looked up. "But you're here now, so you can explain everything to her and make it right. We can be a family again." He frowned. "Well, mostly."

Though Zadok seemed to be in better spirits, I was still hesitant to press him about the particulars regarding Lasha's death. I had only been reunited with my son for a short period. The last thing I wanted was to push him into a place he did not feel comfortable going.

My hope was that Myra might be able to fill in the details where Zadok could not.

"Did things get any easier after Uncle Uriah died?"

"No. You would think so since there were fewer ways to split the food and we didn't have to worry about him drinking all the time. But after they found his body, the people Ma used to do work for asked her not to come around anymore."

"Why?"

"Because they got to thinking that something was wrong with us on account of her."

"What!"

He kicked the dirt again. "Yeah. They said it started when your Pa died just a few weeks after you married Ma."

"A rattlesnake bit him," I said cutting in. "That had nothing to do with your Ma."

He shrugged. "They said we were cursed like the farm. Grandpa died. You went off to the army, and everyone thought you died too. We lost the farm after three generations of nothing but prosperity. Uncle Uriah hanged himself . . ." He sighed. "Ma kept looking for work, but no one would hire her. Not even to wash clothes or scrub floors."

"What did you do for money?"

"We had no money. We slept in the woods and mostly foraged for food. Even with the few things we managed to trap or catch, we were always hungry. Myra was getting pretty angry then. She used to ask Ma why we didn't just go live with her family down south. But Ma said it was too dangerous to travel that far alone, and besides, how would we pay to travel."

"Then what happened?"

"Well, we had been living like that for months. It wasn't ideal, but we got by. But that was during the warmer months. Early that winter, before it got too cold, we huddled around a small fire trying to stay warm. I was shivering hard. Ma started crying. She got real angry and began stomping around the fire, swearing. That was the only time I ever heard her curse. It kind of scared me. Finally she stopped, kicked out the fire, and took us by the hands. She dragged us back to town in the middle of the night without a word."

"To go where?"

"Somewhere she said she should have gone a long time ago, but pride wouldn't let her. She said alive or dead she hoped you'd understand she had no other choice. After that, we all shared her room at the Soiled Dove. Well, except when Ma had to use it to work. Then me and Myra would have to try and sleep behind the stairs in the common room."

Zadok stopped talking then. I'm not sure why. Perhaps he saw something in the look on my face that begged him to.

I fought hard to keep the tears at bay, figuring the last thing he needed to see was his Pa cry for the third time in one day. Despite my best efforts, more than a few escaped. I couldn't stop thinking about how I had failed everyone I loved.

His hand slipped into mine. I squeezed it, remembering how it felt to hold his hand years ago when things had been so much simpler.

We walked in silence away from town toward Jareb's plantation. Buzzing cicadas from the surrounding fields drowned out our footsteps.

* * *

The cicadas stopped and only the gods know how long we walked with no sound but our feet scraping dirt.

Those were the same gods who I had always cared little about, and in light of what I just heard, cared less about than ever before. Their existence and influence no longer mattered to me. My dislike of them turned to hate. It would take a proverbial miracle for me to ever show them the respect their priests demanded.

However, even if the gods existed only in the minds of men, I'd curse their names and every bit of their attributes. I figured that if they were indeed real, cursing them was the least I could do to recompense them for all they had done for me.

People held different opinions on the role the gods played in our lives. Some felt that they intervened only when necessary, and took a passive approach to our lives. Others believed everything we did, down to the smallest detail, like wiping our noses on a sleeve instead of a handkerchief, had already been predestined by the deities who looked down on us.

Both viewpoints had their flaws. It either meant the gods let bad things happen to people or actually made them happen.

Thinking of all that my family and I had been through with not even the support of each other to lean on pushed aside some of the despair welling inside of me. Anger took its place. Before long, my jaw ached from clenching it.

"Pa? Are you going to be all right?" Zadok asked.

The sun had finally begun to set, bathing the rolling countryside in reds and purples. The bruised appearance of the landscape mirrored the ache coursing through my insides.

Was I going to be all right? I didn't know. But saying as much wouldn't have done Zadok any favors. So, I lied.

"I will be soon, son."

"What are you thinking about?"

"Your mother." I decided to take a small chance. "Someone killed your mother at the Soiled Dove, didn't they?"

"Yes." Zadok put his head down. "It was a . . . customer . . . as Ma used to call the men. He was drunk and . . ."

I let go of his hand, and placed an arm around his shoulder. "It's all right. I don't need you to tell me everything about that night. I just wanted to know if my suspicions were accurate."

I felt him relax slightly.

"Do you remember what happened to the man who killed her?"

He nodded. "The sheriff gave him ten lashes and ordered the man to pay restitution to Omri for damaging his best worker for future money lost. Omri is the owner of the Soiled Dove."

I felt sick again, bile creeping upward. I managed to swallow it back down. My throat burned. One of the last conversations I had with Ava came to mind. "What if that had been Lasha?" she had asked me when referencing a whore who had been beaten by a soldier.

At the time, Ava had been making a point about the women working our camp. Lasha had not made the decision to enter that life easily, or selfishly. She did it to care for our children. Pressed with a tough decision, she gave herself away like a piece of meat so that Myra and Zadok could survive. Did that make her a whore? Gods, my head spun just from thinking of that word in association with my wife. Or did it make her a dedicated mother whose unselfishness continued to shine even in the darkest of moments? Did it just prove that she had been every bit as remarkable of a woman as I always knew she was?

"How much restitution did you and Myra receive?" I asked.

"Nothing."

"Nothing!" I said, louder than intended, causing Zadok to jump.

I cursed softly. Ten lashes and restitution for Omri. Nothing for my kids. A cattle thief would receive harsher punishment. Is that how everyone viewed Lasha for what she had become? Worth less than cattle?

"What happened to you and Myra?"

"Omri let us stay in the room for another week. But that ended when he brought in another worker. When she arrived, he kicked us out.

We asked if we could keep sleeping behind the stairs, but he told us no." He paused, head hanging. "Omri said that in a couple of years if we were still around, he'd give us a room of our own if Myra was interested in working for him. Said she had much of Ma's look, and customers always paid more for satisfying their curiosity about the exotic."

Omri had not been the owner of the Soiled Dove when I left town. Stranger or not, I hated the man. I thought about having a talk with him, but knew that I couldn't trust myself. The last thing I wanted to do was get arrested for killing him and abandon my kids all over again. Besides, I was more interested in seeing Myra at the moment than avenging Lasha.

"What did you and Myra do next?"

"We tried to find work, but no one was interested. We were getting pretty bad off again, sleeping where we could, eating whatever food we could steal."

He looked ashamed. I couldn't fault them. Sometimes you did what you had to in order to survive.

He continued. "Eventually Jareb offered us the jobs we have now."

"I didn't think he would still be alive. He was old when I left."

"What? Oh, wait. You mean Jareb Senior. No, he died. Jareb Junior took over everything his father owned."

I grimaced. Jareb Junior had a year on me. Unlike Jareb Senior, Junior had been a donkey for as long as I could remember. I had put him in his place a couple of times when we were children and I caught him picking on Ava. He had backup for our last fight. I was not successful in defending my sister that time.

That's when Ava's powers first manifested. It was also how I discovered my resistance to sorcery, as the only way to stop my sister from killing Jareb and his friends, was to hold her tight until she calmed down. It took weeks for them to recover. Pa had to do a whole lot of explaining so the town wouldn't lynch and burn Ava as someone possessed with a demon.

I grunted. Of course Ava had wanted to avoid Denu Creek.

Anyway, Jareb junior didn't strike me as the kind of person who'd change with age.

But, ten years was a long time.

We left the road a couple miles from town and walked the path leading to Jareb's house as the sky continued to darken. The first stars began to appear in the clear night sky.

"I thought we were going to see Myra," I said.

"We are."

"Oh. Is it common for her to work through dinner like this?"

"Every night. If we're awake, we're working. Myra in the house. Me in the barn or fields. Sometimes we're even woken up in the middle of the night if something needs doing."

I frowned. "That seems harsh."

He shrugged. "When we became indentured to him, those were the terms he offered. At least we have food and a place to stay."

My eyes looked at his bare feet. "But not shoes? Or better clothes for that matter?"

"Jareb said money is tight. Maybe he'd get me some shoes next season."

I eyed the three-story home with columns and a wraparound porch. Light from oil lamps shone brightly in each window. Two burned on the porch near the door. Using such a large amount of oil served no other purpose than to flaunt the fact Jareb had the money to burn it. Money he could be using to buy shoes for my son.

As a boy, the house had seemed enormous to me. As an adult, it was still impressive.

"Yeah, I bet Jareb's hurting for coin," I muttered.

"What was that, Pa?"

"Nothing. Do you know the terms of your contract?"

"Yes, sir. We've got eight more years to fulfill, but there is a buyout in year five if we manage to scrape together the coin to take advantage of it."

"So, he pays you too?"

"No, sir."

"Then how does he expect you to afford to pay the buyout?"

Zadok shrugged. "It's the same terms he's offered the other servants."

Servants? I'd have called them slaves.

"How much is the buyout?"

"Forty gold pieces."

I staggered. "That's over two year's pay in the army. I guess it's good I've been wise with my money."

"That's actually the amount for each of us."

I spat, brows furrowing in anger. With contracts like that it seemed Jareb indeed hadn't changed at all. I'd be able to cover their buyout though I'd have only a little left.

But, at least I'd have my children. I could figure out the money problem later. Making us a family again was most important.

We reached the steps to the porch. I took them two at a time while Zadok pumped his legs to keep up. My palms actually began to sweat, nervous to see Myra again.

Zadok knocked.

"You can't just go inside?" I asked.

"They don't let the field workers in the house."

The door swung open.

"Yes, may I—"

"Myra!" Zadok shouted, grabbing her hand and pulling her onto the porch.

Zadok began speaking so fast and with such excitement that it was hard for me to make out half of what he said. Myra understood though. She wore the same look of shock that Lasha would get. Same dark eyes, brightening in recognition. Same pursed lips as if ready to speak, but unable to find the right words to say. The short hair worn just as Lasha had only added to the eeriness I felt looking at my daughter, not seeing the little girl from ten years ago, but the young woman she was becoming.

The only difference between mother and daughter was skin color. The dark chestnut associated with Lasha's people, mixed with my pale skin gave Myra a coppery hue.

Myra and I stared uncomfortably at each other as Zadok yammered on. I saw she could also stand to gain a few pounds to her wiry frame. Myra shook her head, turned to Zadok, and shushed him. "That's enough."

The boy stopped.

Myra's eyes narrowed in a way that Lasha's never had. I knew where she had inherited that look from. It had worked wonders for me in the army.

"You're supposed to be dead," she said. Her tone was flat and even, not shaky in the least.

"So, I've heard. The letter you got was wrong."

"Obviously."

This wasn't going as I hoped.

"I know this is a big surprise, but I've been discharged. I'll explain everything later. Right now, I just want to take you and Zadok home."

"We don't have a home anymore," she snapped.

"We can find a new one."

She pulled Zadok to her. "Zadok and I already found a new home. What makes you think we want to leave with you?"

"Because I told him we do," said Zadok. "Why are you acting like this? You hate it here more than I do, especially with Jareb—"

"Zadok," she hissed. The boy clamped his mouth down.

I frowned. "What is it?"

"Nothing," she snapped.

"All right. Look, I know you've both been through a lot. Zadok's told me only some of it. I can never make that pain go away. And I can never make up those years I was gone. But, I still want to try anyway." I held out my hand. "Please, let me try."

Her face softened, but not completely. She stared at my hand and I could see her struggling with what to do—slap it away or take it.

Gods, they had been through so much.

"What's taking so long, Myra? I asked you to get the door some time ago," said a voice I recognized.

Jareb stepped into view. Other than a poor attempt at a mustache, he hadn't changed much in my time away. Brown hair, green eyes, defined jaw.

He recognized me immediately, the surprise hindering his ability to speak for only a moment. He cleared his throat, stepped out of the doorway, pushing himself in front of Myra and Zadok.

"Tyrus? By the gods, I thought you were dead," he said. He looked over my shoulder, a bit nervous. "Ava with you?"

I held back a smile. A decade later and he still hadn't forgotten that thrashing. "No. She's in Hol studying with Turine's High Mages."

Jareb relaxed. His eyes went down to my boots then rose until they met mine. "You look like hell."

"I feel like it." I nodded at his clothes—clean and wrinkle-free. You would have thought a tailor had made them that day. "I see you're doing well for yourself."

A thin smile tugged at his face. "I certainly try to make it seem so. People have a way of not showing you the respect you desire if you don't look like you deserve it." He paused, looking down at the children who hadn't said a word since he'd shown up. "I'd ask what brings you here, but I guess that's rather obvious. They are doing well as you can see. Clothed and well-fed."

I wanted to refute that claim based on Zadok's appearance and my own assumptions from Myra's weight, but honestly, I didn't have the time or inclination to argue. I just wanted to get my children and leave.

"I'm ready to take them home. Now that I'm back, there's no need for them to work for you. That's not to say I don't appreciate the chance you gave them," I said, doing my best to keep the peace.

Jareb clicked his tongue. "They have contracts with me."

I reached for my money pouch. "I know. I'll buy them out. Zadok told me the amounts."

"The buyout in their contract isn't an option for another five years."

My voice went low. "What are you saying?"

"I'm saying that I can't just let them leave at that price. It would set a bad precedent. If I allow this for Myra and Zadok, who's to say one of my other servants might not try the same thing."

"What is it going to take for me to buy out their contracts, Jareb?"

He appeared thoughtful, then sighed. "The best I can do is give you Zadok for double his buyout amount. But Myra will need to stay. She's too important for me to part with."

My jaw clenched. "Are you crazy? You want me to pay twice the amount of Zadok's buyout and then leave Myra here?" I opened my money pouch, counted out the amount of their original buyouts, added ten percent, and shoved it into his hand. "This is more than fair." I held my hand out to Myra and Zadok. "C'mon, let's go."

"No!" Jareb snapped. "Myra stay where you are."

Neither she nor Zadok moved. Both looked confused.

"I'm not leaving here without both of my children."

"Kush. Amalek." Jareb called over his shoulder.

I cursed inwardly recalling the names of Jareb's childhood friends.

The two men stepped out of the house where they had obviously been hiding on the other side of the entranceway. In the last ten years, they had put on quite a bit of size. Some fat. Some muscle. Either way, they occupied a lot of space. Swords hung at their waists.

At our last run-in, they had both held me down while Jareb worked me over. That was when Ava's powers first manifested. Both Kush and Amalek still bore the faint scars on their arms and neck from my little sister's wrath.

I fought off a snicker.

"Don't do anything stupid, Tyrus. Your sister isn't here to watch over you this time."

Was that supposed to scare me? I was pretty good fighter before I joined the army. I more than knew what I was doing now. I had faced both people and things scarier than the three of them. The three of them put together didn't elicit the response the sight a single D'engiti brought.

"A good thing she isn't," I said. "Her temper has only gotten worse over the years. You'd probably be dead if she was here watching you prevent me from taking her niece and nephew away."

"Take your son and leave."

"Why is it so important that Myra stays?"

Jareb eyed each of his friends who had moved up beside him, hands on the hilts of their swords. A dumb move since there now wasn't space to easily draw the weapons. The thin smile from Jareb grew wider.

"Well, it's because she reminds me so much of her mother. I still think about Lasha, you know. Best piece of tail the Soiled Dove had. But I'm sure you know that already. Gods, I never saw a whore who enjoyed what she did as much as her." He chuckled, gesturing to Myra. "I'm hoping what they say about the apple not falling far from the tree holds true."

My right fist came up so fast, it snapped Jareb's head back, mid-laugh. He fell backward into the open doorway.

Both Kush and Amalek started to draw their swords, each realizing too late that quarters were too close. Kush stepped back to make more room, so I turned my attention to Amalek while throwing Myra and Zadok back with a sweep of my arm. My heel slammed into Amalek's instep. I followed it with a kick to the inside of his knee. He tumbled forward in a screeching heap.

Kush had managed to get his sword loose and swung it wildly at my head. I ducked under the sweeping blade. It thudded into the side of the house. I stepped into him and pushed his still extended arm against his body, pinning it before he had a chance to recover. Both hands locked on his shoulders and I yanked him down as my knee came up. He expelled a gust of air and dropped the sword. My elbow connected with his nose. Blood sprayed as he fell. He rolled into a ball on the porch.

I turned around quickly as Amalek tried to stand. A boot to the head knocked him out cold.

I walked over to Jareb and looked down at his splayed form. That pretty face looked a mess. Blood oozed from nose and busted lips. The defined jaw crooked. His unconscious body lying in a heap only upset me more. I had wanted him to get up if only to knock him down again. Doing anything more to him while he was out just didn't sit well with me.

I didn't believe for one moment that Lasha had enjoyed what she had to do at the Soiled Dove, but that didn't keep the image of him on top of her from my mind.

"Gods be cursed," I muttered.

Looking up, Zadok and Myra stared at me wide-eyed and wide-mouthed just off the porch.

"That was amazing!" yelled Zadok.

I cleared my throat, suddenly self-conscious. "We need to get moving before some of the workers come by to see what's been going on."

"If they do, I doubt it would be to help," said Zadok.

"Even still. Let's go."

Zadok grabbed Myra's hand, pulling her forward as I stepped around the bodies and joined them on the lawn.

"What about the money?" he asked.

"Leave it," I said. "I think it was wrong how he treated you and your sister, but there were contracts in place. As much as I hate giving Jareb anything more than his life, I won't be called a thief for reuniting my family. The mayor's a good man. He'll see things from my perspective if I leave the money. If I just take you two and run, we'll have more trouble to deal with."

"I don't know, Pa. There's a different mayor than when you were here last, and he's close to Jareb."

I paused, reconsidering. "We leave the money anyway."

We started off the porch as a few curious field hands appeared around the side of the house. They took in the damage and gave me a nod as if saying they approved.

Same old Jareb.

"There's money lying around for Jareb." I said. "It's the money to pay for my children. See that he gets it. If not, I'll be angry. Understand?"

One of the workers, a big man, nodded.

"Good." I tossed him one of my few remaining coins. That might have seemed like a dumb move, but since I thought to take care of him he might be more inclined to leave what still lay on the porch alone.

We hurried toward the main road. Myra and Zadok were complete opposites. She walked in a daze. He wore a smile and dragged her along by the hand.

A bright crescent moon hung in the clear night sky interlaced with countless stars. It was the sort of night Lasha and I used to admire on our porch after the children went down for the night. The memory began to calm me until another image of her and Jareb took over. I cursed and picked up my pace.

"Where are we going, Tyrus?" Myra asked in a huff.

"Tyrus?" That jarred me.

"That is your name."

I looked back at her. "Did you call your mother 'Lasha?'"

"No. She earned the right to be our Ma."

Ouch. That might be the worst thing anyone had ever said to me.

Zadok shoved Myra. "Stop it. He just saved us from Jareb."

"Appearing after ten years and beating on a few people doesn't make up for all the time he's been gone," said Myra.

"Shut up! You're going to make him angry. He'll leave us again."

"No," I said. "The first time I left, it wasn't my choice. It was the king's. But that doesn't matter. Regardless of what either of you say or do, I'm not leaving you again. Ever."

"You never answered my question," said Myra. "Have you been away so long, you've forgotten where town is?"

"I know where town is," I said, trying to mask my frustration with her. "I thought it might be wise to keep to ourselves tonight since it will be late when we would get there." That was only part of the truth. The rest was that I was barely thinking straight after everything that I learned in the last few hours and the last place I wanted to be was around more people who might try to do me harm. Gods, I hoped Dekar and Ira would have a better go of things in Tamra.

I continued. "Don't worry, I know a spot in the woods that will give us what we need."

"Do we have to?" asked Zadok, voice shaky.

"What's the matter?" I asked.

"He's scared," said Myra. "The woods don't hold good memories for us."

I thought of Zadok's story about how Lasha had them living there for a few months.

I put my hand on his shoulder. "It's just for tonight, and I'll be with you. All right?"

He nodded.

CHAPTER 13

We managed our way through thick undergrowth and low hanging oaks thanks to the starry night. It took less time than I thought it would to find the place Ava and I used to spend our free time as children. Surprisingly, it looked undisturbed after all the years away.

Wild blackberry bushes lined the clearing between tall pines. A lean-to that Ava and I had built out of old logs still stood in as good of condition as it had when we were younger. Later when Ava's sorcery manifested, she managed to figure out some minor spell that added strength to the logs, preventing rot and repelling bugs.

I recalled that a quarter mile north stood a giant walnut tree and another half mile past that ran a small creek. At the low point, the water was only a foot deep. When younger, I remember snatching fish right out of the water while they maneuvered through the rocks.

Shelter, food, and water all within easy walking distance. Had I thought about it, I would have shown Lasha the spot long ago. Such resources might have stayed her decision to work at the Soiled Dove.

Maybe a part of me had just wanted to keep it a secret between me and Ava. As children, it was our refuge from the world when we decided we had enough of it. We had built plenty of good memories in our little hideout.

But with what Lasha and the children had gone through . . . those memories seemed unimportant.

It took me less than ten minutes to pull away the vines and brush that had grown around the lean-to. Next I cleared out the leaves littering the ground inside, replacing them with tall grass for Myra and Zadok to sleep on. In the meantime, I had Zadok and Myra gather firewood.

By the time they returned with their fourth load, I had gotten the area squared away for the night. I started a fire in an old pit Ava and I had lined with river rock. It too had stayed intact.

We said very little while we worked. Myra's sour mood hung over us, dampening the easy conversation Zadok and I instantly had.

Once I had the fire going well enough, I stepped away.

Myra and Zadok sat inside the lean-to.

"Do you both know how to keep this going?" I asked.

Myra rolled her eyes. "Of course."

"All right. Good." I started rummaging in my pack which I had set off to the side earlier.

"Why?" she asked.

I pulled out a couple of hard biscuits and my last apple. "Because, I'm going to go work on getting us some supper." I handed the food over to them. "This should hold you over until I get back." I also handed Myra a knife. She gave me a look. "So you and Zadok can share the apple."

She hesitated before taking it, looking nervous. "If this is all you have, we can split it with you."

"No, that's yours. I've actually got some jerky, oats, and a few more biscuits in the bag in case I don't come back with anything. I just thought it might be nice to have something fresher." Her eyes darted about, searching the dark woods like a monster might run out of it at any moment. I realized I was leaving them, even if it was only for a little while. "If you're more comfortable with me staying, I will."

The frightened look vanished, replaced by a mask of hardness. "No. It's fine. Go," she said.

"Can I come, Pa?" asked Zadok through a mouthful of biscuit.

A bit of that worried look returned to Myra.

"Well, you could, but I really need you to protect your sister for me."

His eyes widened. "Oh, of course." He paused. "But how am I supposed to do that?"

Good point. The boy was skinny as a whip and without a weapon. I couldn't do much about the former and I doubted he'd be much use with anything fitting the latter. Still, just holding a weapon can bring as much comfort to a person as being able to actually use it. I unstrapped one of the daggers I kept on my body and gave it to him sheathe and all.

"Here you go."

His eyes got even larger. "Is this mine?"

"Sure, a boy your age should have one. I'll start teaching you how to use it soon. But for now, only pull it out if you have to. And no play fighting with that, especially around your sister. If she tells me you have, I'll take it back."

"He'll be fine, Tyrus. He's knows what not to do with a dagger. He's not five," said Myra.

"No. He's not," was all I could say. Neither one of my children were quite adults, but they were also so far from what I remember them being, I didn't really know how to talk to them. "No one knows about this place or that we're out here," I added. "Besides, I won't be far off."

"You can go whenever you want," said Myra, cutting into the apple.

I realized that I had been just standing there, not sure how to part. I took her cue as the hint I needed. I grabbed some twine out of my bag, waved awkwardly over my shoulder and disappeared into the woods.

The sudden lack of anxiety I had from not being in my daughter's presence brought on a burden of guilt I had not expected. I paused, inhaled a few deep breaths to calm myself, then drifted deeper into the trees.

I somehow managed to spot a set of fresh rabbit tracks thanks to the bright moonlight. I narrowed the well-used path by jamming sticks into the ground on either side of it. At the end of the narrowing, I set up a noose with the twine the rabbit would have to pass through. The other end was tied at the base of a nearby bush.

At best, the noose would tighten around a passing rabbit's neck, killing it. At worst, the noose would tighten around the body. The rabbit wouldn't die from that, but it would be stuck where I could finish the job later.

After the first trap, I discovered several other paths. With that sort of traffic, I was probably near a den. Either that or a very active rabbit. I made four more snares, optimistic I'd catch something.

Next I set a couple of squirrel traps using slip nooses around large tree branches resting against tall pines. The idea was that the squirrel would run itself up the branch like it would the base of the tree, not see the loop, and . . . dead squirrel.

I probably spent about an hour setting the traps up. Under normal circumstances, my mind would have been unfocused with that much time to myself. However, the past few hours had just been too much to handle and my mind took a break, emptying itself. I thought about nothing but the task at hand.

It wasn't until I finished setting traps and sat on a fallen tree to wait that I truly began to recover from the day's shock. Unfortunately, the first thing that clouded my thoughts was Lasha working the Soiled Dove. Angry tears formed in my eyes.

I decided to check the traps. I knew I should wait longer, but I couldn't face those images yet. Gods be cursed, I doubted I'd ever be able to face them.

My impatience was rewarded with two rabbits. My hunch of there being a nearby den seemed likely. I pulled both free, and reset the traps in hopes of catching breakfast in the morning.

Despite the number of squirrel traps I set, I only managed to kill one. Not surprising since they are rarely seen moving around at night. Still, between the three kills, I had enough for a good meal.

I re-entered the clearing with animals in hand, hoping that fresh meat might endear me to Myra who could stand to gain a few pounds.

"Get some spits ready, I got—"

I froze, words cutting off at the empty clearing before me. The fire had been allowed to burn down. Myra and Zadok were not where I left them. I dropped the animals and withdrew my sword. The only sound that reached my ears was that of the crackling wood in the small flames. The only smell foreign to the woods itself was the smoke it produced.

Scanning the clearing, I saw no sign of a visible struggle which was good. However, that meant nothing. Armed or not, anyone in my unit would have been able to snatch Myra and Zadok away without disturbing anything.

My pack looked as it had when I left. Thieves would have gone through it looking for money. I felt like I could eliminate the possibility of someone taking them. That meant the alternative, which in some ways was worse.

I sighed long and hard. The first chance they had, they used it to rid themselves of the man who had abandoned them.

Sheathing my sword, I walked over to the lean-to, examining their tracks. I might not be as good of a scout as Hamath, but I was better than most, and definitely could track a couple of children.

"You won't get rid of me that easily, Myra," I said under my breath. I figured the idea to run off had been hers. Zadok had given no indication that he would do anything like that on his own.

I heard some shuffling in the woods and rose to my feet, unsheathing my sword out of habit as I did. Myra and Zadok entered the clearing. She carried more firewood while Zadok had an armful of wild potatoes.

Myra paused, gaze immediately going to my sword. She looked up to my face and then walked past me to dump the armload of wood next to the rest. "You can put that away. We're back."

I blinked, sheathed the sword, then said. "I didn't know where you were."

"I thought that would be obvious. I didn't think we had enough wood for the night," she said throwing a stick on the fire and stoking the flames.

"And I saw these while we were out," said Zadok about the potatoes. He pulled out his dagger and began peeling them.

"Be careful while you're doing that," I said.

"Don't worry, Pa. Ma showed us how to do this. Do you have a pot to put them in?"

"In my bag." I was still trying to recover from the shock of them returning to camp. I had been so sure they ran away.

Zadok ran over to my bag, pulled free the pot and also a skin of water. He went back to peeling the potatoes, putting the cleaned ones in the pot after a quick rinse with the water.

"Any luck?" Myra asked while stacking firewood.

"Hmm?"

"With getting a fresh supper."

"Oh. Yes." I went back over to my kills, and grabbed them. "Not too bad for such a short amount of time."

Zadok looked up. "Wow, two rabbits and a squirrel!"

Myra walked over with her hand out. I stared at it with a confused look.

"I can help you clean them," she said.

"Oh." I gave her one of the rabbits. We each walked just outside of the clearing to skin and gut them. I kept glancing at her, impressed with how comfortable she seemed with the task. We finished at roughly the same time, though I'll admit, she cleaned hers better than mine.

Apparently, they had been busier than I realized during the short amount of time I was setting traps. Besides gathering more wood, Myra had anticipated me returning with something and made a couple of spits to hang the rabbits on. She grabbed mine and set them both over the flames to cook while I cleaned the squirrel. By the time I propped up the squirrel next to the rabbits, Zadok had the potatoes simmering.

While our supper cooked, I closed in the sides of the lean-to as a cool breeze flitted through the trees. Myra said nothing while I worked, but Zadok talked almost constantly. To be honest, I had trouble following his seemingly random thoughts. However, I dared not ask him to stop. The sound of his voice was enough to keep the thoughts of Lasha away.

Once finished, I noticed Myra had retreated inside the shelter. Huddled closer to Zadok, she shivered. Though her clothes were in better shape than Zadok's, neither was fit for spending nights out in the elements. I grabbed a blanket from my bag, leaned in, and draped it over them.

Zadok paused his latest story long enough to smile. Myra clutched at the blanket and pulled it around them without a word.

I checked the food. It smelled great. If it tasted half as good, I'd consider our first meal as a family again a success. At least from a food perspective.

The rabbits and potatoes both appeared done. The squirrel was done twice over. I gave each of the kids a rabbit while I took the blackened rodent. Zadok dove into his. He pulled away quickly, grimacing at the sizzling meat, then went right back in. Juices dripped from his chin.

"Slow down," said Myra. "No one's going to take it from you."

That gave him pause, and he slowed his attack considerably.

Myra tried to be more subdued in her approach, but even she burned herself a couple times with impatience.

I nibbled at my squirrel, intent on letting the thing cool first. It was dry and overdone, but at least well-seasoned. I followed it with a few of the warm potatoes, giving Zadok and Myra the rest just as they finished their rabbits, sucking the last bit of meat off the bones. They went at the potatoes with more restraint.

Barely.

Both wore a satisfied look when finished.

With a full belly, Zadok was talking again, though this time he asked questions about my life in the army. I did my best to focus on stories about lighter times in camp rather than the hell on the battlefield.

". . . I figured out what Hamath had planned pretty quickly. Especially when I realized Ira was involved. Neither could ever bluff me. Dekar is Ira's brother. He was different. The man could remain completely stone-faced while telling the most outrageous lie. Anyway, once I realized they were up to something, I brought your aunt in to figure out a way to get them first. We decided to feel Dekar out to see if he knew anything. We figured he'd likely go along with anything that might make one of Ira's plans fall apart. The three of us got to work."

I paused for a moment to make sure I hadn't lost my audience. Zadok seemed genuinely interested, leaning forward with elbows on knees. Myra didn't look as interested as her brother, but she also didn't appear annoyed by my story. That was good enough for me.

"We first rigged the watch schedule, then stuffed our bedrolls, getting Ava to put a glamour over mine so it looked real. Right when the rest of my unit was coming to make their move we pounced on them from behind." I started chuckling as I thought about it. "Ava did something to make them move real slow. Then I doused everyone with honey. Dekar followed, with these containers of ants we gathered from a nearby mound. Ava waited a few seconds and then removed the spell. They both hollered at the top of their lungs while jumping into this muddy river we had camped beside."

I was really laughing now as I recalled the looks on their faces when they came back, covered in tiny, red welts. "Man, that had to be the angriest I'd ever seen Hamath. But he got over it eventually."

Zadok chuckled at the story, but not as hard as I did. I guess there was something to be said for being there. Plus, I really wasn't as good a storyteller as others in my unit. Hamath especially. I told a few more tales until he interrupted.

"Was Hamath your best friend?"

"Yeah. We were all close. However certain people gravitated toward others over time. Your aunt and I always stayed close."

He frowned. "Why didn't Aunt Ava come back with you? Did she not want to see us?"

I shook my head. "It wasn't that. She had an opportunity that was hard to pass up. She did want to see you both, but . . ." I started to say something more, but stopped.

"But what?" asked Myra. It was the first time she'd said anything since before dinner. I had wondered if she had even been listening.

"Well, I hate to say it, but your aunt doesn't have the best memories of Denu Creek. She got picked on by Jareb and a few others growing up. Then one day her powers manifested when she was trying to protect both of us. After that, people were scared of her. She always felt like an outsider."

Myra grunted. "I know how she feels."

"Oh?"

"I told you people thought we were cursed, Pa," said Zadok.

"Plus, we have no money," added Myra. "And on top of that we look different than everyone else."

"Your appearance mattered?"

"Yes. Nobody really mentioned our skin color until the curse nonsense came up. But it got bad after that, especially when Ma went to work for Omri." She snorted, though her voice lacked any mirth. "It's almost funny, people made fun of us because we looked different, but that's also why all the men passing through town wanted Ma more than the others. Of course, that only angered the other women at the Soiled Dove since she was taking so much of their business. Always outsiders. Like I said, I understand why Aunt Ava didn't want to come home. I wouldn't have either."

"I'm sorry," I whispered, unsure what else I could say and trying to block out Lasha's time at the Soiled Dove.

Myra's comment sucked the life out of the conversation. Zadok's attempt to revitalize it didn't help.

"Hey Pa, did you ever kill anyone?" he asked, excited.

I grunted. "Hard not to."

"I bet you killed a lot of people, huh? Tell me some of those stories."

I forced a smile. "Maybe another time, Son. It's getting late and you've had a long day. Why don't you get some sleep?"

"Oh c'mon."

"He's right, Zadok. Go to bed. We won't be far behind."

"Fine." He shot Myra a look, then climbed farther into the lean-to and lay down. Myra gave him the blanket to sleep with. Within seconds, a faint snore floated out to us.

"That was fast."

"He was more tired than he let on. But he would have stayed up all night if you hadn't said something." Myra shook at a chill. I undid my cloak and held it out to her.

"I'm fine," she said, trying to dismiss me.

"No, you're not."

"What about you?"

"My clothes are warmer than yours. Take it."

She did, reluctantly wrapping herself in it. I smiled. "You know, you used to wear my cloak all the time when we'd sit on the porch in the evenings. I used to enjoy that time together."

She cleared her throat. "I'm glad you didn't answer Zadok's question about killing. I know he's been through a lot, but I still think he's too young to be hearing that stuff."

I frowned, both because of her refusal to admit the relationship we had in the past and because of where the conversation had turned. I threw a small stick into the fire. "I don't know if you ever get old enough to hear about it. Definitely not to experience it."

Myra cocked her head to the side. "The way you were going on before, made me think you enjoyed being in the army."

"I enjoyed the friendships I made, especially those that lasted long enough to see me out of service, but not much else. Don't get me wrong, I was good at what I did. Real good, actually. But that doesn't mean I enjoyed all the killing. Soldiers used to joke that men like me only survived for as long as I did by being good at killing or being good at hiding." I shrugged. "Hiding never suited me, I guess."

"But you do miss those you served with?"

"Sure. They became like a family to me."

"More important to you than your real family I'd wager."

I frowned. "What makes you say that?"

She looked away. "Because it took you ten years to come back."

"I had no choice. If I had deserted to come home, they would have just sent someone to hunt me down and fetch me back. If I had refused, they would have killed me to set an example to others wanting to desert. They likely would have taken the farm away too in order to make the point stronger."

She snorted. "Well, we lost that anyway. Zadok said he told you everything that happened while you were gone."

I nodded. "I'm sorry. I know that means little to you now, but that's all I can say."

Silence stretched.

"When you got back from trapping, did you think someone took us?"

"At first. But after I examined the evidence, a more likely scenario was that you ran off."

"Were you going to come after us?"

"Of course. I was just ready to leave when you came back."

She stared at the flames. "You know I wanted to. Even with little in the way of a plan, I wanted to run away."

That hurt. "Why didn't you?"

"Zadok refused to go."

"Why not just go by yourself?"

"Because he's all I got." She met my eyes. "I'm not going anywhere without him."

Without another word she moved into the lean-to, laid down and draped an arm over her brother.

I watched them until Myra's breathing matched Zadok's and I knew they were both asleep. "Because he's all I got" still rang in my ears.

I stoked the fire, and settled down beside it in order to compensate for the lack of cloak or blanket. Lying on my back, I stared up through the tree canopy into the starry sky.

The last thing I remembered before closing my eyes was hoping that in time Myra might see things differently.

It was definitely not the homecoming I had expected.

CHAPTER 14

"Now?" Zadok whispered.

He squatted just above the creek's surface. Straddling two large stones protruding from the water, he stared down at the fish playing as though it wanted to go through the narrowing between the stones.

"No. Not yet," I answered, voice just as low. I stood in the shin-high water, squatting almost as low as Zadok. The cold water sent a chill up my spine I tried to suppress. Shafts of morning sun flitting through the tree canopy illuminated our potential breakfast.

"But he's so close."

"Not close enough." I watched the fish decide his path downstream. "Remember, this takes patience."

"Now?" he asked, excitement trying to break free as the fish finally made its move.

"Now!" I yelled.

Zadok's hands darted into the water splashing it up into my face and bare chest. The jerking motion caused him to lose his balance. He pitched forward. My arms shot out to catch him. The shift made my foot slip on the algae in the river bed. We both crashed into the chilly water. If I hadn't been awake before, I definitely was after that.

I sat up gasping, soaked head to toe. Above my labored breathing came Zadok's giggling laugh. He was jumping up and down on his way to the bank. "I got it, Pa! I got it!"

In his hands squirmed a ten-inch long, striped yellow fish.

I forgot the cold, jumped up, and dashed toward him, laughing just as loud, partly because of how the catch had occurred and partly because of his reaction to it. I grabbed him in my arms and gave him a big hug. "I'm so proud of you, Son. That was unbelievable."

"Thanks Pa, you're a good teacher."

In that one perfect moment, I got a glimpse of the life I had always imagined I'd have—a life filled with moments that I had taken for granted before I joined the army. Teaching my kids how to fish just as my pa had taught me and Ava had been something I just knew I would do. Never did I think something so insignificant would hold the importance it did now.

I put Zadok down, but we were still jumping around and laughing like fools when I heard Myra's voice.

"Zadok! Zadok! Where are you?" She sounded almost frantic.

"I'm over here!" he yelled back.

She emerged through the trees a moment later. One hand held the unsheathed dagger I had given her the night before. The other she used to keep my cloak pulled tightly about her. Sleep still haunted her eyes.

"What in the name of the gods are you doing? I was worried something had happened to you."

"Why?" he asked. "I was with Pa. He's teaching me how to fish." He showed her the wriggling catch.

"We've got three more over there," I said pointing. "Enough for breakfast after we clean them. No more luck with the rabbit traps last night, so I thought this would make a good alternative."

"Why didn't you wake me?" she asked.

"We tried," said Zadok. "But you wouldn't budge."

"I'm sorry," I said. "I didn't mean to scare you. It just looked like you could do with the extra rest."

She gave me a look, then turned her attention back to Zadok. "Why are you soaking wet? Did you catch the fish with your whole body?"

"I slipped. Pa tried to catch me, and we both fell in." He chuckled.

"Well, at least you've got your shirts off," she said grabbing them off a low hanging branch.

"Yeah, Pa was worried they might get wet."

"He must be a soothsayer," she said sarcastically. She took off my cloak and wrapped it around Zadok. "Go back to the clearing and get out of those wet pants until they dry. The last thing you need is to catch a cold."

"But the fish—"

"Myra's right," I said. "I'll take care of the fish."

"No," she said. "I'll take care of the fish. You should go do the same and get out of your wet clothes. You can stay under the blanket until they dry by the fire."

"I'll be all right."

"You don't need to be getting sick either," she said, giving me a look, head cocked, mouth puckered. Her expression softened. "What?"

I blinked. "You remind me so much of your mother. You even sound like her."

She looked away.

That had been the wrong thing to say.

"I'm sorry. I didn't mean—"

"Go back to the fire, Tyrus," she said, voice melancholy.

I thought about pressing. "All right."

With my entire body damp, and the day still trying to warm, the comfort of the blanket was a welcome relief as Zadok and I huddled around the fire. He was still going on about his catch when Myra called out. "Everyone decent?"

"We're covered," I said.

She entered the clearing with four cleaned fish. Grabbing the skillet from my sack, the only other significant piece of cooking equipment I owned, she began cutting the fish up and placing them inside. I directed her to the salt and pepper I kept in a small pouch. I hadn't realized how hungry I was until the buttery smell of the fish hit my nostrils. I swallowed the sudden outpouring of saliva before I resembled a house dog waiting for scraps.

The yellow fish cooked quickly. Within minutes of their cooling, we sat near each other eating communally out of the one skillet. I made a mental note to pick up a couple of plates to make meal times in the future easier.

After a few bites I began to slow. Myra gave me a look. "Eat."

"It's all right. I'm not that hungry."

"Don't lie to me, Tyrus. I woke up to your stomach growling during the night. I know you skimped on what you ate for dinner so we could have more. Don't do it again. There's more than enough food, and you feeling weak isn't going to do any of us any good."

I nodded at the sound advice, noticing the stark contrast between my children. Almost twelve, Zadok still acted and spoke very much like a boy at times, somehow maintaining all the excitement and even a bit of the innocence associated with childhood. Myra spoke like a grown woman. In fact, she spoke like a mother. I didn't have to ask why. Given what they had been through, Myra had likely become the mother to Zadock that Lasha could not have been as she tried to keep them fed.

I followed my daughter's advice, though I still held back some. Zadok after all, seemed to have a bottomless pit. By the time Myra disposed of the bones and cleaned up the skillet, our clothes had mostly dried and she was in a better mood.

Zadok and I threw our clothes back on. I made sure to hide my boiled leather under my shirt. It wasn't going to fool anyone up close. However, I hoped I might appear less threatening.

Zadok chattered away to his sister about his catch, going over every detail to her for at least the third time. The affection she had for her brother was obvious. She acted just as excited and in awe with the third telling as she pretended on the first. When the story came to a conclusion, she looked my way before Zadok could start again.

"What's your plan? I presume we aren't going to spend the rest of our days here. Then again, if that is your plan, let me suggest we build a more substantial shelter before winter sets in." She nodded toward the lean-to.

"No. Once you're ready, I thought we'd go into town."

"Why?"

"Well, for starters you and your brother could use some better clothes." I nodded toward Zadok's feet. "And shoes. After that, I thought I'd start looking for a job. Once I secure a source of income, then we can look at renting a room or something at one of the inns for winter." I sighed, thinking about the money I left at Jareb's in order to buy Myra and Zadok's freedom. "In time, I should have enough money to get a place of our own. I don't know if we'll ever be able to get our old home back, but the more I think about it, maybe that's for the best. A new house might be a good symbol for a fresh start."

"The best place to have a fresh start would be somewhere other than Denu Creek."

I blinked. "But this is our home."

"Not by choice." She grunted. "I wanted to leave years ago. It offers nothing for me. Or Zadok."

Zadok didn't voice an agreement with his sister, but he didn't speak a differing opinion either.

"Besides," Myra continued. "Jareb won't let go of what happened. You should know that."

I looked away, thinking.

No father wanted to listen to advice from his children regardless of how sound it seemed. Especially, when it was not only sound, but something I should have considered myself. The problem was that I was letting emotions cloud my judgment. But then, how could I not? Every dream I had in the last decade involved me returning to Denu Creek, and reuniting with my wife and kids. Now, my wife was gone. As dumb as it sounded, leaving Denu Creek meant I had to completely face the fact that those dreams would never come true.

I sighed and began packing my things. "You're right. We should probably leave."

"Good."

"However, we aren't ready to go anywhere just yet. You and Zadok need clothes and we're pretty light in the way of supplies. I don't have a whole lot in the way of coin left, but I should have enough to get what we need before heading out."

"Couldn't we just go to Tamra where your friends are, and buy our stuff there?"

I snorted. The girl was smart. "We could. However, I don't want to go to them completely empty-handed. Especially, since they're just getting settled in themselves."

I wouldn't say it out loud, but a part of me wasn't eager to see Dekar and his wife cozying up to each other with Lasha's death fresh on my mind either. Even still, I'd get over it if I felt it would keep my kids away from danger. I guessed I had a full day, if not more before Jareb got his act together and tried to come after me. He had always been slow in making a decision and I hadn't left him and his friends in the best of conditions for any speedy action.

Regardless, I'd have more than enough time to get the things I needed, and also check in on Nason. His reaction to me entering town still stung quite a bit. I needed to see what was going on there for my own peace of mind. Maybe he was in trouble himself?

I stood and slung my bag over my shoulder. "Zadok, put out the fire. We're leaving."

CHAPTER 15

We reached the edge of town late in the morning. By that point, my clothes had long dried and then begun to dampen anew with sweat.

Though a few people patrolled the streets, for the most part, the town sat empty. As was usually the case in towns the size of Denu Creek, early morning, midday, and late evening were the times it bustled most with life. Time in between was spent working in the fields or in the shops lining the main street.

Few noticed us as we veered to the left side of the thoroughfare. I hoped my worries from when Ira, Dekar, and I had first ridden into town were an overreaction. I doubted it, but hoped all the same that just maybe the idiocy that had plagued other towns on our way home hadn't completely reached Denu Creek.

I was taking in the town's changes in more detail when I came to an abrupt halt in front of a local apothecary not yet open for the day.

"I thought you were taking us to a tailor," said Zadok

"I was. . . ." But the tailor wasn't where I remembered it.

"Oren retired almost six years ago. He sold the space to Irad who turned it into an apothecary," said Myra, reading my thoughts.

I frowned. "Gods, I never thought Oren would retire. So, who's the tailor now?"

"We actually have two. Gadiel moved into town right after Oren retired. He's next to the feed store."

"What's he like?"

"Oh, he's a jerk. He's apparently from some town near Hol and likes to remind everyone any chance he gets. Looks down on most people."

"Is he good?"

"Yes," said Myra.

"Who's the other one?"

Zadok pointed. "Sivan is a few doors down. He opened up just a year back."

I looked to Myra. "Any good?"

"From what I hear. Nice too. Problem is Gadiel has been dropping his prices in an attempt to drive Sivan out of business. He over charged everyone for so long he can afford to do that now."

My hand ran across my money bag. Although I didn't have much to spare, a part of me felt pulled to at least start with Sivan. I never liked bullies. "We'll try Sivan first."

That warranted a smile from Zadok and a slight nod from Myra. I guessed I had made the right decision. Score one for me. I needed all the help I could get where Myra was concerned.

I took note that on our way to Sivan we passed the cobbler. That would be our next stop. Poor Zadok was walking around barefoot. He didn't seem to mind, but I did. Thankfully Myra's footwear was actually in good shape. So long as she didn't incur a massive growth spurt I felt they could easily last her through the winter.

A large window adorned the front of Sivan's shop. Full ankle-length dresses, shades of blue and brown, hung in the window. Various shirts and trousers lay beneath them on the bottom of the display.

A small bell sounded as I opened the door.

"I'll be with you in one moment," rang a woman's voice. It came from an open doorway in the back of the shop behind the counter.

"Take your time," I said, not so much because I meant it, but because it seemed like a courteous reply.

I scanned the inside of the shop while waiting. More displays sat against the wall to the left with a large, full-length mirror between them. A box about two hand widths high rested on the ground in front of the mirror. To the right, shelves held stacks of fabric in various colors. A privacy shade stood in the back, obviously used by customers to change. One chair sat not far from the privacy shade.

I faced the doorway in the back of the shop as footsteps against the wooden floor grew in volume. A small woman appeared with hair as bright as the morning sun. Her skin was without blemish or wrinkle even though she looked near my age. I thought the reason for my guess at her age might have had to do with the warm smile she wore, or possibly the way her hair was pinned up in a bun, but then I realized it had more to do with what lay behind her eyes. There was something there that said she was not simply a young, pretty face to be treated like window dressing in order to attract customers.

"Good morning. My name is Damaris. What can I do for you today?"

"I was hoping you and your husband could fit my children with a new set of clothes, something warm for winter."

"I'm sorry, I didn't catch your name."

"Tyrus. This is Myra and Zadok.

She smiled. "Well, Tyrus, I'm actually not married. I help my father run the place. He's in the back working on a recent order."

"My apologies."

She waved me off as she walked over. "You aren't the first to make that assumption." She changed subjects. "What about something for yourself? Perhaps a new shirt, something dressier? We've just received this great material that—"

"No," I said, cutting her off. "Nothing for me. My clothes might not be much to look at, but they serve their purpose."

She nodded and turned to Myra. "How about we size you up first?" She took Myra by the hand. "While I'm taking your measurements we can talk about what style you want your new dress to be."

I thought about Myra shivering last night, and frowned. "No dress."

"What?" Myra asked, giving me a dirty look.

"I'm sorry, but we need to be practical. You'll be warmer in trousers and shirt. Plus, trousers are less cumbersome which may be important to us since we aren't sure how things will play out in the coming days."

Her shoulders hunched forward, wearing a look of defeat. She saw my reasoning, though she didn't like it.

I put a hand on her shoulder. "Maybe we can get you a dress in time for next summer," I said, trying to brighten her mood.

She shifted her stance so my hand fell away. "It doesn't matter."

I saw it did.

She probably hadn't owned a nice dress since I was bouncing her on my knee. I made a mental note to make that up to her. My list seemed to grow by the minute. I clenched my jaw. I had been careful with my money for ten years so by the time I made it home I wouldn't have to wait any longer to make things up to her.

Jareb's contracts changed my plans.

Damaris watched the exchange without interrupting, something I appreciated. She smiled wider, and spoke to Myra. "There are still plenty of things we can do with trousers and shirt. We can cut it differently so it still has very much a feminine quality. I actually have an outfit like that myself for traveling."

Myra looked up, hopeful. "All right."

I breathed a small sigh of relief. "Myra, would you mind letting Zadok go first? I need to visit the cobbler to see about getting him some shoes. I can do that while Miss Damaris is fitting you afterward."

"Sure."

"Go ahead, Zadok."

"Do I have to, Pa?"

I saw his trepidation. "Miss Damaris isn't going to bite you. It's fine."

"I'll be as quick as possible. And it's just Damaris," she said to me, walking over to Zadok. "I'm not ready for the Miss part yet. Maybe by the time my hair turns gray." She gave me a small wink before putting her arm around Zadok and leading him to the mirror.

Myra stood next to me, quiet and sullen. I thought to say something more in an effort to make things right, but everything that came to mind seemed like it would do more harm than good. I chose to focus my attention on Zadok who looked as uncomfortable as a stable hand at the king's court. I'm pretty sure I saw him blush a few times during the measuring process.

Damaris could obviously sense his discomfort as she kept her smile present and made small talk in an effort to distract him. She moved quickly between measurements and jotted down notes on a nearby chalkboard.

When Damaris announced Zadok could step down, he jumped off the box and ran over to me. I patted him on the back and leaned down as Damaris was making the last of her notes. I whispered. "One day you might not mind having a pretty woman jostle you around like that."

"Pa!" he said in a low whisper, face growing red.

Damaris turned. "All right, Zadok. That should do it. Myra, are you ready?"

Myra nodded and walked over. Zadok was out the door before I even had a chance to turn. I decided not to tease him anymore. I may have pushed it too much already. Sadly, my children were still strangers to me and I didn't know when to tease or when to be serious. I had to remind myself that these weren't soldiers. I needed to talk to them differently.

Like most other businesses, including the tailor we just left, the cobbler had his own window display. The display showed shoes of varying styles—mostly black or brown with the exception of a green pair I'm sure no one but an actor or a playwright would buy.

I led the way inside again, greeted by the overwhelming smell of leather and hide. A middle-aged gentleman looked up from a work station in the back where he hammered on the sole of a boot. A large, twisting mustache spanned his face.

The small twinkle in his eye at first evident when we entered, faded as he looked us over. He rose from his seat and approached.

I guess our physical appearance was beneath his usual clientele. "Can I help you?" Skepticism laced his voice.

"Yes, I need to get my son fitted for some boots, something warm, but comfortable."

The man looked Zadok up and down. "Payment is required up front."

"That's fine. I'd like them by this afternoon. The nights are getting cold."

"That shouldn't be a . . ." his voice trailed off as his eyes rested on the sword at my hip. He seemed to notice the dagger at my thigh next. Then the boiled leather peeking through the collar of my shirt. "You know, come to think of it, I doubt I could get your order fulfilled anytime in the next few days."

I frowned. "Is that so?"

"Yes, I'm actually behind on my work."

"Is there another cobbler in town?"

He shook his head. "No. You might try Tamra though. It's only a day's ride away."

"Which means I'll get the boots two days too late."

"I'm sorry, I—"

"What's your angle? Are you trying to work me for more money? If so, let's get to it."

"You were in the army, weren't you?"

Ah, the crux of the situation. "I was."

"There are stories about—"

"So, I've heard. Most are completely inaccurate."

"Regardless. If someone saw me doing work for you it might impact my business."

"It's not for me. It's for my son." I pulled Zadok forward. "Look, I just got back to town and I learn that my boy's got nothing for his feet. I know you've been outside recently. The air's getting colder and unless he gets something to wear by the time the first snow hits, he's liable to start losing toes. I can't let that happen. You don't want to be seen with me. Then I'll leave out back once we're done here. But first, you need to size him up and promise me his boots will be ready by the end of the day. How much do you charge for something like that?"

He told me the number.

I blinked. No way it cost that much for boots. But I didn't have time to argue and I could see he was going to be hardnosed about it. I clenched my jaw, fighting the urge to strike him. I knew that wouldn't get me or Zadok anywhere.

"Fine."

I walked over, counted out the money from my pouch and set it on the counter. My pouch was getting light far too quickly.

He counted the money, meticulously examining each coin for authenticity. I began to wonder if he was in the wrong profession. Moneylender seemed more apt considering his scrutiny.

"We have a deal?"

He paused for a moment, thinking. "Have your son sit there," he said pointing to a chair. The man walked over and locked the door.

After that he hurried over to Zadok, squatted, and grabbed a foot. He scrunched his nose. "A bath might do him some good," he offered.

"No doubt," I said, trying to make light of the comment rather than let the cobbler's rudeness get under my skin. "But one step at a time."

The cobbler measured Zadok's feet, then had him stand to determine where he placed most of his weight.

He scribbled notes quickly, calling out without looking up. "Come to the back door after sunset. I'll have the shoes ready for you then."

"We'll be there. C'mon Zadok, let's go."

The man got up and walked to the back of his shop. "Follow me."

He peered out the window of the back door. When satisfied, he opened it quickly. "Make sure you're here on time. I won't wait around."

"We'll be here." I held out my hand, hoping to end on good terms. "I'm Tyrus."

He looked at my hand, but refused to take it. "If anyone else from town is with you or sees you come, then the shoes stay with me. I can't take any more chances."

He slammed the door, leaving us out in the alley.

"This isn't what I expected at all," I muttered.

Zadok said nothing.

"C'mon, let's go see if your sister is ready."

We got back to Sivan's and Myra was sitting in the only chair, waiting. Damaris was in the back, but came out at the jingle of the bell on the door.

I requested to have their clothes ready by the evening as well. After the cobbler, I expected a battle or at least some extra fee tacked on for such a request. However, Damaris surprised me.

"That won't be a problem. My father is already working on Zadok's trousers now. I only ask that you allow a little extra time when you return for the final fitting. You can pay for the clothes then."

I smiled, genuinely. ."Thank you."

It was nice to be treated with some sense of courtesy. I had almost forgotten what that was like.

On the street, Zadok asked. "Where to next, Pa?"

"The blacksmith."

"Why there? You need some work on your sword?"

"Not exactly." I turned to Myra. "Is Joram still running the smithy?"

She shook her head. "No. His place burned down when one of his apprentices got careless. I don't know the new smith's name, but he's over on the corner, there," she said, pointing.

It looked nothing like old Joram's place. Twice as large with two chimneys, each billowing smoke. A large sign painted with a hammer and anvil hung over the wide, open door capable of fitting a horse and carriage.

I sighed. Had anything not changed?

The rhythmic banging, clanging, and pounding of hammer and anvil served as the backdrop to my conversation with the new blacksmith at a table in the middle of his shop. I allowed Myra and Zadok to wait outside rather than suffer through the heat.

Sered went about five and a half feet. However, what he lacked in height Sered made up for elsewhere. His sleeveless, leather apron exposed thick arms, neck and shoulders bulging with rope-like cords of muscles. Shaking his hand felt like trying to squeeze a wooden beam.

"My apprentice said you're looking for a sword." He nodded to the youngest of three boys running around the place, busy with various duties. He stoked the forge and a wave of heat pressed against my face.

"I am. Two if possible."

He gestured to my waist. "Something wrong with the one you have?"

"No. I'm actually looking to give something to my children. We're about to do some traveling and it would make sense to give them something for protection. I'm not looking for anything special, something more workmanlike. Needs to be light with good balance since I don't think either have used one before and I don't want them hurting themselves."

He grunted, still studying the hilt and scabbard of my sword. He gestured to one of my daggers. "Those markings look familiar. Where were your blades made?"

I frowned. It seemed odd for a business owner to be more concerned with what a potential customer already owned rather than what the person was willing to buy. "Might I ask why?"

"The markings on the hilt look like something you might see out of Hol." He grunted. "High quality, but cheap. A common choice among those in the military." He met my eyes. "You served?"

I smiled, trying to appear as nonthreatening as possible. I was not ashamed of my time in the army, but it seemed like most people took issue with it. I wanted to come across as friendly as possible in the hopes it would contradict any of the rumors he had heard over the years.

"I just got back home yesterday, actually. Denu Creek is where I grew up."

Sered stared without emotion. My smile faded as he worked his jaw, like he was reaching a conclusion he didn't like.

"I'm going to have to ask you to leave," he said.

"What about the swords?"

"I don't have any for sale."

I glanced over to more than a dozen laid across a table on the right. "And those?"

"Spoken for."

"What about a couple of good daggers?" I asked.

His brow furrowed. "I can't do that."

"Can't or won't?"

"Can't. It wouldn't be good for business if word got out that I helped someone like you."

"You mean a soldier?"

He nodded.

"And why is that?"

He paused, fighting with what to tell me. "I can't get into the details."

I scowled, voice rising in frustration. "Why? Tell me, and we can talk through this."

Sered shook his head. His hand slowly drifted to the hammer laying across his anvil. "I'm sorry. I wish I could help you, but I can't. I think you should leave."

Despite Sered's obvious strength, I wasn't intimidated. Still, that was no reason to get into a fight.

I walked away without responding, heading for the exit.

Once outside, Zadok asked, "Did you get what you needed?"

I shook my head, noticing Myra's furrowed brow as she stared into the smithy. "What's wrong?"

She faced me. "Nothing."

I followed her gaze, seeing that the apprentices had been staring back at her with a mix of lust and disdain. They looked away as I met their eyes with a sergeant's gaze.

"All right," I said. "Let's go. We still have several more places to try before we circle back to Sivan's."

* * *

"Why in the name of the Molak not?" I yelled at the town physician.

The bristled old man gave me the stink eye while standing with arms crossed. He jutted his cleanly shaven chin out with arrogance which made it tempting to slap that chin right off. A lesser man might have.

"This is my business and I can choose to do business with whomever I desire," the physician said.

I was in his place seeking some herbs or potions to take on the road in case we got into trouble. I had tried the local apothecary first, but the owner never opened for the day. I learned that he was going through some nasty sickness and couldn't make it in. Not sure how highly that spoke of the man's work that he hadn't known how to cure his own ailments.

"But you know nothing about me. You haven't asked me anything."

"I don't need to ask you anything. I can see what you're about and I don't want your kind in my town."

"This is my town too! I grew up and lived here for over twenty years before being pressed into service. My family ran a farm for three generations just down the road. I've got more of a claim to this town than you or half of the other people who are here now!"

"Maybe you did at one point, but not anymore. This place has changed. This town is no longer yours. It's ours, and we don't want your kind here."

I kicked a chair across the room in anger. "My kind?"

"Yes. The kind of person who burns the countryside so families starve. The kind of person who rapes women and kills children."

It was the same story once again.

I wanted to explain all that I had before to the old man, but I knew I'd be wasting my breath. People like him didn't understand. They liked to believe that if everyone adopted their moral insights the world would be a better place. They would never understand the world just didn't work that way.

In fact, it never had.

The world would be a better place without violence. The problem was that it was hard enough for only two people to agree on all points. Asking an entire population spanning countries, cultures, and religions to find common ground was, in many ways, a fairytale of the highest order.

I left the physician's shop, trying to find a positive to take with me from the encounter.

There wasn't one.

Shouting greeted me as I stepped outside. At first I thought they were directed at me. Then I saw they belonged to a handful of young kids a short distance from my children. Myra and Zadok had drifted off down the street, going against my instructions to stay where I left them.

Zadok said something to the group, acting like he was going to take them all on despite being outmatched and outsized. I admired his guts, but not his thinking. Myra looked visibly upset, but did the right thing in trying to separate herself and Zadok from the others, one eye always watching their movements.

I started walking toward them, at first thinking the situation stemmed from kids just being kids.

"Better watch out for him," one said, mocking Zadok. "Father's a baby-killer they say. Gods know what that makes him."

"He's not a baby-killer," said Zadok. "He's a hero!"

They laughed.

"Look at them. They're both trash, just like their ma," said another. Spit flew from his mouth with the insult.

"Hey!" I boomed, picking up my pace as I stormed toward them.

They wheeled, didn't like what they saw in my eyes, and spouted curses as they took off—all before I could add anything. It was probably for the best. I was so hot I would have either made a fool of myself or done something I would have later regretted.

I turned to Myra. "What happened? Why weren't you by the door where I asked you to stay?"

She turned away without answering.

"It was my fault, Pa," said Zadok, jumping into my line of sight. "They asked me if I wanted to play a game of dice. But it was a joke. Myra was trying to bring me back when you came out."

I tilted my head in the direction the kids ran off. "Does that sort of stuff happen a lot?"

"Well, we hardly ever come to town anymore since Ma died."

"But when you do?"

"Yeah, mostly."

"And what do you normally do when that happens?"

He shrugged. "Walk away if we can. But sometimes we can't. So, I talk back."

"And you fight too?"

"I try, but I'm not very good at it. I haven't won one yet."

I thought about those five boys, all older and stronger. "Against those odds I'm not surprised." I looked to Myra. "Is this all true?"

"What?" she snapped. "That everyone treats us like dogs? Of course it is. The choices you and Ma made aren't exactly ones people would approve of. Why do you think I don't want to stay here? Even for another day."

I noticed she had dodged my question, but given the venom spat at me, I decided to ignore it. It really didn't matter what had caused the confrontation with the boys anyway.

I scanned the town, three quarters of it unlike anything I remembered and most of it populated by individuals I didn't know and had no love for. Most of the people I knew in my youth had either joined the army and died, gotten old and died, or just moved away. Even then, they weren't without fault. Ava's complaints of her childhood came to mind.

"You're right. And considering the luck I've had in getting what we need to travel, maybe we should have gone straight to Tamra as you suggested."

"We did get some food from the feed store though," said Zadok as he tried to look on the bright side.

I snorted. "We did. And we're already here now so we might as well continue on while we wait for your clothes to be ready. C'mon. We still have a couple places left to try."

"And if they act the same as most others?" asked Myra.

I tried to make light of the situation. "Then we won't have to worry too much about our burden as we travel, right?"

She scowled. She wasn't buying the joke.

I sighed. I hoped Ira and Dekar were having it better than me.

* * *

The pungent smell of limed cowhide permeated my nostrils as we neared the tanner. A blacksmith was always far from any inns due to the noise generated there. But a tanner was kept far away from just about anyone because of its reek. Strong winds would move some of the stench toward the town center, but at least it would have a chance to dissipate by then.

I stepped from the wooden sidewalk to the dry earth. The kids were a step behind. With a glance down the side of the building I saw large hides hanging on hooks, drying like laundry on a line. Except in this case, lines were replaced by thick dowels of wood to handle the extra weight. Big barrels sat nearby—some empty, some filled with water, some filled with lime. I wasn't sure I wanted to know what filled others.

After crossing the fifty feet separating the last building to the tanner, I stepped up to the small porch preceding the door. Unlike many businesses in town enticing customers with the latest fashion, potion, or tool, there was no window to lure shoppers. Anyone who went to the tanner did so out of necessity.

I grunted to myself, eyeing the exterior. Not even a sign. The stink announced the business on its own.

The door abruptly swung inward causing me to jump. The slender man I had recognized when I entered town with Ira and Dekar stared back at me. Nason looked unsettled and frustrated, different than the man I had seen the day before.

"It's about time," he said.

"Huh?" A befuddled look was the most I could manage.

"Quit gaping," Nason said sharply, "and get inside."

I entered, not sure what else to do. Myra and Zadok followed. Nason closed the door quickly.

"Gods, it took you long enough to get here," he said, as he locked up.

I gathered myself. "Well, the way you ignored me when I came into town, I didn't think I would be welcome."

"So you didn't come because you thought I was mad at you?" he asked, turning. "That's ridiculous. We were best friends when we were kids."

"I thought so too. But most everyone else is ignoring me or berating me because of my time in the army. It seems like doing business with me drives customers away. I figured I'd wait to see you until less people were around so not to make you more angry with me."

He smiled. "I appreciate you considering me like that. I really do. And I'm sad to say there is a bit of truth to what you said. I'm not mad at you by any means, but I do need to be careful with how I talk to you. Showing kindness to you is a sure way to bring trouble. Jareb has been the most vocal in his opposition to the war and those who served. He's the most powerful person around here now. I'm sorry, but I can't afford that trouble. I got a family now," he said, nodding to Myra and Zadok. "I have to think of their safety first." He paused. "You know, some people have started going around warning others you might stop by just so they'd have a time to think of how to turn down your business."

"Well, I'm glad to know that your reaction wasn't because you wanted nothing to do with me."

"C'mon Tyrus. Like you said, we were best friends growing up. Gods, I had a crush on your sister."

That staggered me. "What? I didn't know that. Why didn't you say something? Ava would have—"

"—likely thought I was lying. Besides, I wasn't about to confide in you about her. You were too much of the overprotective big brother." He paused, finally taking a breath. "Where is Ava anyway? She didn't . . ."

I shook my head. "She chose not to return."

He nodded. "I understand." Finally, a small smile formed on Nason's face. He came in and embraced me tightly. "It's good to see you, Tyrus. The stories were that you died."

"So, I heard."

I embraced him back. It felt good to connect with an old friend, someone familiar from my past. It also felt good knowing that not everyone in town held an awful view of those in the military. They just simply did not have the guts to stand against the popular opinion and Jareb.

He pulled away, looking at the kids. "Apparently, you haven't heard everything," he said, walking away. He began digging in drawers. "Otherwise, you'd be gone by now."

"Huh?"

"That thing you pulled with Jareb just reached town a couple minutes ago. If anyone was feeling sympathetic toward you, it's going to be harder to show it with what you did to get your children back. Not that I can blame you. But you shouldn't be here. The sheriff is at Jareb's farm now talking to him about you stealing his servants."

"I stole nothing. I paid him more than what was called for in the contracts."

"But he claims you broke them early."

"Details. I did what I had to do to get my children back."

"Like I said, I don't blame you. In your position, I'd like to think I would have done the same." Nason grunted. "Also, Jareb and his friends were pretty bad off according to what I heard." He shook his head, grinning. "Same old Tyrus."

He continued. "Listen to me. I'm sure you can see that Denu Creek is a shadow of what you remember." He closed the drawer he had been searching, carried a small bag over to me. "You need to get out of town. When the sheriff gets back, Jareb will likely be with him. You don't want to be around." He thrust the bag into my hand. "Since you paid so much to Jareb, I figured you could use some coin. That's all I can afford. It should help you along your way though, wherever that is."

Nason spun me around and pushed me toward the door. "Now, I hate to push you out so quickly, but what I said earlier still holds true. I love you like a brother, Tyrus, but I can't have you here if Jareb shows. Only the gods know what he'll do to make me or my family miserable."

"I understand."

He unlocked and opened the door with one hand while pushing me through it with the other. "Good." He paused, then sighed. "You take care."

"You too, Nason."

He nodded, then closed the door, leaving me standing on his porch, dumbfounded, staring at the small pouch of money in my hand.

I looked at my kids staring back at me with uncertainty. "Let's get our stuff from the cobbler and tailor, and get out of here."

I looked back once at Nason's place as we walked off, thankful at least one thing in Denu Creek hadn't changed after all.

CHAPTER 16

It was evening. The streets and sidewalks were slowly filling with people. After my conversation with Nason, we kept our head down and did our best to keep to the shadows as we walked.

Zadok hurried up beside me. "So, you were good friends with Nason, Pa?"

"Yes."

"Hmm, that explains a lot."

I cocked my head. "What does it explain?"

Myra cleared her throat. "When things got bad for us, Nason tried to help Ma and Uncle Uriah out as best as he could. After a while, Uncle got resentful though and ran Nason off. Even still, when the rest of the town wanted nothing to do with us, he'd somehow find us and give us a bit of food or a couple of coins when he could spare it."

I squeezed the money pouch in my hand again while feeling a tug in my chest. "I wish I'd had known that."

Nason pushed us out in such a rush, I never had a chance to even thank him for his help, let alone for looking out as best as he could for Myra and Zadok.

Maybe one day I'd be able to repay him.

With still half the town to cover, we started to draw notice from passersby. I guided the kids into an alley, then had them jog behind the buildings to the cobbler's shop. I looked around quickly to make sure no one was following us, then rapped my knuckles on the door.

Nothing.

I knocked again, louder and with a greater sense of urgency. Footsteps from inside followed.

The door cracked open. "You're early. It's not sunset."

He was right. The sun was dropping quickly, but had not yet fallen out of sight. "I know. But we're in a hurry."

He mumbled. "I figured you might be. I was just finishing up when you knocked. Wait here. I'll be back."

He went back inside, returning after a few moments. The man thrust a pair of boots out the door. I noticed a pair of socks stuffed inside them. "I almost didn't open the door after what I heard you did to Jareb. He'll come down hard on anyone helping you."

I looked up. "Thank you."

"Don't. I only did the job because the shoes weren't for you. It isn't your son's fault who his Pa is."

The door slammed before I could respond. Locks turned quickly afterward.

I turned around wearing a frown. Myra and Zadok wore expressions that matched. I handed the shoes over to Zadok. "C'mon. Let's get your clothes and get out of here."

We skirted around the cobbler's place, moving through an alley to Main Street in order to approach the tailor from the front. The hard jingle of the bell tied to the door announced our arrival as we hurried inside Sivan's place.

Damaris appeared, smiling.

"Perfect timing," she said, coming around the counter. "Father just finished Myra's trousers." She came over to grab Myra's hands. "Come this way and I'll help you change so we can determine what the final adjustments will be."

"No." I glanced out the window at the front of the shop, looking for potential trouble. "I'm sorry, but we won't have time for that."

She tilted her head. "But it will only take a few moments, and it is crucial to ensure the clothes fit properly."

"They'll just have to do as is." I moved away from the window. "We're in a hurry."

I tried to keep my expression neutral, but I couldn't hide the tone in my voice. Damaris let go of Myra's hand. "Just give me a moment, and I'll be right back."

As she ducked inside the back, I turned to Zadok. "Get on those socks and boots while you have the chance."

He ran over to a chair and hurried along. When finished, he stood and took a few steps, almost awkwardly—like a boy unused to wearing footwear.

"Well?" I asked.

"They're more comfortable than I thought they'd be. Though they're also a little big."

"You'll grow into them."

Damaris reappeared carrying a bundle in her arms that she plopped onto the counter. "Father is wrapping up your boy's clothes. He'll be out shortly."

I walked over and began pulling the agreed upon amount from my money pouch when a voice called out from the back. "Here is the other bundle. I wish I could persuade you to stay sir. A better fit is—" An older man with a bald pate and neatly trimmed salt and pepper beard came out.

I paused in my counting and looked up at his worried expression. Damaris turned around and frowned.

"What's wrong, Father?"

Sivan cleared his throat. "I wish you would have told me who this man was, Damaris."

"What does it matter?"

"Because I'm a soldier. Or was. You won't do business with me either, right?" I grumbled, growing ever more tired of this routine.

Sivan shook his head. "No. I understand what it means to be in the army. I fought in the Byzan wars in my youth. I also lost a son in the early years of the Geneshan conflict."

I felt a tug in my chest for him. I had lost a lot of friends, but I couldn't imagine losing a son. "I'm sorry to hear that."

"What is it then?" asked Damaris.

"Sered came by earlier when you were sweeping out back. This is the man who struck Jareb and stole his property."

"News travels faster than I remember," I muttered.

Damaris frowned.

Sivan nodded to my children. "I'm assuming they are the property in question."

I nodded. "I stole nothing, though I could have. I paid more than their contracts called for. Things only got physical when he refused to release my daughter."

Sivan tightened his jaw. "I'm not surprised." He looked over his daughter's shoulder at the pile of coins resting on the counter. "That should cover the cost of materials. No other payment is necessary." He handed over the other package.

"Father," Damaris snapped in a hushed voice. "We can't afford to give our goods away."

He reached under the counter and came up with a wool blanket, throwing it on top of the pile. "We don't have the money to make our next payment to the bank anyway, Damaris. If we're going to lose the place. Might as well do something good first."

Damaris stared, dumbfounded, looking like she didn't know how bad things were for them.

"Sir, I—" I started.

"Just say thank you. Then take it and go. Jareb will be here soon if what I heard from Sered was true. Come on, now isn't the time for pride."

I nodded. "Thank you. Both of you," I added, looking toward Damaris.

I picked up the packages and left, quickly hugging the shadows.

The sun was rapidly descending, its remaining light showed hues of dark purple and red. More legitimate places of business like the tailor started closing up for the day, while those places dependent upon the nightlife prepared to entice everyone coming in after a hard day in the fields.

We passed a youth changing the lettering on the sign outside of the local theater, detailing the start time for the show tonight.

Women appeared in the doorway at one of the newer pleasure houses. They had dressed themselves in exotic paints and powders, while wearing as little as possible, despite the cool weather. They suffered for their trade.

I wondered how they got away with presenting themselves like that. Before I left for the army, the women in the town, as well as the more religious men, would have never put up with that sort of spectacle on the streets. It was one thing to have a whorehouse. All towns did. It was another thing to flaunt one so openly to all who passed.

Watching how the women advertised their services made me shake my head in disgust.

Then I imagined Lasha having to do the same thing for Myra and Zadok. My disgust shifted to sorrow.

The debates Ava and I had so many times before ran through my mind. I still had no idea why many of those women did what they did. Sure, some were just out for money, but more than ever I understood some were not.

And even if they were out for money, who was I to judge them?

I tore my gaze away from the women as I needed to be alert. I felt the stares from people as we walked and I stared right back at several. Few had the courtesy to appear embarrassed by their gawking. At this point, everyone knew who I was. I just hoped that no one would decide to find their courage and act on their own to win over some influence with Jareb before he got into town.

Shouting and cursing from half a dozen voices roared inside a saloon just up ahead. The doors to the place swung open with such force they slapped against the outside walls. A body flew into the street as if hurled. With the door open, the clamor rose even higher in volume and I wondered if someone was about to get lynched. A man similar in size and appearance to the one who'd been thrown into the street exited the saloon, walking over to the first. Their blond hair was instantly recognizable.

The yelling died down and the doors closed. I came to a halt, dumbfounded.

Ira climbed to his feet. He looked almost like he was ready to fight his brother as he dusted himself off. "What did you go and do that for?"

"To save you," said Dekar, in his calm, even voice.

"From what? We could have taken those fools easily. By the gods, I could have probably handled them without you."

"Maybe. But I don't need you getting injured. You said you were only going to have one quick drink."

"So, I had two more. Three mugs of ale ain't nowhere near drunk. You know that. Besides," Ira inclined his head back at the saloon, "they're the ones that started it. I only—"

By that point, I had recovered enough to interrupt. "By the gods."

They both whipped their heads in my direction.

A wide grin formed on Ira's face. He slapped his brother in the arm. "And you were worried we wouldn't find him."

We all embraced. It had only been a little over a day since I last saw them, but it felt like half a lifetime considering all that had happened to me since. The stress and worry of what would happen next eased in the presence of friends.

"What are you doing here? I thought we said we'd meet up in a month or so."

Dekar looked away, somber.

I frowned as Ira's smile faded. "Things ain't what they were, Ty." He paused and eyed his brother. "Dek's wife thought him dead and remarried. She saw us and more or less told us to go back to being dead." He spat. "Man, the stuff they're saying about us and what we did in the army. It's like they have no idea what war's like or what we all gave up for them." He spat again. "All that crap from Damanhur followed us too. That didn't help things."

I sighed. "Yeah, things aren't any better here."

Ira nodded back to the saloon. "We figured out as much. We came here looking for you after we stopped at your farm and learned someone else owned the place now." He chuckled. "I take you were the cause for him being all hunched over and groaning."

I winced, feeling bad for having taken down a man who really had done nothing wrong.

Dekar raised his head upward and closed his eyes. "They all threw us a big send off in support when we left Tamra. They told us to make Turine proud. The women had shouted they'd treat us like heroes when we returned." He gritted his teeth. "Adwa had told me in private I already was a hero in her eyes and nothing would ever change that." He swore. "It was all a bunch of crap. They've forgotten everything. They've forgotten us."

That took me aback. Dekar must have really been hurting inside. The man wasn't known to say a whole lot about himself. Actually, he wasn't known to say a whole lot, period.

"Just a bunch of forgotten soldiers, Ty. If we had stayed in Tamra that's all we'd ever be." Ira paused. "Well, if they didn't get sick of our company and kill us first."

"Anyway," said Dekar, composing himself. He nodded to Myra and Zadok. "We figured you might be dealing with similar stuff and considering you have a family to look after, we thought you might need a hand if trouble started."

At a time when it felt like most of the world had turned against me, it nearly brought tears to my eyes when I thought about them considering my situation in spite of the stuff they both had dealt with.

"We've been hearing something about a fight between you and some guy named Jareb," said Ira. "That's what I was discussing with them folks in the tavern when Dek thought to intervene."

That name jarred me away from my reunion among friends. "I'll explain later, but yeah, things could get ugly. We really need to get out of town."

Ira pointed. "We still got the wagon with us over there."

"Where do we need to pick up Lasha?" asked Dekar. I saw him eyeing the kids.

I cleared the lump from my throat. "Nowhere. She's dead."

His eyes widened. He put a hand on my shoulder. "I'm sorry, Tyrus."

"Me too."

A meaningful "I'm sorry" offered more support to someone grieving over the loss of a loved one than some long speech or thin philosophical phrase ever would. Unfortunately, too many people hadn't yet reached that conclusion. I was especially thankful then for Dekar being smarter than most people.

"Let's just get out of here." I nodded to my kids. "I'm taking with me the only things I can't leave behind."

* * *

Ira and Dekar led the way through town toward the wagon. Knowing we had a quicker way to travel than simply huffing it on foot, did wonders for my mood. Only Molak knew how far we'd have to go to find a place like Treetown.

Good old Captain Nehab sure had it made.

Zadok eased up beside me. "Pa, these are the people you were telling us about last night?"

"Some of them. They were in my unit."

"I imagined them to be different."

I raised an eyebrow. "How so?"

"I don't know. Less dirty and more heroic."

"They aren't any less dirty than I was before we fell in the creek. And I'm no more heroic than them."

"That's not true."

"Why not?"

Myra muttered from behind, "Because then Zadok would have to admit that all those crazy things he's imagined you doing in the war were wrong. If dragons weren't just some mythical tale, he'd be convinced you had slain one."

"Shut up," Zadok hissed.

I rested a free hand on the boy's shoulder. "I hate to tell you this, son, but I'm not a hero." I felt him deflate. "That isn't to say I haven't met my fair share of them."

"Really?"

"Yeah, they aren't the sort of people you might have heard from fairy tales though. Each and every one of them had their own sad tale to tell. The heroes I knew dug ditches and sharpened stakes until their hands bled in order to quickly fortify a position against the enemy, only to die from some infection brought on by the broken blisters. The heroes I knew stayed up for almost two days straight, keeping watch and protecting their injured friends, only to later die of a bug bite. The heroes I knew stepped in front of a sword stroke so that their friend might live, not because of the promise of glory or the possibility of having songs written about them."

Zadok frowned. "But those can't be heroes. They all died."

"So?"

"Heroes are supposed to win."

"No. Heroes are just supposed to do the right thing."

"Hey, Ty. If you're done being all philosophical with your boy, we got trouble."

I looked up. Ira had paused at the corner of a building. Dekar stood next to him. I slowed.

"What is it?"

"Look for yourself. Friends of yours?"

I peered around the side of the building. Illuminated by the evening sun, two men waited at the wagon, looking over the supplies strapped in the back. Both were of medium height and build. Other than the long, thin beard worn by the man on the right, neither stood out.

"Never seen them before, but that doesn't mean anything. There are few people I know here anymore."

Dekar grunted. "Think they might be working for that Jareb fellow?"

"It's possible."

"If so," said Ira. "They hadn't learned much from last time. They only sent two to bring you in."

"They could just be there to keep an eye out and slow us down in case we met up with you," said Dekar.

"How would they know we planned to meet up with Tyrus?"

Dekar gave his brother a look. "You weren't exactly discreet in that saloon."

"Oh, yeah. Well, all we're doing is making their life easier by waiting around like this."

"You're right," I said. "Let's go."

Ira led the way, carrying a bagful of attitude that would have weighed most people down. "Can I help you two dung heaps with something?"

The men wheeled, neither making a move for a weapon. They didn't seem worried. That behavior confirmed Dekar's assumption that their purpose had not been to apprehend us so much as to keep an eye on the wagon.

"Hey, I'm talking to you two idiots," Ira said in the hopes of eliciting a response.

With each step we took forward, they shuffled two back. The man with the beard shifted his glance away from us and to a spot behind him on his left.

"Ira. Bushes," I said.

We all drew our swords, forgetting about the two men who retreated in a run. Ten people emerged from the bushes. Another attempted to stay hidden. I recognized three of them right away—Jareb and his two friends. All looked pretty bad off, Amalek on a crutch. Jareb's face was swollen and darkened with bruises. A bandage covered half of it.

The others I hadn't seen before though I could piece them out.

The man to the far right wearing the king's crest on his chest was obviously the sheriff. The two men next to him probably deputies. The small man behind those three didn't have a weapon. But that didn't stop him from thinking himself something special by the way he carried himself, thrusting out his dimpled chin. I guessed him to be the mayor.

The others gravitated more toward Jareb, watching his movements. Likely more men that worked for him. The last person, who realized hiding was useless by the way I stared at her, came out of the bushes. She carried no steel, and her fingers twisted and turned about themselves as her lips mumbled. She looked right at me, growing ever more frustrated as she did so.

I grinned at her and then Jareb who shot the mage a look. She shrugged, dumbfounded. It was obvious she had never come across anyone resistant to sorcery before. The fact that I didn't even feel her attempts made me think she knew little more than a few parlor tricks. Because of that I wasn't worried about her trying anything on Ira or Dekar. They had faced far worse.

I glanced over my shoulder at Myra and Zadok. I wasn't sure if they had any experience with sorcery, but I doubted it mattered. Jareb wouldn't waste any of his mage's efforts on them.

We all stared at each other. Each side waited for the other to start things off.

I got tired of waiting. "Mayor? Sheriff?" I asked looking in the direction of the men I pegged. They focused on me. "Would one of you mind telling me what's going on?"

The sheriff cleared his throat. "I'm gonna need you to put your sword down and disarm yourself." He gestured to Dekar and Ira. "All of you."

"That ain't gonna happen," said Ira.

"Shut up, Ira," snapped Dekar. "Let Tyrus handle this."

"Sorry, Sheriff. As my friend said, that's not going to happen. I know everyone's heard stories about the war and even about Damanhur, but none of you know the facts. We did nothing wrong."

"That's for me to decide," piped up the mayor before shrinking back down.

The sheriff nodded. "What Mayor Rezub means is that your friends will be able to go free. However, you've got some things to answer for unrelated to what happened in Damanhur." His eyes flicked to Jareb.

Jareb spat venom, shouting and jabbing the sword in his hand at me. I couldn't make out much of what he said since his jaw and nose were so swollen.

Ira chuckled. "Gods, you did a number on him, Ty. Can't understand a thing he's saying."

That shut Jareb up, but it just made him stare daggers at Ira as well. Ira returned the look with a wide grin. He lived for these sorts of moments.

I took the silence to address the sheriff. "I paid for my kids' contracts and then some."

"That's not what Jareb says, and he has witnesses."

"I'll bet he does," muttered Ira.

"My word means nothing then?"

No one said anything, but I guessed they didn't need to. The silence said a multitude of things.

My ears caught the whispering of Myra's voice as she spoke to calm Zadok.

I knew that if I went along with the sheriff, I'd likely hang or at the least spend Molak knows how long in the town jail. Either scenario would condemn the kids to return to Jareb's land where he'd continue his mistreatment of them. Probably worse than before.

I sucked in a breath.

"Tyrus?" asked Dekar, pushing me to make the call.

"Counting them out," I said. Ira and Dekar relaxed, waiting for assignments, not doubting for one second that despite having a disadvantage in numbers, we'd win. A man might think he knew how to use a sword from running drills on a post in his barn or sparring with a neighbor, but none of that meant anything in a real fight. I'd take a veteran of war over a town champion any day.

Everyone else looked confused as I fired off orders. "I've got eleven first." By eleven, I meant the mage. "After that, I'll move to ten, nine, and maybe eight. Shouldn't be hard considering their state." After all, Amalek was on crutches. "Ira, one, two and four since I don't expect three to do anything but run." Three was the mayor. "Dekar, five through seven."

I looked at our opponents. Despite the cold air, a sheen of sweat appeared on the faces of most. Several looked jumpy. They had probably expected us to lay down arms on account of their numbers. Jareb and his two friends had worn the ugliest smiles imaginable, obviously finding the situation comical until they also realized we planned to stand our ground.

"On three?" Ira asked.

"Yeah," I said. "One."

We charged before I said "two," throwing our opponents off guard. I made a beeline for the mage, who was once again trying to work some spell on me. The faintest tingling sensation tickled my ears. The fact that I felt anything at all meant it was likely her strongest spell.

Jareb's eyes and the lazy way he held his weapon betrayed the confidence he felt in stepping in front of me as I ran toward her. Obviously, he expected the mage he had with him to do her part. Obviously, he was an idiot.

I dodged his swipe at my head and slammed the hilt of my sword into his face. I heard a crack, followed by a wheeze and gasp. Blood sprayed once more as he fell backward.

The mage's eyes widened as I continued toward her. She yelped, turned tail, and sprinted off into the brush. I opted to let her go, in part because I doubted she'd be back any time soon and also because Jareb's two friends, Kush and Amalek, had made it over to me.

I kicked out Amalek's crutch before he could raise his blade. He fell.

Kush came in fast, hoping to make up for his friends' failures. He spat angry curses, wanting to seek retribution from our confrontation yesterday. His anger made up for his sloppy blows. He moved with such strength I backed away and deflected the first half-dozen strikes. He overreached himself on the seventh, raising his arm higher for what he probably imagined to be some act of intimidation before raining down a stroke with all his might. It never came as my blade sank into his side just under the armpit.

I walked over to Amalek as he tried to rise and kicked him in the face. He fell back next to Jareb. Both rested, motionless, unrecognizable and covered in blood.

It was too good for them.

With my three men down, I turned my attention to Dekar and Ira. They stood over four injured men. Ira had a sword raised, ready to plunge downward.

"Wait!" I called out.

Dekar grabbed his brother's arm as it started to descend.

Ira looked up, confused "What the heck, Ty?"

"Just wait."

I looked over to Myra and Zadok. Both stared in disbelief. Zadok especially seemed unsure about what to make of things. I doubted that the ugly clash of steel reflected anything he had heard before in his fairy tales. There was no chivalry and majestic sweeping of blades, no swearing of long-winded oaths in real life.

"Myra. Myra!" I repeated, louder. She blinked. "Are you both all right?"

She nodded.

"Good. Stay there a moment." I turned back to Ira and Dekar. "Where are the others?"

"You were right about the mayor running," said Ira. "However, the sheriff and one of his deputies decided to join him when they saw things get out of hand."

"Figures." I nodded to the four groaning bodies. "Let them be and let's get out of here."

Ira gave me a confused look. "Seriously?"

"Yeah. We've made our point." I thought of some of the accusations consistently made against me and others from the army. "We defended ourselves and won. We're not cold-blooded killers."

"You know they'll just likely be part of some party coming to hunt us down inside of a couple of days."

I knew he was probably right, remembering a lesson my old drill sergeant once told me. 'Never let your enemy live, unless he's living in chains.' However, when I looked over my shoulder and saw the looks on Myra and Zadok's faces, I couldn't bring myself to kill the men lying helpless on the ground.

I knew I'd likely regret the decision.

"Let's just go." I faced my kids. "Hurry and jump in the back of the wagon."

Myra led Zadok by the hand, making as wide a circle as possible to avoid the men on the ground. She reached the wagon bed and climbed in back. I piled in behind them and took a seat.

"I'm sorry you had to see that."

"It was so much different than I thought it would be," said Zadok in a monotone voice.

I nodded while blowing out a slow breath, scanning the bushes in order to make sure that mage hadn't found the nerve to return. I neither saw nor heard anything. "That's usually how they all go."

Myra gasped. I turned. "Tyrus, you're bleeding."

I looked down and touched my side with a free hand. "Not mine."

"Oh," she said softly in recognition. "Shouldn't you clean it up or something?"

"Later. Maybe I can find a place come morning to take care of that. For now, we need to get moving. Speaking of," I began, realizing that neither Ira nor Dekar had climbed onto the front of the wagon. "Hey, let's get a move on! We give the mayor enough time, he's likely to come back with a mob." I called out.

Ira snorted. "Funny you should mention that. Ty, can your kids fight?"

"What?"

Dekar said. "What Ira means is you might want to think up something quick."

I cursed, stood, and looked past Ira and Dekar. About three dozen townspeople carrying everything from old swords to shovels and pickaxes walked toward us. None of them looked friendly. Worst of all they blocked our only way out of the area short of turning the wagon around, and maneuvering through uncleared terrain. Not exactly an ideal solution.

"Molak be cursed. We're not taking them all out," I said. "Quick, get in the wagon and take off."

They both ran back. The mob didn't speed their approach. I guess they assumed there was no need to rush with us pinned as we were.

Dekar called out as he climbed in. "They're blocking us."

"Then make them move," I said.

"Now we're talking," said Ira, drawing his sword once again.

I had still had mine in hand and shifted the grip. I looked down at Myra and Zadok. "Climb underneath the seat quickly and tuck yourselves in tight."

They did so without question just as Dekar seized the reigns and flicked them hard. The wagon lurched forward, nearly rocking me off my feet. We didn't have a lot of room to build up speed in our charge, but my hope was that the sight of the animals barreling down on them would be enough to have them second guess their decision to make a stand. Maybe they wouldn't realize they could strike at the unprotected flanks of our horses. If they did gather themselves in time, my hope was that they'd strike the wagon, which could take the punishment.

The mayor was smarter than I was hoping. He screamed for everyone to hold their ground. Funny how he did so from the edge of the mob rather than the center. He probably thought he'd be safe.

Dekar angled the wagon toward him.

A series of loud, rapid pops followed by a magnificent burst of bluish-white light exploded in our path. Dekar veered the wagon away and pulled up on the reigns. The sudden stop pitched me forward and I just barely stopped myself from falling over the side. Several more pops sounded again, and the transfer portal closed.

I was still working hard at blinking and rubbing my eyes with my free hand when a woman's voice yelled "Get Back!" in the direction of the townspeople.

Through blurry, yet slowly clearing vision I called, "Ava? That you?"

"Yeah, it's me. You want to tell me what in the name of the gods is going on?"

My vision started to return, and I saw that she was standing in front of the mob all by herself. With wide eyes and nervous glances, none moved.

Ava wore white robes rather than her black leathers. In any other situation, I'd give her a hard time about that. She had her hands on her hips daring the crowd to try something stupid. None of them wanted to take that dare. They had most likely never seen anything like a transfer portal before.

The mayor might have been able to work the crowd into a big enough frenzy to stand their ground against a charging wagon, but I doubted he could convince them to attack a mage, especially since it was obvious she knew more than the few parlor tricks like the woman I ran off earlier.

"Long story," I answered. "The gist of it is that our homecoming has been anything but what we all thought it would be. We had a bit of trouble early on that's only gotten worse. We're no longer welcome and the townspeople want to imprison me."

"Been busy, I see," she said.

"Yeah."

People still looked for the mayor to take the lead, but unsurprisingly, I could no longer spot him. The sheriff seemed the next logical person to command the crowd, but he was as dumbfounded as the rest. Without a leader present, everyone just stood and watched.

"Where are Lasha and the kids?" Ava asked over a shoulder.

"I've got the kids covered in the wagon." I paused. "Lasha's dead."

She flinched at that, eyed the crowd one last time and gave them her back as she walked toward us. Ava always liked to flaunt her power. "How?" she asked before giving Dekar and Ira a nod.

"Another long story." It wasn't the time or place.

"I'm sorry."

I nodded. "What are you doing here?"

That question jolted her. "Gods, yes! I got distracted when I walked into this. We have to get out of here now! I don't care where, but it needs to be far away."

"No argument from me," said Ira.

Dekar grunted in agreement. "That was our plan before the mob came along."

I jumped as a giant burst of light from far off in the distance brightened like a hundred setting suns, bathing the land in a hue of red and orange. A towering cloud rose from the ground in the direction of Hol, widening as it ascended. A deafening roar that could only be described as the loudest thunder imaginable echoed, changing in pitch to a high shrill at the end. A warm, heavy breeze blew against my face as the shrill reached its crescendo.

"What in the—" I started only to be cut off by the moaning and wailing of everyone around me, including the horses.

The townspeople were on the ground, some convulsing. Ira and Dekar had fallen over in their seats, grunting and whimpering in pain. Ava had hit the dirt, limbs shaking like she was caught in a seizure.

I looked down to Zadok and Myra. "Are you both all right?"

"Yeah," said Myra. "Mostly just a sudden headache. But also warm and something like a tickling sensation across my skin."

"Me too," said Zadok.

"Sorcery," I muttered as if a curse.

"What?" asked Zadok.

"That eruption was tied to a large amount of sorcery. You and your sister must have some level of resistance like I do to not be affected like the townspeople."

"You mean we could fight sorcery?" asked Zadok, eyes wide.

I could only imagine the thoughts running through his head. Probably imagining himself fighting some evil wizard from his fairy tales. "We can talk about it later. Help Ira and Dekar by keeping a hand on them. Your resistance will also draw out sorcery from others. I'll see to Ava."

I jumped down and touched her forehead. It felt like fire, but then began to cool as I came in contact with her skin. I left my hand there and the shaking subsided slightly. Her eyes flicked open.

I checked on the townsfolk. They were all in bad shape, which from my point of view was a good thing. I didn't need them trying to attack us now.

The faintest whisper came from below. I looked down and shushed Ava as she struggled to speak. "Just rest. We're safe for now. Whatever you want to tell me can wait."

She shook her head and swallowed. "I was trying to warn you about this," she said in a low voice. "This is why I wanted you to leave."

I frowned. "You mean you know what that was?"

She gave a faint nod. "The end of the world."

CHAPTER 17

I always assumed that if the world ended, it would be immediate and filled with crazy visuals. Most people would be tortured and burned while a select few were whisked away to whatever afterlife ended up being the true one amongst the hundreds of religions in the world. All life would end in a matter of moments and those unlucky enough to see it happen would be kicking themselves for choosing the wrong god or gods to have paid homage to during their meaningless lives.

I wasn't even close.

For a few short moments after Ava told me the distant eruption had been the end of the world, I thought I had been right. People writhed and moaned in pain. The hellish vision of dark clouds in the distance and the evening sky changing to hues rarely seen in the hour before a sunset seemed to only validate Ava's proclamation.

No one around me was lifted up to some majestic afterlife, but that could be easily explained. Maybe no one around here had the correct god or faith.

I dismissed my natural inclinations, realizing quickly that as bad as things appeared in that moment, the progression of this possible disaster would probably take longer to develop than I expected it might. I reassessed what was going on with a clearer mind. The darkest clouds seemed to stay in place over the site of the explosion. I couldn't be certain from this far away, but they didn't appear to be spreading. At least not yet.

I swore.

The explosion had occurred in the direction of Hol. I remembered the conversation I had with Balak about the Geneshan artifact, and I suspected the Council of High Mages did exactly what they said they wouldn't do and used it.

One more reason not to like them.

Ava had passed out. Though the shakes had lessened, her breathing remained erratic and her skin felt warmer than it should have. I kept a hand on her temple as I glanced over my shoulder to Myra and Zadok who tended to Ira and Dekar. My two friends had mostly come out of their stupor. I couldn't say the same for the townspeople. We were certainly safe from an attack at the moment.

I raised my voice above their moans. "Dekar. Ira. Talk to me."

"We're doing better," said Dekar.

Ira leaned over and retched near the front wagon wheel. "I'm all right now, Ty."

"Do either of you have enough strength to get us out of here?"

"I can manage," said Dekar.

"Me too," said Ira.

"I don't think that's going to happen, Pa," Zadok said.

I turned my gaze to him. "Why not?"

Myra gestured to the horses. "That's why."

As if on cue, one of the mounts unsteady on her feet, slammed into the other. Both careened to the ground, snapping one of the harnesses and rocking the wagon in the process. We wouldn't be using them or probably any other animals anytime soon.

"Can everyone walk?" I asked.

Everyone but Ava nodded.

"Good. We gotta get Ava somewhere to recuperate. You two could also use the rest," I said, nodding to Ira and Dekar as they swayed on their feet.

"What about going back to our camp in the forest?" asked Zadok.

"That's a couple miles away, son. Without the wagon, only me, you, and your sister have the strength right now to do that kind of walking. And that's with me carrying your Aunt the whole way. I don't even know if it's safe to move her that much." I glanced back at the sky where the eruption originated. Clouds swirled and lightning pulsed. It wasn't getting any better. "Besides, no telling if that's done. Getting indoors is probably the best move to make right now."

"And if there's trouble again?" asked Ira. He pointed toward the townspeople. Some tried to right themselves, but most didn't have the energy to bother and lay helplessly on the ground.

"I'll figure something out. Based on the way everyone's acting, we got some time before that's a problem." A man cried out. "I doubt they got much fight left in them right now anyway. Grab what food and supplies you can manage. Meet me at the Hemlock Inn. It's across the street from the theater. The kids know where to find it."

I bent down and slid an arm under Ava's shoulders, the other under her legs. With a grunt, I scooped her up, trying not to jostle her more than necessary.

Zadok helped Ira out the wagon, allowing the soldier to use his shoulder to steady himself.

Though I tried not to think about it, seeing my sister in her current state, long limbs swaying without resistance, scared me more than her prophetic statement about the world's impending destruction.

I started walking toward the afflicted townspeople. The moans of pain had died down to dull groans. Two people managed to sit up. One had the strength to lift his head and meet my stare. I doubt he knew who he was looking at as his eyes rolled around in his head. He blinked rapidly trying to focus.

I maneuvered my way back onto Main Street. More people lay on the ground, dazed and hurting. I ignored them and made my way toward the inn.

About a hundred feet from the inn's door, I shifted Ava in my arms. Her swinging limbs grew more cumbersome with each step. Thankfully, she had always been on the lean side. Her head rolled around a bit as I hoisted her higher, exchanging the strain in my back for burning in my arms.

Stepping off the dirt street and onto the wooden sidewalk, my boots resonated over the whimpers of a middle-aged man from across the street slumped against the wall to the theater. Vomit covered his shirt. A puddle between his legs leaked between the sidewalk's boards. He strained to extend an arm toward me. I ignored him.

Molak cut me a break for once. The door to the inn was slightly ajar. I swung it open with the toe of my boot.

Inside, a fire crackling brightly in a large hearth against the back wall cut the cold from the autumn breeze outside. However, after the exertion of carrying Ava I quickly grew uncomfortable.

Maroon-colored, plush chairs surrounded three round tables in the center of the space with matching curtains over the window. Oil lamps hung over three paintings on the walls.

I didn't see any patrons or employees. The silence in the space felt unnatural. A faint whine came from the left. With Ava still in my arms, I avoided a large oaken chest and stepped behind the counter.

Slumped on the floor with his back against a wall, sat a thin, light-haired man, face absent of even the slightest of stubble. He wore clothes more refined than what was common. Based on dress and location, I took him for the inn's manager.

"Hey, I need a room."

His head flopped to the side and his eyes rolled up. His lips moved, but nothing came out.

I swore.

I had no clue what rooms were available. I guess I could have just walked upstairs and busted into the first room I came across, kicking any current occupant out. However, I figured why borrow more trouble.

Squatting down, I eased Ava to the floor. I relished the sudden relief to my arms, shoulders, and back.

"Hey, can you talk at all? I need a room," I repeated while reaching out a hand.

The man's unfocused gaze continued to slide around the room until I touched his arm. He gasped for air and blinked rapidly. I pulled my hand away in surprise at such a fast response. He started to tumble over in a groan. I grabbed his arm to catch him, feeling a shirt damp with sweat. His eyes widened and his breathing picked up. I helped him sit straighter and within moments, his condition seemed drastically improved.

"What . . . happened?" he asked.

Trying to explain my hunch about the Geneshan artifact would be lost on the man. "Something big. Most in town are as bad as you."

He looked me over, brow furrowed. "But not you?"

I shrugged. "Lucky, I guess. Look, I need a room. Do you have one available?"

He blinked hard, still trying to clear the cobwebs. "Just the suite. Top floor." A deep breath. "Two bedrooms and a sitting area."

"I'll take it," I said thinking the room's size would be ideal when the others caught up. "Where's the key?"

"I'll get it," he said, starting to rise.

I let him go, and he immediately dropped to one knee. My other hand reflexively left Ava as both darted out to steady the innkeeper. "You all right?"

"Yeah, sorry. I'm better now. It's weird but when you let me go, I felt sick again. Not as bad as before, but enough to make me dizzy."

"Just tell me where the key is and I'll get it."

"Top drawer of that cabinet," he said, pointing. "It'll be marked."

I started to rise when a commotion on the floor started behind me. Turning, I saw that Ava had begun to shake again, her boots clicking on the wooden boards. I rushed back to her. The moment I touched her, the trembling ceased.

"Is . . . she all right?" the innkeeper asked.

"I'm not sure." I frowned, having noticed the quivering in his voice. He had slumped against the wall again.

"Are you feeling bad again?"

He nodded. "Some."

"Reach over and touch me."

"Huh?"

"Just do it."

The innkeeper scooted over gingerly and extended an arm. My eyes never left his face as I felt him wrap his fingers around my wrist. His face gradually gained more color.

"That's strange. I'm feeling better again." His eyes widened. "Are you a priest? A healer? What gods do you serve?"

I snorted. "I don't serve any gods. And I'm not a healer."

"But how—"

The door to the inn opened, cutting off the question.

"Where in the name of Xank did he go?" I heard Ira mutter.

"Behind the counter," I called out.

They came around the side carrying far more from the wagon than I thought they'd be able to manage. Myra and Zadok still had a hand on Ira and Dekar. Both looked better.

"What are you doing back there, Pa?" asked Zadok.

I quickly explained the last couple minutes. Then I decided to test how well everyone was recovering. I had Myra let go of Dekar to fetch the key to the suite for me. I had a suspicion that my kids' resistance wasn't as strong as mine based on their comment about headaches. Still, I expected Dekar to be further along than before.

"How do you feel?" I asked Dekar.

"Not as bad as earlier. Groggy though. Like I just woke up."

I nodded. "The symptoms lessen the longer you're in contact with someone who has a resistance. They'll probably go away all together before long."

Dekar looked at Ava and frowned. "So, because of your sister's connection to sorcery, it's harder on her."

"Possibly. It's as good a guess as anything."

It meant I wasn't leaving her side.

Myra found the key and led the way upstairs. I picked Ava up and we followed. The extra time the innkeeper had in contact with me seemed to do him wonders. He managed to keep his feet under him without assistance before we left. With a clearer mind, he became panicky as he thought of his family. He disappeared through a swinging door in search of them.

The suite ended up bigger than I had expected. We entered through a sitting room that separated two bedrooms. It held a wood burning stove, a small table, and enough chairs for four people. The floor space provided enough room for rolls to be laid out for those not sleeping in beds.

I didn't linger and headed for the bedroom on the right with Ava.

A four-poster bed with white sheets sat against one wall—nightstand and a sitting chair flanking it. A window looked out from the wall across from the bed. Under normal circumstances, I imagined sunlight streaming into the space. The only thing visible now was a murky gray interrupted by the faint, orange, red, and purple sitting over the land in the distance. A dresser stood to the right of the window. A chamber pot on the left.

I was reminded that the room was twice as large as my old bedroom on the farm. I had always promised Lasha I would get a place like this for a night or two when we had the money and the time.

Another promise I'd never fulfill.

Myra followed me into the bedroom. She pulled the sheets back as I lay Ava down on the bed. Keeping one hand on her shoulder, I started pulling the sheets up.

"Wait." Myra closed the door.

"What's wrong?"

"Shouldn't we undress her? No telling how long she'll be out and we don't want her soiling her clothes."

"I didn't even consider that."

I made a move to slip off her robes and then froze as it suddenly struck me what I was about to do. I hadn't seen Ava without clothes since we were children sharing a bath.

We weren't exactly kids anymore.

It may sound dumb considering Ava's circumstances, but the idea of undressing my sister made me uneasy. Still, it needed to happen.

I gritted my teeth and began to pull one of her arms through the sleeve of her robe.

Myra must have noticed the difficulty I was having, both mentally and physically, as I kept one of my hands in contact with Ava's body at all times, worried the shaking would return.

She walked over. "Let me do it. Just focus on staying in contact with her."

I nodded. "Thanks. For multiple reasons."

She shook her head and muttered. "All of them obvious."

Myra got Ava's robes and the leathers worn underneath off quickly before drawing the sheets over her body. She searched the drawers of the dresser and as luck would have it found a suitable bed pan to slip underneath Ava.

Relatively safe inside our room, the potential of losing my sister struck me again.

I swallowed hard. I loved my kids and couldn't have been happier to have them back in my life. However, with Lasha's death, no one knew me better than Ava. There's something to be said for the connection you share with your sibling. No one else gets to see you at your best and worst as you enter and exit each phase of your life like they do.

"Tyrus!"

I sat up to Dekar's voice. "Yeah?"

He entered the doorway. "That innkeeper is at the door. He wants to see you."

"Why?"

"He says his daughter is really bad off. He's worried she's going to die."

I could hear the innkeeper arguing with Ira about coming inside to talk to me. I knew he wouldn't win that argument.

"I'm not leaving Ava."

Dekar nodded. "I'll tell him."

"Wait," said Myra. "Why can't you help him?"

I gave her a sour look, one because of how guilty I suddenly felt having to face the question, and two because her asking it surprised me. "I thought Zadok was supposed to be the one with the high morals in the family now."

"I'm serious, Tyrus."

"I'm not leaving Ava. Too much can happen."

"Let me take care of her. You already said I have a resistance too."

"It's not as strong as mine."

She turned toward the door. "Zadok! Grab a chair and come in here!"

The boy came running in holding one of the chairs from the sitting room. "Yeah?"

"Go sit on the other side of Aunt Ava and put your hand on her arm." Myra faced me. "Together we should be able to come close to matching your resistance, right?"

Zadok did as his sister said.

I grimaced. "I don't know. It's all a guess at this point."

"We could go help instead," Zadok offered.

"No. I don't want you two running off without me. You can stay here with Ira and Dekar. That way I'll know where you are and that you're safe."

"So that means you're willing to give my idea a chance?" Myra asked. "It shouldn't take but a moment."

"A lot can happen in a moment," I said, still not ready to give in. "Besides, why do you care so much about the innkeeper's daughter?"

"Because she's just a child. Completely innocent. Unlike the rest of this town."

She had me there.

"All right. We'll test things out." I stood. "Take my seat. Put a hand on her. If I let go and nothing visibly changes, I'll see to the innkeeper's daughter. If anything negative happens, I'm staying."

Myra did as I said. I slowly lifted my hand, one finger at a time. My eyes drifted from Ava's face to her chest, and back again, looking for any sign of change. Nothing happened.

I grunted. "I guess you were right."

"Then hurry and go," said Myra. "The girl needs your help."

"Don't worry, Pa. We've got it," said Zadok.

"All right." Passing by Dekar on the way to the door, I told him. "If her condition changes at all, you come and grab me, understand?"

He nodded.

By the time I got to the door, the innkeeper was literally jumping up and down. To Ira's credit, he hadn't laid the man out, despite his frantic behavior. The innkeeper saw me and started rambling at such speeds I only understood maybe every third word. The gist of it was that he would give me anything I wanted or do anything I desired so long as I came to look at his little girl.

"Take me to her."

He reached inside the doorway, latched onto my arm like a vice, and started dragging me through the hallway toward the stairs.

In the midst of everything, I managed to get his name.

Boaz brought me to the basement, past several sacks of flower and barrels of ale. In a corner, sat his wife and daughter next to a tray of spilled limes.

"They were down here getting supplies for the kitchen when whatever happened, happened," he said.

His wife, Dinah, looked rough, but she at least was awake, even having enough strength to lay a hand on her daughter who quivered unconsciously next to her. The lucidity of Boaz's wife had me adding to my theory that although my resistance to sorcery would heal people faster, many might get better on their own. It would just probably take them longer.

I kneeled next to the young girl, probably around eight, and placed both my hands on her. I felt a slight vibration, common when my resistance drew away sorcery. Her shuddering ceased.

"Hold your wife up and put her hands on me while I stay in contact with your daughter," I said.

Boaz quickly obeyed. His wife's breathing improved significantly. "You too," I told him. "I can tell you still aren't completely recovered."

He touched my other shoulder.

"Thank you," Boaz's wife whispered between quiet sobs. She chanced removing one hand from my shoulder to stroke her daughter's cheek. "Why is she so worse off than us? Is it because she's so young?"

"Possibly." I glanced over to Boaz. "Does she have any talent?"

He gave me a look. "Talent?"

"You know, sorcery?"

"By the gods, no," said the wife, appalled that I would even suggest such a thing.

I ignored her and stared at Boaz, waiting for his response.

"None that we know of."

"What about a penchant for good luck? Predicting the weather? Anything odd like that?"

Boaz grunted. "She's always had a way with animals. It seems they do whatever she tells them to, wild or not. Why?"

"Because only my sister acted anywhere near as bad as her and that's probably because she's a mage. Your daughter might have some hidden talent you aren't aware of."

"Don't say that!" Boaz's wife began to cry harder at that news than she had before. "What will we do?"

I thought about all the hardships Ava had suffered during her life—the looks, the names, the ridicule. . . . The tone of horror this little girl's mom held in her voice for her daughter made me sick. My initial inclination was to slap her. In the end, I opted for a more tactful approach.

"What's your daughter's name?"

"Abigail."

I stared at Abigail's innocent face. Smooth skin framed with long brown hair.

"This is what you're going to do," I began. With head down, my voice took on the quality I used in the military when disciplining a member of my unit. "When Abigail comes around, you're going to tell her how much you love her and that she means everything in the world to you. Then you're going to protect her and raise her as you had before. You're not going to make her self-conscious of her talent and you sure aren't going to make her ashamed of it. If she has questions, you'll help the best that you can. If you can't help her, then you're going to find someone who can. In the end, you'll let her make her own decisions regarding her gift once she's old enough." I looked up and shifted my stare between Boaz and his wife. "Am I clear?"

Boaz nodded. "Yes, of course. All of that goes without saying."

Dinah seemed embarrassed. "I didn't mean that—"

"I don't care what you meant," I said. "I'm just telling you how things better be."

No one said anything after that. I might have been harsher than needed, but I had enough of the "better than you" attitude I had been witness to since leaving the army.

I lost track of time, but eventually Abigail came around. By the time she did, Boaz and Dinah were no longer showing any symptoms. Seeing their genuine relief and love at Abigail's recovery, eased the bitterness I had from earlier.

"We can't thank you enough," said Boaz.

"Don't worry about it."

"No, my husband's right. Thank you," said Dinah.

"You and your family can have the suite for as long as you like, free of charge. It's the least I can do," added the innkeeper.

I nodded. "I appreciate that. Don't take offense by me saying I hope our stay isn't long. It would be in everyone's best interest if we were on our way as soon as my sister recovers. Maybe tomorrow, if we're lucky."

We still had to contend with the rest of town should they come around and chances were they'd be upset with Boaz for helping us.

"I understand." He paused. "You know, not everyone is as bad as you might think us. Not everyone thinks you and your friends are monsters because of the war. I never held that view."

"I appreciate that, but it does seem to be the most popular opinion."

He sighed. "Sadly, it is. Probably because it is the opinion of Jareb and few people are brave enough to disagree with him."

"Some things never change," I muttered. "Thank you again for the room. I need to go check on my sister."

* * *

Ira and Dekar lay sprawled out asleep on the sitting room's floor. I was about ready to kick one of them awake, angry for neither keeping watch on the door until I heard hushed whispers coming from Ava's room. The conversation broke off when I bumped into a chair to my right as I tried to squeeze between it and a small table. Myra leaned back, head visible through the doorway I had been moving toward. She looked at me as if I had caught her sneaking candy.

I entered Ava's bedroom, and noticed no change in her.

"Did you help her, Pa?" asked Zadok.

I nodded. "She'll be fine. Turns out she had a small talent for sorcery like Ava so the eruption affected her more." I walked over and rested my hand on Ava's brow. "How is she?"

"The same as before," said Myra.

I sighed and looked out through the window at the night sky. "Why don't you two take a break and get some sleep. It's getting late. I'll stay up with her."

"Actually, we were thinking we'd stay up so you could help others," said Zadok.

"What? The innkeeper's daughter was one thing, but I'm—"

"Shh," said Myra. "You'll wake up Dekar and Ira." She gave Zadok a look. "We didn't mean everyone."

"Good, because it's not happening."

"I did," Zadok said sternly.

"Well, I didn't," said Myra. "And the idea was mine." She eyed me. "I was just thinking that since you were able to help the innkeeper's daughter, then maybe you should go check on Nason and his family considering how much he helped us over the years."

I thought of what they told me earlier about Nason giving them food or money while I was away in the war. He once was my best friend. The weight of the money he had given me jangling in the pouch at my belt suddenly became heavier.

I looked at Ava.

My daughter gave me a smug look that once more reminded me of Lasha when she knew she had me.

"Fourteen going on thirty," I muttered under my breath.

"What?" she asked.

"Nothing. I'll go see about Nason."

"What about the tailor and his daughter?" asked Zadok.

I raised an eyebrow at him.

"They helped us too even after they knew the trouble they could get in because of it. And they weren't so harsh about it like that cobbler was with my shoes."

I sighed. "I'll stop by Sivan's shop on my way back from Nason's place."

"And then maybe—" started Zadok.

"And then nothing. I've got too many things to worry about without adding town savior to the list." Especially after the way they treated us, I thought. I walked to the bedroom window and gave Myra a look that said, "See what you started?"

She ignored me, but I could tell she regretted taking Zadok's side as well.

Her morals more closely matched mine than Lasha's. I would bend over backward to help family, friends, and even strangers in most situations. However, once someone did me wrong, it took a lot for me to overlook it.

On the other hand, Lasha had always been the person ready to give someone a second chance and was constantly on me about that particular character flaw of mine. It seemed Zadok was every bit his mother's son in that department. Based on Myra's look, I imagined that Zadok had a way to lay down the guilt on his sister just as Lasha used to do to me.

Don't get me wrong. In hindsight, Lasha always had the right of things. And I'm a better person because of her. It's just that sometimes it's easier to be a less than likeable person.

I peeked through the window. Last night the moon had barely been a sliver. Tonight, it was close to half full. That didn't make sense. Of course, last night there hadn't been the explosion either.

By the light of the moon, I saw people still sitting or lying in the streets. Some improved faster than others. Some crawled about. A few climbed to their feet long enough to take a couple steps before falling.

I held back a curse. That wasn't good. The faster they recovered, the less time I had for Ava to get better and to get us all out of town. No telling if the townspeople would blame her for everything. I doubted they would chalk it up to coincidence that she appeared right before the explosion.

I drew the curtains.

"Leave the curtains closed and the light of the lamp down," I said while dimming the wick. "I don't want to draw any more attention to ourselves. Some of the people are slowly recovering. They don't need to know where we are."

"Won't people see you leave the inn?" asked Zadok.

"I plan to go out the back." I paused. "I'm sure you know this but I'm going to say it anyway. Don't open the door for anyone except me. No matter what. If someone comes knocking, have Dekar handle it."

"We've got it, Tyrus. Go," Myra said.

My stomach soured at her using my name yet again. I wondered if I'd ever get used to it.

I left the suite. I had no clue if any of the other rooms in the inn were occupied, but I acted as though they were anyway, tiptoeing my way downstairs to the main floor. I didn't see Boaz or his family so I took it on myself to find an alternative exit. I found the rear entrance by way of the kitchen.

Once outside, I took a moment to study the sky over Hol. The devilish hues of red and orange pierced the black clouds like a sunrise fighting against a raincloud.

However, unlike a sunrise, the demonic colors started in the middle of the sky rather than at the horizon. The spot seemed to brighten slightly and then fade. I blinked, unsure if my mind was playing tricks on me. I didn't notice it again.

"The end of the world," I muttered to myself while staring at the anomaly.

Molak be cursed, I hoped Ava was wrong.

CHAPTER 18

One minute my unit was slinking through an overgrown field, the next we were caught in the middle of an ambush.

A flight of arrows peppered my unit, thudding into hastily raised shields. I barely managed to avoid a sword swept at my face. A spear pierced the gut of the man next to me before I could warn him of the incoming attack.

His high-pitch scream shook my bowels.

"Not even hell could be this bad," a voice whispered in the back of my mind.

I grit my teeth to stave off the pounding headache brought on by my racing pulse. My sword crashed down, severing both hands of the spearmen. My backswing slid across the chest of a man carrying a morning star. The man fell back as a spray of crimson sprouted from his torso, the spinning ball of metal clipping the man next to him.

I screamed and ran forward, eager to meet the enemy on my terms.

"Ty! Wake up!"

I sat up quickly, hand darting to the dagger at my side. Someone grabbed my arm tightly so that I couldn't move it.

Waking up is never an easy thing.

Waking up in a hard chair, hunched over the bed that your unconscious sister is lying in doesn't make it easier. The harsh memories of war haunting my dreams made the entire process infinitely worse.

Ira stared into my face. "Calm down, Ty. You were dreaming. We ain't in the field anymore. We're in Denu Creek. Remember?"

Slowly, my mind relaxed. Visions of the men under my command dying began to fade. Memories of the last day in the present took their place, essentially replacing one hell for another.

My chest tightened when I remembered Lasha.

"Sorry. I'm all right."

I checked on Ava. There was still no change in her condition, but at least she looked peaceful. That didn't stop me from saying a quick curse to Ao though. The goddess of sorcery had to have some sort of hand in this mess. I figured Ava's lack of improvement probably stemmed from a closer connection to it than Abigail's.

I finished my inner tirade and added a quick curse to Molak for good measure. In my opinion, there was no such thing as saying too many curses to the father of the Turine gods.

"Which one was it?" asked Ira.

"Huh?"

"You were talking in your sleep. Sounded like a battle."

I wiped the sweat from my brow with the back of my hand. "The ambush on the Safed Plain."

He closed his green eyes, blew a deep breath, and rubbed his hands through his blond hair. "Xank, that was brutal."

I nodded, thumb and forefinger moving down to rub my tired eyes.

Ira snorted. "You know I can barely distinguish where my dreams take place. The gods-forsaken things all run together. One blood bath after another."

"Yeah, it's getting that way for me too. Not sure what else to say to that."

Ira pulled up a chair and sat. "You don't necessarily have to say anything more. I know what you're going through and just trying to let you know you ain't alone. Anyway, Zadok told me you went to check on some people you knew in town. What time did you get in?"

"Just before dawn I think. What is it now?"

"Still early morning. Your kids are still asleep in the other bedroom. Dekar went downstairs to get an idea about what's going on outside." His voice lightened. "You hungry?"

Only then did I notice the smell of cooked oats. Ira held a bowl. "Starved."

"Figured as much." Ira placed the bowl on the bed, next to Ava's arm. "The innkeeper's wife brought some breakfast up a few minutes ago. Said it was on the house, as is the room, on account of what you did for her daughter."

I began spooning the warm oats into my mouth with my free hand while the other stayed in contact with my sister. The honey sweetening the dish was a welcome surprise.

"Her daughter's still doing well then?"

"I guess. She didn't say otherwise."

That was encouraging. Since Abigail had recovered, I held out hope that Ava would eventually do the same. She just needed time.

"Do you have a water skin?" I asked, noticing Ava's lips had begun to crack.

He raised one.

I set the oatmeal aside. "I'll lift Ava up and tilt her head back. Slowly pour a bit of water in her mouth. Just a little at a time."

It took a few minutes to get Ava in the right position without exposing her, but eventually we managed to get a few sips down her throat without completely soaking her pillow in the process. I eased her back down just as Dekar returned.

"I asked the innkeeper's wife to bring up some broth when she had the chance," he said, entering the room.

"Good. Water isn't going to cut it."

I wolfed the rest of my oatmeal between sips of water. During the process, Dekar filled us in with what he had learned.

"For the most part, everyone's still in really bad shape. Most of the people from yesterday are still in the streets. A couple might even be dead. Those that can stand on their own, are trying to drag others inside. The way they're moving reminds me of watching people affected by a confusion spell."

I grunted. "Well, as long as they're busy with each other, then maybe they'll leave us alone while Ava recovers."

"About that . . ."

I set the empty bowl aside. "What?"

"Well, the innkeeper and his family are out there helping people. I also saw an old man and a younger blonde down the street doing the same. I guess that's that tailor and his daughter that Myra told me about?"

I nodded.

"What do you think the likelihood that your friend Nason and his family will start helping too?"

Nason had gone out of his way to help both me and the kids, despite the risk. "Pretty good, I'd say."

"That's what I figured."

I cursed. I hadn't considered what would happen as a result of my kindness.

I muttered a few swears to Molak when it dawned on me what Dekar was getting at. I could never curse Molak enough as far as I was concerned.

"What are you so upset about? Who cares what they're doing?" asked Ira.

"Because eventually people are going to start asking why the innkeeper, the tailor, and the tanner aren't as bad off as everyone else," said Dekar.

"And then it's only a matter of time before it comes back to me." I shook my head.

"You mean us," said a voice.

We turned to Myra standing in the doorway. Her black, curly hair looked a mess. Her eyes, red and puffy with sleep, stood out against her copper skin.

"Sorry, if we woke you," I said. "You can go back to sleep. We'll keep it down."

"I'm up now, but you can keep it down for Zadok." She walked over to the edge of the bed. "So, what are we going to do if people figure out where we are?"

I looked at Ava and sighed. I had hoped she would be better by morning. Conscious, at least. In her current state, there really wasn't a whole lot we could do except make our stand in the inn and hope the innkeeper, Boaz, might make a case for the rest of the town not to burn us out.

Of course, if it came down to losing his inn, I couldn't fault the man if he had a change of heart and decided to side with the rest of town.

A knock sounded before I could express those thoughts. "Must be Boaz," I muttered.

Dekar left. "I'll get it."

A brief and muffled conversation followed.

A smell I couldn't quite place hit me.

The door closed and footsteps followed. Dekar reappeared.

"Got rid of him?" Ira asked.

"Depends what him you're talking about," said a voice I hadn't expected to hear.

Nason came in behind Dekar. The smell made sense now. Lime and leather. The smell of a tanner.

"I think you should hear him out, Tyrus," said Dekar.

I nodded. "Give us a few minutes."

Ira gave me a disappointed look which I ignored. It was likely he had wanted to be a fly on the wall. Dekar cuffed him for taking his time in exiting.

Myra quietly followed, but not before lingering to rub Ava's leg. The gesture gave me pause, as it was the only time I'd seen her convey any sort of care to anyone besides Zadok. A part of me was jealous at being upstaged by my unconscious sister, someone Myra knew even less than me.

Of course, Ava had something going for her that I didn't. Myra didn't blame her for ten years of pain and misery. I got to carry that blessed burden.

Nason took a seat as the door clicked shut. Smudges of dirt covered his face, his brown hair tussled after what looked like a hard day's work. He let his arms hang off the sides of the chair and stretched out his legs.

"You look tired."

He snorted. "No worse than you, I'm sure." Nason nodded toward Ava. "How is she?"

"Alive and breathing. Beyond that, I have no clue.

He leaned over. "I always forget how much you two look alike."

It was true. We both took after our father. Same square jaw. Same brown eyes and hair which we both kept short. Both tall and lean, but neither skinny.

"Don't say that when she wakes up. You remember how much she hates hearing that."

He frowned. "I think it's the hair that really makes it obvious. I never understood why she cut it so short. Don't get me wrong, she still looks cute, but . . ."

"Ma used to tell her the same thing. Naturally Ava kept it short to spite her." I let the silence linger for a moment. "So, why are you here?"

"A couple reasons. One, you left so quickly last night I barely had a chance to thank you."

"Sorry. I needed to be here."

His gaze flicked back to Ava. "I understand. But regardless, thank you. Other than a lingering headache, the family is doing well."

"Glad to hear it. It's the least I can do considering what Myra and Zadok said you did for them before Uncle Uriah became a hassle."

He hung his head. "By the gods, it's a shame what they went through. Lasha too. Tyrus, I'm sorry I couldn't do more."

"What's done is done." I cleared my throat, not wanting to dwell on that. "Why else are you here?"

"To ask you to help the rest of town."

I snorted. "Not you too."

He gave me a confused look.

"Zadok tried to get me to do the same last night," I explained.

"I wish you would have listened to him. There doesn't seem to be any pattern to how people are affected. Some are far worse than others. A couple have died, many more could go at any minute. Lots of people are sick."

"Why should I help them? To repay them for the wonderful way they treated me and my family? For trying to kill me? Or should I do it to thank them for making sure Lasha didn't have to get a job that involved her working on her back? Or how about repaying them for the kindness they showed in preventing Myra and Zadok from becoming slaves to Jareb just so they could eat a few pathetic meals each day?"

Nason had leaned back in his chair and I realized I was practically out of my seat, yelling.

"Not everyone in town is as bad as you think they are. There are still some good people here. You've seen some of that with Boaz and his family. Sivan and Damaris too."

"Then why didn't anyone help?"

"They're scared of Jareb. Scared that they might end up . . ." His voice trailed off.

"Scared they'd end up like my family?" I asked.

Nason frowned. "Yeah."

I laughed, though there was nothing pleasant about it. "And you want me to help these people again, why?"

"Because it's the right thing to do."

Just what I needed. Another moral compass in my life.

I shook my head. "I'm not leaving Ava."

"You did it last night. Myra and Zadok can watch over her."

"It's not the same as me being here."

"You don't know that for sure, do you?"

I sat back in my seat.

Nason leaned forward. "Look, Boaz's wife slipped up and told several people what happened. They know you're here and they know you can heal them. Some of the townsfolk might lack the strength to do anything now, but if you stay up here while their loved ones die, well, it'll be worse than the small mob that the mayor cobbled together yesterday."

"Go away, Nason, and let me be."

"Tyrus."

"Go."

Nason sighed. "All right." He stood. "I'll try to make up some excuse and hold them off as long as I can. Maybe Ava will get better by then and everyone can sneak out of town before they try something. But if I can't, the next person that comes to talk to you might be leading a group with pitchforks and torches. Then what will you do?"

As Nason left I watched my sister's chest steadily rise and fall with the same unchanging rhythm as before.

"I don't know," I answered under my breath.

I spent ten years being in command where I was used to making decisions on the fly. Never did I hesitate. Yet, right then, I felt completely helpless.

"I just wanted to come home," I whispered. "I just wanted my life back."

The door to the suite opened and closed. Soon afterward, everyone drifted into Ava's room. Zadok was up, joining Myra, Ira, and Dekar.

"Well, that was a bunch of garbage, eh, Ty? Who in the name of the gods does he think he is trying to guilt you into helping these people after what they did to you and yours?" asked Ira.

"I see you were eavesdropping again."

"Didn't really have to, as loud as you were."

I sighed. "He means well."

"He makes a good point," said Dekar.

"What? Are you crazy too?" Ira said.

"It's true. Some of these people might have done us wrong, but until Ava's recovered, we're stuck here. If Tyrus heals some of them, it would go a long way toward building goodwill."

Ira spat. "Xank can have them all. We don't need goodwill."

"I think we do," said Myra. I looked up at her. "Unless you believe that the three of you can take on a whole town by yourselves."

"We faced worse odds," said Ira, though his comment lacked conviction.

I saw where this conversation was going.

"It's the right thing to do, Pa," Zadok said. "If Ma was here, she'd want you to help."

I sighed again, much heavier than before. That did sound like Lasha. Zadok had mastered his mother's unselfish nature.

"Myra and I can help if you don't want to," he continued.

"No. I still don't want you to leave this room until I say so. I don't trust anyone out there." I paused, thinking. I eyed Myra and Zadok. Except for new clothes, they looked more worn than when I first met them. Given our situation, it made me wonder if I was doing them any good at all since returning home. "All right. I'll go. Dekar, go grab Nason. Tell him I'll be down in a minute."

* * *

Apparently Dekar didn't have to run far to catch Nason. He had taken his time getting downstairs. I'm not sure if it was because he didn't look forward to telling the townspeople the answer I had given him or if he figured I'd change my mind.

Regardless, I went to meet him in the hallway after giving instructions to everyone once more about Ava and what they should do if I didn't come back.

Ira told me none of them was in swaddling, and that I should leave before he put a boot in my mouth to shut me up. I expected a rebuttal from Dekar, but for once the two brothers were in agreement. Apparently, I was being overprotective of everyone, not just Ava.

I took the hint and left. The quick hug I got from Zadok took a bit of the sting out of Myra's cold goodbye.

Nason led the way down the stairs. Another whiff of the lime on his clothes made me wonder if I should have taken the lead.

He looked over his shoulder. "I figure we'd start by the feed store if that's all right with you. Most of the families are there."

"Sure," I said, not caring one way or the other.

We took another flight of steps and low groans and garbled voices rose in volume. I heard Boaz's wife, Dinah, holler over the lot of them.

"Just be patient. I'm sure he'll be down any moment," she said.

Nason reached the bottom of the stairs and paused. I eased down beside him.

Townsfolk packed the inn's common room. Some sat on the maroon chairs, while most lay sprawled out on the floor, struggling to find enough energy to keep living. Hollowed eyes framed by pale, damp skin turned my way. Mouths gaped with moaning pleas. Desperate parents barely able to support themselves stood and tried to drag their children toward me.

"These are the worst. I guess they couldn't wait," said Nason.

The scene left my throat dry. Flashes of the horrors I had looked upon too many times over the years in the infirmary hit me. Maybe it was because of the lack of sleep or the stress I'd undergone since returning to Denu Creek, but my nerves were shot. Though weak, those panicked faces struck fear into me in much the same way the first time I went toe-to-toe with a D'engiti had. My heart started racing.

"Tyrus. Tyrus!"

Nason looked me in the eyes. "It's all right. We'll calm them down."

I relaxed, berating myself for being so jumpy as Nason joined Boaz and his wife in organizing everyone in the common area.

To my left, I noticed a young mother and father holding their two children in their laps. The young girl and boy looked near the same age Myra and Zadok had been when I left for the war. Both parents sobbed and whispered into their children's ears. I saw that the effort to fight against the eruption's symptoms had been brutal on their own physical well-beings, but as parents, they found the resolve to push through the pain in order to comfort their kids.

My chest tightened, imagining me and Lasha in a similar situation while someone who could easily help just stood by doing nothing.

Shame washed over me.

Zadok had been right about his Ma. Lasha never would have turned someone away and she never would have allowed me to deny help to others. As I had already done. My stomach knotted as I remembered Nason saying a couple of people had already died.

I walked over to the family and dropped to one knee. "May I help?"

"Yes," rasped the father.

"Our children," whispered the mother.

I placed a hand on the shoulder of each child then asked the parents to grab my arms. They complied. Just as before, the change in their condition started immediately. Others waiting in the room saw this and anyone strong enough to put up a fuss did so.

Nason came over quickly. "By Prax, we almost had them organized."

"Take off my clothes, will you? I don't want to move."

"What? Why?"

"Because the fewer clothes I have on, the more surface area people can touch."

His eyes widened. "Oh. But uh . . . I don't know how to remove all that stuff you have on. I've never worn leather armor before."

"Boaz!" I called out over my shoulder.

The innkeeper hurried over. "Yes?"

"Go upstairs and tell Dekar to come down here right away." He'd get me undressed quick enough and without all the dirty comments Ira would make.

"Yes, of course." He took off.

The two children I touched began to stir, showing more promising signs of life. Tears streamed down the cheeks of the two parents as they thanked me.

I worried about all those I wasn't helping. "Nason!"

"You don't have to yell. I'm still here."

"Start bringing people over here. Drag them if you have to, but find a free spot on my body until Dekar gets down here. Pull off my boots or something."

"You got it." He took a step.

"Nason."

"Yes?"

"Thanks."

"For what?"

"For coming to get me."

He patted my shoulder. "Just doing what Lasha would have done."

* * *

I was in the middle of Main Street when a hand touched my shoulder.

I didn't have to look to see who it belonged to. I smelled its owner.

"Nason, when this is all over, I'm going to buy you a bar of soap."

He ignored my jibe, just like when we were kids. "Tyrus, you need to stop and eat."

I had left the inn not long ago after spending hours helping all that had made it there. I figured leaving would save people the trouble of coming to me.

I shook my head in response to Nason, concentrating on the old woman before me. I didn't really know if concentration would do any good. I doubted I could increase my resistance just by thinking about it. It never seemed to make a noticeable difference before when I drew away sorcery. But I tried anyway.

"Tyrus, you need some water at least. You've been at this all day."

They brought the old woman to me just a few minutes ago. I had worked on her grandson earlier and once he recovered enough, he took off in a sprint to retrieve her. I don't know how he managed it, but he carried her all the way back to the center of town on his back. He collapsed from exhaustion in front of the feed store.

The old woman's gray hair had begun to fall out around her ears. Even her wrinkles had wrinkles. Most marveled that she hadn't yet died when others much younger had.

Her grandson wasn't surprised at all. He said that his grandmother had always been a fighter. She had raised him after his parents died, and had outlived three husbands and four children. He was all she had left and it was obvious the reverse also held true.

I pressed more firmly with my hands against her brittle skin, mumbling curses to Molak.

"By the gods Tyrus! You aren't going to do anyone any good dead."

My head bobbed.

"Look at you, you can barely support yourself."

"Just give me some water."

I tilted my head back and opened my mouth as someone poured water down my throat. I hadn't realized how thirsty I was until then. I started to cough. My dry throat wasn't ready for the liquid.

Why was I so worn out? It's not like I was on a thirty mile march. I guess I had never combated sorcery for so long before. I wondered if the healers in the army felt this way when working on us. Especially when dealing with me.

The grandson began to sob. He sniffed and wiped his nose on his sleeve. "I guess she didn't have enough fight left in her after all."

My brows furrowed, confused for a moment until I realized what he was saying. The old woman's chest had stopped moving and no air passed through her lips.

Dead. I hadn't noticed the change.

I pulled my hands away and looked at them in disbelief. Others had died during the night before I had a chance to treat them, but this old woman who was the center of her grandson's world, was the first to die after I had come into contact with them.

"I'm sorry," I whispered.

"It's all right. I know you did your best."

Had I really?

He continued. "You move on to someone else, Mister. Someone who still has a chance."

Panic hit me when I thought of those who still needed help. I couldn't let anyone else die. Too many had died under my command and I couldn't fail the people here like I did those in the army. I couldn't fail Denu Creek like I had failed Lasha by not being here for her. I rose to my feet quickly and nearly passed out as the town spun. I shuffled several steps, not regaining my balance until a set of soft hands grabbed hold of me.

"Take it easy," came a voice I hadn't expected to hear. "I have you."

My eyes stopped dancing, and I stood straighter, gaze drifting down to Damaris's hands, one on my arm, the other on my bare chest.

I had been trying to heal people for so long, I had forgotten that I was shirtless. With trousers rolled up to my knees, I wondered how foolish I must have looked.

Damaris pulled her hands away, her cheeks going rosy.

I cleared my throat. "Where's Nason?"

"He said he was going to get one of your friends to come talk some sense into you. He asked me to make sure you didn't hurt yourself."

"Oh. Who's next?" I asked.

"No one here."

I gave her a puzzled look. The streets of Denu Creek were eerily void of people, a stark contrast to the morning when it seemed like beaten earth was the place to be for the dying and dead to reside.

Gods, I guess I was more tired than I thought.

"Where is everyone?"

"Home. Most needed food, water, and sleep since they were in too much pain to do those things before you helped. Some also needed time to clean up since they were unable to move and accidently soiled themselves."

I turned back to the young man in the street who I left by his grandmother.

Damaris's father, Sivan, was at the boy's side. I overheard the faint prayer he led to Xank, the God of Death. It seemed the only time people ever prayed to Xank was in the time immediately following the death of a loved one, hoping he might watch over their soul. A part of me wondered if people quit cursing him during their days and prayed to him instead, if he would stop taking so many lives.

Such a thought seemed contradictory to my incessant cursing of Molak. I wondered if instead of devoting most of my swears to him, maybe I should give Ao her due.

I let out a sigh.

"What are you thinking about?" asked Damaris.

"Since I don't know your religious inclinations, I'll keep that to myself." I turned away from Sivan. "I guess I must have gone into a trance because it seemed like there were more people who needed my help."

"Well, there was. Jareb and several of his people weren't as affected by the explosion as others. Or at least they recovered quickly on their own. They convinced quite a few people not to come to you. They blame you for what happened, saying everything in town was fine until you showed up. They keep talking about some curse on your family."

My hands balled into fists, remembering what Myra had said about such nonsense. "That's ridiculous."

I cursed Molak. Then I cursed Ao. They took an old woman who meant everything in the world to her grandson, but let Jareb and his goons not only live, but barely suffer.

"I know. They've holed themselves up in the Soiled Dove where the physician is looking after them."

"Is he well enough to even care for them?"

"He was one of the first people you healed today. Apparently, he suspended his prejudice toward you just long enough to suit his needs."

"That's usually how it works." I shook my head. "I should have done more sooner. Jareb might not have been able to convince them that I was the problem if I had."

She stepped in front of me, grabbed my chin and pushed it up where I had been staring at my feet. Up close, our difference in height became more noticeable. The top of her head barely reached my chest.

"You can't dwell on that. You saved a lot of people today."

I grunted, suddenly uncomfortable with taking credit for what I had done. It felt insincere to become puffed up with something I should have done sooner and without convincing.

"One thing has been bothering me all day though."

I inclined my head, curious by the shift in her tone.

"You left last night before I had a chance to ask you why you helped me and my father. All we did was sell you clothes."

"You didn't treat me or my children differently. After all Myra and Zadok had been through and everything I had experienced since leaving the army, that meant something to me."

"Well, thank you." She smiled in a way that made me suddenly aware of how close we stood to each other. I took a step backward.

Dizziness returned to me the second my foot found earth. Damaris reached out to steady me once more, but was a second too late.

I fell. Hard.

"Gods be cursed, Ty. What's the matter with you?" Ira's voice rang out as footsteps pounded the dirt.

Rough hands reached under my armpits and yanked me to my feet where they held me firm.

"Nason said you were pushing yourself, but I didn't realize you were this bad off." Ira flung one of my arms over his shoulder. "Let's get you back upstairs."

"I'm fine," I mumbled.

"Yeah, I bet." Ira leaned in and whispered as we walked away from the feed store. "Not many people can say they literally fell for a woman, Ty." He snorted.

"Gods, that was bad even for you."

"You're just tired. After a few hours of sleep, you'll wake up laughing."

"Not likely. Tell Dekar the line when we get upstairs and see what he thinks."

"What would be the point of that? The moment's passed. Besides, you can't judge the quality of a joke by his standards. The man barely smirked that time we got Caleb drunk and tricked him into wearing that old dress we found."

"Caleb? Man, that's a name I haven't heard in awhile." I chuckled. "It was pretty funny though." A sigh followed.

"What was that for?"

"Just thinking about Caleb now."

"Oh?"

"He was a good soldier." I felt a tickle in the back of my throat. "Then the fool had to go and save my life. Now, he's dead like thousands of others. Just another name that only a few will ever remember."

Ira swore. "You sure killed my mood quick."

"Sorry. It's just aggravating that so many like him won't be remembered. Everything they did will be forgotten."

Ira spat. "I ain't going to forget. I doubt you will. And you know good and well Dek won't. That man remembers what we had for breakfast twenty years ago to the day. I'm not sure what happened to Hamath or what's going to happen to your sister, but I reckon they aren't the kind of people to forget a man like Caleb either. I guess it's up to us to make sure others hear about their deeds so they live on. Right?"

I nodded. "That's some deep stuff coming from you."

He laughed. "Dek's been my brother for almost thirty years. The man's bound to have an influence on me after that much time."

We reached the porch in front of the inn and our boots hit the wooden planks with a thud that reminded me of my Pa fixing boards on our barn when I was a kid.

I froze as a thought struck me. I threw Ira off and turned back toward Nason who was talking to Sivan and Damaris in the middle of the street. My footfalls came quickly thanks to a sudden burst of energy.

"What's wrong?" asked Ira, coming up behind me.

"The farms!"

"What?"

My shouting caught Nason's attention and he hurried over.

He eyed Ira. "I thought you were getting him upstairs."

"I tried to but—"

"Do you have enough healthy animals to pull a wagon?" I asked.

Nason started. "Maybe a couple."

"Get them harnessed. We've been so busy worrying about those here in town, we've forgotten about the farms."

He swore. "You're right. I'll try to organize some people to pick up those really bad off and have them brought in."

I thought of the old woman I lost. "No time for that. They could be too far gone to heal by then. Just take me to them."

"You're in no shape to travel," said Nason.

"I can sleep in the wagon."

"Don't be ridiculous. You're swaying on your feet now. You need more than a few minutes of rest in the back of a bumpy wagon."

"Molak be damned, Nason! You talked me into helping these people. Don't try to talk me out of it now."

Something happened then. I'm not sure what. One moment, I was all set to get into a shouting match with Nason, the next my eyes opened to Ira slapping my face. I was on the ground.

"All right, stop. I'm awake."

Ira hit me again, this time harder.

"By the gods, I said I was awake!"

"I know," said Ira. "That was for being so hard headed. I'll drag you upstairs if I have to, Ty, but you're not going anywhere until you get some rest. I'm not about to have you pass out again."

"But by then it could be too late . . ."

"I'll go."

All heads turned back toward the inn. Zadok stood on the edge of the porch looking at us.

"I thought I told you to stay upstairs," said Ira.

"You were taking too long. I was worried about Pa. And Aunt Ava is doing all right without me." He left the porch and walked toward us. "I heard what you said, Pa. Let me help those people on the farms. I know my resistance isn't as strong as yours, but it's better than nothing."

I shook my head. The thought of Zadok going off without me made me sick to my stomach. If he went off into the country, I'd have no way of knowing how he was doing until it was too late. "No."

"Why not?"

"It's too dangerous."

"Too dangerous? What's dangerous about riding in a wagon and putting my hand on people who need my help?"

"A lot can happen."

"A lot can happen here too. I could trip and fall. The inn could burn down. There could even be an explosion," he said, gesturing toward the ugly sky that hovered in the direction of Hol.

My son, the jester.

"That's different."

"Why?"

"Because if something does happen while you're at the farms, I'll be too far away to help you."

"I'll go with him, Ty." Ira's face had taken on a look of stone. "I promise not a hair on his head will be harmed as long as I'm breathing."

Ira didn't make declarations like that often and when he did, he took them seriously. Still . . .

"Please, Pa."

I sighed, realizing he was right. "You can go, but so help me you better not do like I did. You need to take breaks to eat and drink."

Zadok gave me a brilliant smile. "I will."

"Don't worry, Ty," Ira said. "I'll be as much of a nag to him as you can be to us."

I shook my head. "All right, Nason. Go get a wagon. I'm going to see everyone off before I go upstairs."

CHAPTER 19

Lasha stood at the foot of the bed and slowly undressed, exposing the fullness of her dark, smooth skin. She wore a smile she saved only for me when the kids had gone down for the night and the house was quiet.

My heart raced and blood flowed to places I had no control over.

Her smile grew wider as she began to glide around the bed, stretching and pretending that she had no clue what she was doing. She looked down and noticed my excitement. "Oh, were you expecting something?" she asked, teasing me as she liked to do.

I loved every minute of it.

I started to speak, ready to fire back some bit of witty banter for her to play off of, but found I could not open my mouth. I attempted to bring a hand to my face, but my arm did not move and neither did the other. I was strapped to the posts of the bed. Looking down, my legs were bound similarly.

I pulled, jerked, fought to break free of the constraints without any success. Lasha stood as naked as her name day at the foot of the bed, smile growing wider by the moment.

The door to our bedroom swung open. Jareb entered. He said not a word. In fact, he didn't even acknowledge me. Why would he? I saw the lust in his eyes. I knew what he wanted. He pulled Lasha to him, kissing and touching her in ways that only

I had ever done. Bile crept into my throat and tears filled my eyes. The entire bed shook, creaking as I pulled as hard as I could against my binds. I felt the straps dig into my skin, cutting my wrists and ankles. Still, I pulled. I could not let him do that to my wife.

My Lasha.

She turned to me. Her eyes met mine and she whispered. "You weren't here for me."

My head slammed back against the pillow as the fight left me. I closed my eyes. Regaining control of my mouth again, I screamed.

* * *

"Tyrus! Xank be cursed, wake up!"

My eyes shot open and I sat up covered in sweat, chest heaving. I swallowed and winced at the grating rawness in my throat.

"What happened?" asked Dekar, hands still gripping my shoulders as if he let go I might slip back into the hell he shook me out of.

My eyes darted about, blinking. I saw the chairs, the dresser, the big window. I was back at the Hemlock Inn.

"A dream," I said.

"About the war?"

I shook my head.

He noticeably relaxed.

In the army, some soldiers began to lose their minds as the things they had seen in the war began to haunt them. It started out while they slept, but over time, they began to dream of the horrors even in their waking moments. It couldn't be predicted who would be affected. A grisly old veteran was just as susceptible as the young recruit. And the worst part was that none of the healers knew how to treat the ailment. Several of the men affected ended up taking their own lives rather than experience those memories over and over.

I was sure Ira had told Dekar about having to wake me from reliving the battle at Safed Plain.

"What was it then?"

"Just a nightmare," I said.

"Do you want to talk about it?" asked Dekar.

"No."

I didn't want to even think about it. I sure didn't want to discuss those images. To me, nothing in the war was as bad as what had entered my mind—especially because there was some truth to the dream. Granted, Lasha likely never enjoyed what she had done with Jareb, but he'd had her. And worst of all, I wasn't there to prevent it.

One more thing that would haunt me forever.

My stomach lurched and my heart raced again, this time in anger. "Let's just talk about something else."

I went to rub my eyes and realized one of my hands was bound. I was in bed beside Ava, my forearm strapped to hers. I guessed that might explain part of my dream.

"What in the name of Molak happened? Last thing I remember I was outside as Nason went off to get a wagon to take Zadok out to the farms."

Dekar reached over and snatched a skin of water off a nearby chair. "Here. Drink."

I took the skin and inhaled the liquid, nearly choking.

"Slowly."

I wiped my mouth. "So, last night?"

"Well, you ended up passing out in the street again and Ira had to carry you upstairs. Zadok came up too and they filled us in on what had happened. It was probably a good thing you were out because Myra was pretty livid at you for saying Zadok could go off by himself. Ira said he'd be there with him. Myra made some choice comment about that and within a matter of seconds all three were at each other's throats."

I took another long swallow, then realized I didn't hear any movement outside the bedroom. "Is Myra asleep?"

"No. She said the only way Zadok was going to leave was if she went with him. But since she didn't want to leave Ava unattended, she suggested we throw you in bed next to her and strap you both at the arm so she'd stay in contact with you. I said that for all we know that might delay you coming around, but she did it anyway."

"I'm glad she was as equally concerned about me," I muttered.

Dekar frowned. "I've stayed in here while you slept. You started screaming and it took me a minute to get you to wake up. You know the rest."

I looked out the window. A night void of stars stared back at me. At least it seemed the night was void of stars since the sorcerous glow continued to do weird things to the sky.

"So, I slept all evening and into the night?"

"Yeah. Dawn's probably a couple hours away."

"And they aren't back yet?"

"Nason said they'd likely spend the night at someone's farm so they can visit more homes first thing in the morning, but only as long as Myra and Zadok were still up to it."

I didn't like knowing they were out there somewhere without me, but I trusted Nason's word and Ira's blade. It'd take a couple D'engiti to take my children from Ira and those monstrosities were but a memory now.

"You hungry?"

On cue, my stomach growled. "I'd say that's a yes."

"Here." Dekar held out a plate containing a roll of stale bread, assorted cheese, and a link of cold sausage. "Dinah brought this up for you a few hours ago in case you woke up before breakfast. She apologized for it not being more, but in light of everything going on she had little time to cook."

I took one more drink of water, set the skin down, and accepted the plate. "The way I feel, I'd say it's a feast fit for the king." Saliva filled my mouth as I took the first bite of cheese.

"If the king is even alive," Dekar said with a grunt. "You'll probably want to eat that as quick as you can and try to get some more rest. You still look like you've been through hell."

"I guess not sleeping much will do that to you." I tried a bit of sausage. It was bland, but not bad. "You look tired yourself. Why don't you take the bed in the other room since the kids are away?"

"I'd rather stay here while you sleep."

I thought of the dream that woke me and shuddered, sausage almost coming back up as I did. "No. Go on. The food is helping. Besides, it will be a while before I get back to sleep anyway."

"Dream, that bad?"

"Doesn't get much worse."

War didn't have anything on imagining someone else having your wife.

226

He grunted, but didn't pry. That was one of many things I liked about Dekar. He listened better than nearly anyone, but he never tried to force you into saying more than you felt comfortable with.

He stood. "All right then. That bed does sound pretty good right now. I'll keep the door open in case you need me."

* * *

I almost called out for Dekar not long after I finished eating. It hit me that I hadn't relieved myself in quite awhile. Yet, I was stuck in bed, strapped to the arm of my sister, while the chamber pot sat in a corner. It might as well have been leagues away.

It took me a few moments to undo the strap, climb out of bed, and maneuver my sore body around to the corner while also managing to keep a hand on Ava's leg. Despite the adventure, I managed to take care of business on my own, but it was close.

Once finished, I stretched to get the blood moving about my stiff limbs. I then tended to Ava by spooning more broth down her throat and cleaned her face with a damp towel.

When I could think of nothing else that needed doing, I settled myself in the chair next to the bed.

My eyelids began to drop. I knew I'd have to face sleep again eventually so it would be better to get it over with. After intertwining my fingers with Ava's and wrapping the leather strap around our wrists I allowed sleep to take me.

CHAPTER 20

Morning arrived for me with a bang. The sound of doors being thrown open and things being dragged across the floor woke me with a start.

"Can you make any more noise?" hissed Myra.

"Maybe if someone got off their high horse and decided to help me bring all this junk inside. Gods, I'm glad you're not my daughter," said Ira.

"Trust me, the feeling is mutual."

Ira started on some tirade when Zadok interrupted. "Will both of you stop? Pa is likely still asleep. Dekar too."

"Not anymore," Dekar called out from the other bedroom.

"I'm up too," I said.

"See what you did," said Myra.

Heavy footsteps followed, drowning out Ira's subsequent curses.

"C'mon kid, help me bring up the rest of this stuff since your sister can't be bothered."

The door slammed as Ira and Zadok left.

I snorted to myself thinking about all the grief Ira had likely put up with. In some ways it made me feel better about myself. Myra wasn't just angry with me or even the people in Denu Creek. She seemed to be mad at the entire world.

I checked over Ava, who unsurprisingly, looked no different than she had hours before.

"Any change?" Myra asked as she strode over to the head of the bed. She placed a hand on her aunt's forehead.

"None."

"When's the last time she was fed?"

"I gave her some broth a few hours ago."

"So she's probably ready for some more then."

"Probably."

She lifted up the sheet on her side of the bed. "I see you didn't change her bedpan."

"Hard to do with only one hand. Besides, it didn't need it last I looked."

"Well, she needs it now. Lift her up." She went back to the bedroom door and closed it for privacy, then threw the sheets off Ava completely. I averted my gaze and tried not to think about what I was doing as I lifted my sister so Myra could empty the bedpan and wipe her down.

"All right. I'm done."

I lowered Ava and Myra threw the covers back on top. To my surprise, Myra wore a smirk.

"What's so funny?"

"I just think it's silly how bashful you are about seeing her naked."

"Are you telling me that seeing Zadok without clothes on wouldn't make you uncomfortable?"

"I doubt it. I've seen him like that when we were younger."

"Things change."

The door to the suite opened again and I heard things being jostled around as Ira and Zadok grunted.

"What are they hauling up?"

"Offerings," she said with disgust.

"Offerings? For whom?"

"Us. You, specifically. The people you healed aren't sure what to make of us anymore, especially you. Some are saying you're a priest or a tool of the gods. Some are saying you're a god yourself, an offspring of Lavi and Prax."

"You're joking."

"Does it look like I'm joking?"

Her eyes narrowed in a way that made it impossible for her to ever deny she was my daughter. It made her look older than her fourteen years. Of course, she didn't speak like any fourteen year old I had ever met.

Given our current situation, she'd start sounding like an old crone before spring.

"I guess not."

"People started giving us stuff in thanks as an offering to you or for you to offer to the gods on their behalf."

"And you accepted it?"

"We healed them despite the way they treated us before. Why shouldn't we get something out of the deal?"

"That sounds like something Ira would say."

"It was his suggestion. But, it makes sense."

"I'm surprised Zadok went along with it."

"He didn't want to at first. But once he saw all the things people wanted to give him—things he had always wanted, but never could afford, he came over to our side." She paused. "I guess you going to help all those people wasn't so bad after all. We've obtained more stuff in one day than you would have earned in a year at any job in town. Even after we split our take with Ira and Dekar, we could go somewhere and maybe buy a place like the one we used to have."

A part of me saw the logic in what she said. And if someone other than Myra had made the observation, I would have agreed with them, not bothered in the least. But something about hearing my daughter speak like a cynical old woman pained me. It was a complete contradiction to the way I knew Lasha would have wanted her to behave.

"You know your mother wouldn't approve of hearing you talk like that."

"Probably not."

"That doesn't bother you?"

"Why should it?" she snapped. "I loved Ma, but helping people out of the kindness of her heart without expecting anything in return didn't help her, or us."

I nodded to Ava who she continued to fuss over. "You've been taking care of her. She never did anything for you."

She paused as if I raised a point she hadn't considered. She pulled away and sat in the other chair.

"I guess I'm just doing it as a favor to you," she said after a moment.

"How so?"

She nodded to our interlaced hands. "It's obvious how much she means to you. And even though I still think it was dumb what you did to Jareb at the plantation, you meant well by trying to help us. Plus, Zadok hasn't been this happy since before we lost the farm. Consider me taking care of her as payment for what you've done for him."

But not her. . . .

I changed subjects, hoping that by doing so the room might warm from the ice-cold words of my lovely daughter. "So, I guess people no longer believe you and Zadok are cursed?"

"Some still do. Those who are still loyal to Jareb think the eruption was all our fault." She leaned back in the chair, stretching. "But in the eyes of those we healed, how could we be cursed when we're apparently the children of a god?"

She had a point.

CHAPTER 21

Doing anything she could to continually show her appreciation, Dinah brought us a hot breakfast of porridge, sausages, and biscuits. Abigail carried the biscuits. Looking at the smile she wore, I'd have never known that just a few days ago, the little girl had been near death. Her current condition gave me some much-needed hope for Ava.

Little Abigail came around a second time with the basket of biscuits and I made sure to snatch up my share before Ira hoarded them. Dinah hadn't prepared anything complicated for us to eat as of yet, so I wasn't sure how far her culinary skills extended. However, with another bite of biscuit, it was obvious she had a firm grasp on the basics.

Seeing the relationship Abigail had with her mother and the way she enjoyed helping her, made me consider the life I might have had if not for the war. I imagined Myra and Lasha with that kind of bond, and my heart grew heavy. The image didn't last long. Even my imagination couldn't hold a picture of Myra being sweet and carefree when her sour demeanor was in my face.

With everyone's mouths and hands full of food, Boaz's wife picked up the trays and headed for the door. Abigail surprised me by running over and giving me a hug, squeezing me with more strength than I would have given her credit for. Then she ran out of the room.

Dinah smiled back at me. "She can't stop talking about you, Tyrus. She calls you her protector and prays for you." She looked at all the stuff people had given us lying around the sitting room. "Some people think you're a god or one of their agents. But to Abigail, you're just her hero."

She closed the door and left before I could find the words to respond to that. How could I have responded to someone calling me their hero?

"Well, Ty. I guess now is as good a time as any to tell you that you've been my hero for as far back as I can remember," said Ira. I could tell from the sound of his voice he was trying to hold back a chuckle. "Something about the way you eat your biscuits like you're doing now where the crumbs park themselves on your lips, or how you look like you've been on a weeklong drinking session when you first wake up every morning. All of that and so much more give me the chills. I am in awe of you."

Dekar snorted between bites of sausage.

I wanted to be angry, but couldn't stop myself from chuckling. That was what friends were for. They brought me down from my perch before my head started to swell. I set my food down long enough to rub at the sleep in my eyes and remove said crumbs from my face.

"Are you ready to start going through all this stuff?" asked Dekar.

I eyed the stacks of crates, overflowing sacks, and random goods that didn't fit into the numerous piles Ira had grouped the items in. Too much of it seemed worthless. "Not especially. There's a lot of junk here."

"Junk?" Ira bent down and began rummaging through a sack. "Look here. We've got some winter blankets, a good hunting knife, some good wooden bowls."

I'd moved to one of the crates. "Yeah, and we have dress clothes none of us will ever use." I held up a shirt with more ruffles than any man had business wearing. "And here's an old, rusty saw, a hammer with a broken handle. . . . What are we going to do with those?"

He shrugged. "They can't all be winners. Some people might not have as good of stuff to give away as others do."

"Or some just used this chance to unload their garbage on us."

"It's not all garbage," Dekar said. I faced him, hearing a bit of rare excitement in his voice. He pulled out a carrying case used to hold the game pieces for Crests. He opened it and smiled. "I've never seen a complete set before."

"See," began Ira, "even Dek sees the promise here. When's the last time you saw him actually show some emotion?"

He was right. Dekar was so busy examining the game pieces he didn't even bother with giving Ira a response.

"He can keep the game and we can keep some of this stuff if we need it, but I don't want to accept anything more."

"Even if it's coin?" asked Dekar.

"Huh?"

"I didn't tell you but that mayor dropped by when you were out last night. Looked like it nearly killed him to muster up the strength to make it over here from the Soiled Dove."

I winced at the name. "What did he want?"

"For you to finish healing him. He had a nice sized bag of money with him, but I turned him away."

"Why would you go and do something like that?" asked Ira.

"Because Tyrus was still out. And considering the mayor had been one of the main people trying to kill us just a couple days ago, I didn't want to make a decision on my own about whether it was all right to heal him."

"You could have just plopped the mayor down next to Ty while he slept." Ira faced me. "You wouldn't have been upset with some coin, right?" he asked.

I was unwilling to entertain the question. I asked Dekar. "I thought the mayor was Jareb's man."

"He is. Or at least was. He didn't handle the sorcery as well as many others in Jareb's camp. And the doctor hasn't been able to speed up his recovery. Apparently one's commitment wanes while suffering in pain and soiling oneself. I guess he finally had enough."

"But not enough to totally turn his back on Jareb?"

"What do you mean?"

"Well, you said he came while I slept which was in the middle of the night. When you told him no, I bet he went right back to Jareb."

Dekar shrugged.

Loud gasps from Ava's room cut off the conversation.

Zadok's voice quickly followed. "Pa! Come quick! Hurry!"

I dropped the biscuit in my hand, hurdled a sack of oats, and dove into the bedroom awash in panic.

Though I had been making plans internally for when Ava woke up, I hadn't realized how little I actually believed that would happen. When I heard Zadok cry out, I just knew she was dead.

Storming in, I found her eyes fluttering open.

Zadok and Myra were out of their seats, grinning. I joined them quickly, gently pushing Zadok aside to get to Ava. I grabbed her hand.

Red, weary eyes stared back at me. I couldn't decide if confusion or surprise dominated her expression. She opened her mouth to speak, but only managed a rough cough.

"Lift her up a bit and tilt her head back," I said.

I looked up and Myra had already grabbed a skin of water, holding it ready. She dribbled the water out like an expert. After a few gulps and a short rest, we allowed Ava to drink her fill. Even though we did our best to keep her hydrated while she was unconscious, I had no doubt she desperately needed water.

I eased Ava back down. She took a couple deep breaths and swallowed again.

"Better?" I asked.

She nodded and started to try and push herself up. She stopped suddenly. "Why am I naked?"

"Well, you've been out for three days. It was either that or have you lay in your own filth until you came around."

"Who stripped me?" She blinked. "Not you?"

"Myra did most of it while I held you."

She gave Myra a glance. "I'm surprised he did even that."

"He was uncomfortable the entire time. He said that no man should see their sister without her clothes on."

Ava snorted. "I can't believe you actually helped."

"Well, it was either I do it or let Ira and Dekar help."

She scowled, glaring over my shoulder to the sitting room where Ira and Dekar moved about. They were giving us privacy.

"Don't even joke like that. Three days. Gods, no wonder I feel so awful." Recognition hit her suddenly and she squeezed my hand, while trying to pull me down to her. "Quick, tell me what happened. We might not have much time and—"

She paused again as if confused. I could tell she was still feeling out of sorts. When healthy, Ava never lost her bearings.

"I'm still close enough to Hol that I thought I'd die when they used the artifact. Why am I alive?" she asked in a hurried manner.

"Slow down." I shook my head. "I figured that whatever happened had been a result of the artifact. It just made too much sense."

"Again, why am I not dead?"

"My resistance." I nodded to the kids. "And theirs. They both have a talent for it as well. Between the three of us, we kept watch over you."

She eyed Myra and Zadok, then clicked her tongue. "Interesting. I should say thank you then."

"You should," I said, grinning. Ava showed gratitude by how she acted toward you. Rarely did she actually say how she felt.

She paused. "Well, thank you."

"That must have hurt." It felt good to give her a hard time.

"Not as much as you think it did." Her eyes widened again. "I keep getting distracted. Hand me my clothes. We need to get on the road. The farther we get from Hol the better."

She started to sit up, but with a gentle push, I flattened her back against the bed. "You're in no condition to go anywhere. Why don't you try to eat something and then get some more rest? We can talk when you get up. Whatever that artifact did, it seems like it's done. "

She shook her head. "I don't think it is." She took a slow breath. "Do you have any food? I feel so weak."

"Zadok. Go get the rest of the breakfast Boaz's wife brought up."

"All right, Pa."

"I'll bring in some more water," said Myra.

Zadok came back with a handful of biscuits and a bowl of porridge. "This is all that was left, Pa. Ira ate the last of the sausage."

"That figures. He's always been as greedy as a pig," Ava muttered.

"I love you too," Ira shouted from the other room.

Ava tried to shout a curse back, but ended up coughing. Their bickering made it almost feel like old times. In a good way.

Dekar peeked in. "I'll go down and see what else is in the kitchen. Any requests, Ava?"

"I don't really care. Just make sure you grab some honey so I can coat my throat."

Dekar nodded. "I'll be back shortly."

He ducked out.

Myra returned with more water.

"Just leave it on the nightstand," said Ava.

"I can help you drink it," said Myra.

"I'll be all right. But if I need help, I'll make your Pa do it. Might as well milk him having to wait on me, huh?" She winked.

Zadok chuckled, but Myra's face remained like a wall of stone.

"How about you give us a little time alone?" Ava asked. "No offense, but me and your Pa have a lot of catching up to do in private."

I saw their disappointed faces. "It'll just be for a little while," I said. "Besides, you both look like you could use some more sleep."

"So do you," said Myra.

"I'll get it eventually."

"Fine," Myra huffed. "Let's go Zadok." She grabbed her brother by the arm and they left again, closing the door behind them.

Ava grunted. "They turned out to be good-looking kids."

"Yep."

"A little on the skinny side though. Zadok has that worships-his-father look about him. I'm sure that makes you feel good. Myra though . . . she's a cold one. Definitely inherited that look you liked to give to recruits when they were on your bad side."

"I've noticed. I think she pretty much hates me."

"Well, what girl doesn't hate their Pa at that age? I remember getting into arguments with ours all the time."

"True. But your arguments were about staying out late or using sorcery as a way to pay back those who used to pick on you. They weren't about blaming him for every bad thing that had happened to you over the last ten years. There's a lot we missed," I said, voice somber.

"There's a lot you missed in Hol too. Here, help me sit up and hand me that food. We've got a lot to talk about. You go first while I eat. Then when you're done I'll jump in. Maybe by then I'll be able to think clearly enough for us to figure out what in the name of Ao to do next."

I pulled her up and adjusted her pillows as she used her free hand to hold the sheet over her chest. "So, where do I start?" I asked, handing her a biscuit.

"How about with what happened to Lasha?"

I opened my mouth, paused, and shook my head as something got caught in my throat. Images of what must have gone on in that room at the Soiled Dove flooded my thoughts.

"Let's start somewhere else. I'll need to build up to that."

* * *

Eventually, I built to what happened to Lasha, but only after telling her about everything else I could recall including all that Myra, Zadok, and I had gone through since my return to Denu Creek. I kept my focus on my hand still wrapped around Ava's through most of it. I just couldn't look her in the eye. I didn't notice my sister's sobs until she squeezed my hand tightly while I began the story of how Lasha had to work as a prostitute to make sure our children survived.

I looked up at Ava's tear-streaked face. My sister, tougher than every other woman I'd ever known, had not cried since she was probably six and had skinned her knee while out in the field. I remember giving her a hard time about it then, a requirement of all older brothers. However, she hadn't so much as sniffled in sadness since then, even when our parents died.

"You're crying?"

She punched my arm with her free hand. It was a weak effort, but the meaning was not lost on me. "Of course, I'm crying. I'm not a piece of granite."

"Sorry, I'm just surprised."

"I'm sorry, Tyrus. For everything."

"Forget about me. Think about Lasha." I nodded toward the door. "And the kids."

She wiped her face. "I guess they had been fighting their own war while we were fighting ours. That explains why your daughter could probably freeze water with that look."

I bobbed my head in agreement.

"How are you dealing with all this?" she asked.

"Not well. But I don't really have a choice. I've got two kids to look after."

"So you been keeping it in then?"

"Well, I'm not about to talk to Zadok or Myra about what I'm feeling."

"What about Dekar? Or even Ira? Have you told them everything?"

"A few things in passing, but not all the details. I'm sure they've been able to put the pieces together, especially if others in town have talked to them. They've been good enough to keep it to themselves."

"Big brother, when will you learn? You can't keep this stuff to yourself."

"Look who's talking."

"True, but I'd talk to you about something like this if the roles were reversed. Gods, I can tell you're feeling better already. I know that's not just from me coming around."

"I was worried about you."

"Still."

I sighed. "I'm not disagreeing with what you're trying to say, but it's not as easy as you think." I thought of my dream with Jareb and Lasha. "Frankly, I don't want to talk about the stuff going through my head, because its images of things no man should have of his wife, you know? I don't want to share that with anyone because I want to forget it myself. Her enjoying . . ." I coughed, then started to laugh bitterly. "I keep thinking about our conversation over that last recruit you hurt when he hit that whore. You asked 'What if that was Lasha?' To think after all this time you had a talent for prophecy too."

She put her free hand over mine and I realized I had started to shake. "I never in a thousand years thought there'd be any truth to what I said. Otherwise, I never would have made the comment."

"I know."

"Big brother, promise me something."

"What?"

"Not to forget that regardless of how genuine those images seem, they aren't real. Lasha worshipped the ground you walked on in a way I never understood. Still don't. She loved you. Just like she loved those kids. I'm sure anything she did she treated like a job. Like you and I would have looked at digging ditches. I'm willing to bet it lacked all enjoyment and love. No way she would have given that part of herself to anyone but you."

"I know," I whispered. "It's just going to take time."

"Then let's drop it. Pull yourself together so we can call in Ira and Dekar. They should be back by now. It will do them some good to hear what I have to say and I'd rather not repeat myself."

"Are you up for more talking?"

"I'm feeling better after that food. Besides, after what you told me, the end of the world doesn't seem half as bad as what's happened already."

* * *

Before I grabbed Ira and Dekar, I helped Ava put on an old shirt we'd borrowed from Dinah so she could sit up without someone helping her hold a sheet over her chest. She wasn't keen on putting her leathers back on just yet. Dekar came in shortly afterward carrying more food—a bit of ham, cheese, fresh bread, a couple of apples, and honey. He took the lone chair in the room and began laying the goods out. Ava went right for the honey, attacking it with a spoon while Ira brought in another chair from the sitting room.

Everyone got comfortable and waited. Ira, as usual, lacked any patience. "Well? What's going on?" he asked Ava.

She glared. "I'm thinking about where best to begin."

Having recovered from our earlier talk, I couldn't miss the chance to poke at her. I gestured to the dresser. "How about that white robe? If I recall, you swore you'd never wear one."

Ira seized on the opening. "Yeah, how long did it take for you to cave in?"

"I didn't cave in, you idiot. It's a disguise. I had never opened a transfer portal before and knew I needed to get to Tyrus. I figured he had made it back here, but without any experience, I knew I'd be taking a risk trying a portal that would cover that distance. So, I needed access to the Sky Tower. It's this place in Hol where the High Mages perform their most complicated sorcery. The wards etched in the stone there make it easier to cast a spell. Only a High Mage can get past the guards, which I'm not. Therefore, I needed the robes so people wouldn't ask questions."

"The Sky Tower? That's a pretty dumb name," said Ira.

"Almost as dumb as Ira, huh?" Ava shot back.

Ira opened his mouth and closed it like he had been ready to agree. Dekar snorted.

"How does that fit into all this end of the world stuff?" I asked.

"Not much other than providing me a way to get here. But you asked the question."

"Fair enough. Start when you're ready."

She took another swallow of honey, set the spoon down, and cleared her throat.

"News of Damanhur hit Hol hard. Everyone agreed something had to be done about the rogue soldiers who started that mess as Damanhur had reported things to the king," Ava began. "No one in the army believed the city's report though. We all knew this wasn't a bunch of green recruits, but veterans. You wouldn't have started killing unless someone had been trying to kill you first. The king knew this too at first, but popular opinion began to sway him. The High Mages took the side of the king. Probably for no other reason than to get under General Balak's skin, who, by the way, was livid. He and the king got into quite the shouting match. Balak didn't back down until the king threatened to remove him as commander of the army."

"I never thought Balak would do that," I said.

Ira grunted in what sounded like disgust. I remembered his story about why he hated the man and wondered if Balak could ever do enough to redeem himself in Ira's eyes. Probably not. Honestly, after hearing Ira's story, I doubted Balak could ever do anything to redeem himself in my eyes either.

"Despite the outcry," continued Ava, "the king ordered Balak to release the next wave of soldiers. Balak did and word is he told them to pass through Damanhur. He was daring the people to try something again."

"Why?" I asked.

She shrugged. "Probably out of spite. Balak was angry and I guess he figured that since that group was triple the size of the group you left with they'd be safer. He was wrong. Damanhur attacked the second group at the city's gates. The city took heavy casualties, more than twice of what they gave, but in the end they had the numbers and wiped that second group out completely."

Ira, Dekar, and I all exchanged curses. More of our brothers had died while just trying to get home.

"Makes me want to go back and kill every last one of the people in that city while they sleep," said Ira.

"Too late," said Ava.

I raised an eyebrow.

"Balak lost it. The same night he got word of what happened, he pulled the entire army out of Genesha and marched on Damanhur while refusing all communication with the king and the Council of High Mages."

"By the gods, he marched on a Turine city?" I asked.

She nodded. "He razed the blasted thing to the ground. Every last man, woman, and child killed. Word is he wouldn't even allow it to be looted. Said he didn't want the taint of those spoils in his army."

Dekar whistled low.

I blinked. "Wow. What happened next?"

Ava took another swallow of honey. "He began slowly taking the army south, following the path that I think he expected you took to get home. It was like he was daring the citizens in other towns to try something similar to Damanhur."

"What did the king do?" I asked.

"He sent a small team of our best High Mages to take Balak down and regain control of the army. The king had a lot of cleanup to do in the public's eyes and there would be no satisfying end to Balak except one that involved his death."

"Considering how much they hated Balak, the High Mages must have loved those orders," I said.

"They did," said Ava. "Until they got there. Balak must have anticipated the king using the High Mages and created a bodyguard of those resistant to sorcery. We received word later that they never leave his side. The High Mages didn't have a chance with their sorcery negated. Only one lived long enough to tell us what happened."

"The world keeps getting crazier," said Ira.

I grunted in agreement. "How does all this relate to the artifact?"

"The king, like everyone else in Hol, was worried Balak would just decide to march on the capital and take Turine for himself. Who could stop him? The king wanted him removed immediately, but the forces he still commanded were too small and the High Mages were obviously hesitant to send more of their own against him. I sat in on those meetings. It wasn't pretty. On top of everything already spinning around, there was a huge undercurrent of what the Geneshans would do once they got word that the Turine army was now under the control of a renegade. They could invade Turine again and we'd be defenseless to stop them if Balak chose not to get involved."

"So, out of options, the king instructed the High Mages to use the Geneshan artifact," I said.

Ava nodded. "The plan was to use the power of the artifact to initiate a massive transfer portal from Hol to Balak's location. They'd bring in the king's personal guard along with every other mage available. The hope was to hit Balak hard and in all the confusion seize him."

"And you left?" I asked.

"Snuck away that morning, right before they attempted the transfer portal. I didn't sign up for that. I felt the power of that artifact. And I sat in on some of the preliminary studies of it. The Geneshans had every right to be scared of using it."

Dekar grunted. "Obviously."

"Well, at least the worst of it seems to be over," said Ira.

"I'm not sure," said Ava.

"What do you mean?" Dekar asked. "People are getting better. You're finally up."

"Yes, but everything we learned about that Geneshan prophecy hinted that using the artifact would be the end of the world. Balls of fire dropping from the sky, earthquakes, and so on. If you can think of something bad, it's supposed to happen after using this thing."

Ira stood. "C'mon. I bet most of those stories are just meant to scare little children."

"Explain the sky then," Dekar said to his brother. "It doesn't matter what time it is, day or night, but you can still see these bright colors over in the direction of Hol."

Ira waved a hand. "Just residual effects from the artifact. We've seen stuff like that on the battlefield before."

"Nothing like this," said Dekar.

"It'll fade eventually." Ira walked to the window, peering out in the direction of Hol. He grunted and then went quiet.

Ira going quiet was never a good thing.

"What?" I asked.

"The sky's changed."

"Changed how?" asked Ava, sitting up a bit more.

"Well, it's pulsing now. Going real bright, reds and oranges getting deeper in color. Then it dims, and it's like its drawing itself back in." He shrugged. "I guess the sorcery is fading already."

"Tyrus, get me to the window," said Ava.

She began to tuck the sheet underneath her legs and nudge herself over to the side of the bed.

"Are you sure? You haven't walked in days. Your legs might give out on you."

"I need to see things for myself."

Dekar came around and helped me guide her to the window. Ava didn't shy away from his touch. Unlike the rift her and Ira always had, she and Dekar got along well.

She put her head down as sunlight touched her eyes. "Tyrus, I need my hand back or I won't be able to see anything. If you're unwilling to let me go yet, then grab my shoulder."

I did, and she used the free hand to shield her eyes.

She stared toward Hol for some time. We all did, actually. Confirming what Ira said about the pulses.

After a minute, Ira couldn't keep quiet. "Well? Was I right?"

"No," said Ava. "It may be pulsing, but it's not going to fade away. It would have done that by now if that were the case. I think its building up for another eruption."

"You mean where we all feel like garbage again?" asked Ira.

"That, and probably more," said Ava. "We need to leave Denu Creek, Tyrus."

"And go where?" I asked. "If this is the end of the world, we can't outrun it."

"Maybe. Maybe not. I'd rather at least try to go somewhere else than just sit and wait for whatever hell that artifact is going to cause. Who knows, if we get far enough away from Hol, the effects might be weaker. Maybe it's just the end of the Geneshans' world, not everyone's."

"I could buy that," said Ira.

"What about you, Dekar?" I asked.

"It's worth a shot."

"All right, then where do we go?" I asked as we all stared toward Hol.

The sky pulsed brighter than it had before, bringing in hues of purple to mix with the reds and oranges. For a moment I thought my mind had played tricks on me, until a small gasp from Ava.

She clicked her tongue. "I'd say as far away as we can, big brother. And soon."

* * *

Ava wanted to stay up longer to discuss our plans, but her lack of strength betrayed her when she needed Dekar and I to hold her up.

We carried her back to bed, forced her to stay awake long enough to eat another biscuit and drink some water. Then I told her to get some sleep.

She never liked being bossed around, which was a testament to just how tired she was since she didn't argue once. As soon as she lay down, she was asleep. She didn't even wake when we started talking about where we should go.

The discussion didn't last long, though, when I remembered that both of our horses had died after the initial eruption so our wagon was essentially useless.

In light of that, I sent Dekar and Ira out to see what sort of animals were available in town. I told them to buy something decent with the junk we had been given.

It wasn't long after that I closed my eyes as well, leaning over my chair, head resting on Ava's bed.

Myra and Zadok nudged me shortly afterward. Both insisted I go sleep in the other room. They said they would take over. I didn't protest. Ava's condition had improved dramatically and my body ached from being stuck in too many awkward positions the last few days.

Worried about what nightmares might plague my dreams, I almost said a prayer to Molak to ease my mind.

Almost.

I fell asleep before I made that mistake.

CHAPTER 22

Two days later and life went on. People kept bringing us stuff, some junk, some valuable. Most of it I turned away only to find later that Ira had brought it back inside while I slept. We got into a couple arguments about that until I decided it wasn't worth the trouble. Whatever was useless, I'd just make him leave behind anyway.

It took over a day to get mounts secured, mainly because Ira had been adamant about inspecting every horse in excruciating detail. He didn't want to take any chances. The two he settled on cost nearly ten times what they normally would, but considering so many animals had died in the eruption, it had definitely become a seller's market.

According to Boaz, normalcy had returned to Denu Creek. Even Jareb and his bunch had recovered enough to return to their homes and jobs. It seemed that Jareb could no longer draw up enough support to have me arrested for taking Zadok and Myra away from him. The town was more than split in our favor now.

I finally stumbled out of bed a couple hours after dawn. That was late for me, but I was still recuperating.

I shuffled over to a basin of cool water atop the dresser. I held my breath and dunked my head, using a hand to rub the water over my neck and head. I came up huffing for air. Reaching for a towel, I threw a few curses at Molak while drying myself. I hated the feeling of first waking up and thought the Father should suffer a bit himself because of it.

After a quick visit to the chamber pot, I dressed, and walked into the sitting room.

Dekar and Myra sat opposite each other at a small table supporting a flat, thin, board covered with military markings and various terrains. Wooden pieces of various colors, shapes, and sizes stood atop it. Each piece represented units a general might have at their disposal such as cavalry, siege equipment, archers, infantry, spies, various levels of mages, and so on.

Dekar had begun teaching Myra Crests.

I scratched the patchy stubble on my neck. "Have you been at it all night?"

"No," said Dekar as he moved one of his cavalry units up into a flanking position. "But we were both up early and she's a determined player."

"You know he's never lost before, Myra."

"Yet," was all she said, staring intently at the game board.

Dekar grinned in my direction. "She's got skill, Tyrus. A good mind for strategy. Might be a natural."

"That's my girl."

Myra whipped her head up wearing a look somewhere between a scowl and a frown. It wasn't pleasant. "Don't call me that," she said.

"Sorry," I said, unsure how else to respond. Any approach I tried at bonding with her had fallen flat, and in many cases only increased the gulf between us.

Fatherhood was much easier when all I had to do was patch her skinned knee or cut up her meat.

She put her head down. "Zadok and Ava are awake. There's leftover breakfast with them."

I could take a hint. "Thanks." I took a step toward Ava's room and stopped. "Where's Ira?"

"Walking the horses," said Dekar. "They're eating better, but they aren't quite back up to full strength yet."

"Shouldn't he be back by now?"

He grunted. "Maybe. I'll go check on him."

I waved him down as he started to stand. "That's all right. I'll go. Finish your game. I can wait to eat."

I left the inn, passing Dinah on the way as I cut through the kitchen. She smiled and pointed me to some food. I grabbed a cold sausage, realizing I was hungry after all. I gobbled the whole thing in three bites. This one had a bit more pepper, which I liked.

I left through the back entrance and cut around an old storage shed. It was where Ira had moved our wagon.

The two horses he purchased were harnessed. However, neither the horses nor the wagon were moving. Ira stood next to them arguing with a handful of people from town. The only one I recognized immediately was Mayor Rezub. He still had the presence of someone who thought too highly of himself. I did have to give the man credit for holding that demeanor while squaring off against Ira. Ira probably had the skinny mayor by at least seven inches.

Given the angle I approached the group, none saw me at first. I wasn't sure what was said next, but Ira's voice rose significantly and included quite a few colorful phrases that were common during our stint in the military.

Mayor Rezub took a step back at the outburst, showing his first sign of wilting. His supporters took two steps back further, much keener on supporting him from a safer distance.

"Everything all right?" I called out.

Heads swung my way. Relief washed over Ira's face, his brow over his green eyes relaxing. "Ty, please talk to these people. I just don't have the patience."

Rezub took the opportunity to jump in. "I was just discussing your future with your friend."

My eyes narrowed as I stopped next to him. "What about my future?"

"Well, we couldn't help but notice that your group has been buying supplies." He nodded to the wagon. "Including those two horses. From what Sered said, you paid him a pretty inflated price for them."

"Supply and demand."

He smiled. "Of course."

"Do you have a point, Mayor?"

"It's just that I've been hearing rumors that you and your group are planning to leave town. And after seeing all this, I realize that those weren't just rumors."

"Again, your point?"

The others exchanged worried looks and began murmuring.

Rezub looked over his shoulder at them, then back at me. "Can we talk somewhere a bit more private?"

"No. Say what's on your mind and quit all this dancing around. This isn't a political debate."

He cleared his throat and forced a smile. "Yes, I guess not. I'll just lay it out for you. We don't want you to leave."

That took me off guard. "Really? Well, as flattered as I am, that's just too bad. Because we are."

"You don't understand. We don't want you to leave and we are willing to do whatever is necessary to make sure you don't."

I stepped closer and leaned in. "That sounded like a threat. I hope that wasn't a threat. You saw what happened last time you and yours tried to stop me and mine from leaving town."

He swallowed hard, but held his ground. He lowered his voice to a whisper. "That wasn't my idea. It was Jareb's. I don't want it to come to that again. In fact, I plan to do everything I can to stop it from coming to that. I know it was wrong then and I know it's wrong now. Especially after all that you and your children did to help us. I know I appreciate it."

"I sense a 'but' coming."

He nodded. "The thing is I am the mayor and represent the people of Denu Creek."

I gestured to the people behind him. "So what you're saying is that this is their idea. Not yours. You're just the mouthpiece."

"More or less. Trust me, they don't want to hurt you either."

"But that doesn't mean they won't if it comes down to it."

"Well, it's just that they're scared. People are trying to go on living their lives as before, but it's hard to do that with the sky as it is and the memories of those who died fresh on everyone's minds. They know we would have lost more if not for your help. Trust me, they're grateful. Plenty grateful. But when it comes to family, people will do drastic things to look out for them. Considering what happened between you and Jareb, I'm sure you of all people can understand where they're coming from."

I understood completely. That didn't mean I cared. Just as they wanted to look out for their family, I wanted to look out for mine. Staying in Denu Creek wasn't an option for us.

I finally answered. "Yeah, I understand."

Rezub noticeably relaxed. "Thank Molak. And thank you too, Tyrus. I'll tell everyone the good news," he said, taking my answer not as I intended it.

I decided quickly that was probably for the best.

Rezub went back to the group and informed them of what they couldn't hear. Smiles and waves flashed my way from the others. They turned and left, walking lightly as if they had won some great victory.

Ira who had stood off to the side, uncharacteristically silent during the whole exchange, gave me a sidelong glance. As usual, he had snuck in close enough to the conversation where I didn't doubt he heard everything.

"Change of plans?" he asked.

"No."

"So you lied? Good for you."

"I didn't lie. I told him I understand their situation. Not that I agreed with their solution for solving it."

"But you let him think that you did."

"Yeah. We're leaving tonight regardless of how ready the horses are. C'mon. I'll help you unharness them. Then we need to go finalize things with the others."

* * *

We made it back to the inn quickly. I let Ira fill in Dekar and Myra while I went to check on Ava and Zadok.

Ava was at the window, fully dressed in her black leathers and a gray shirt. I bought the shirt from Sivan the day before. Zadok stood next to her as they gazed in the direction of Hol. Neither turned as I entered the room.

I wondered what had them so engrossed. Ira was making a ton of noise in the common room, taking too much enjoyment from interrupting Dekar's game of Crests.

I cleared my throat and finally got a response. They both jumped, wheeling.

"Gods, you could have said something," said Ava.

"I didn't think I needed to shout. What are you looking at?"

"The sky, Pa," Zadok said. "It's doing all sorts of crazy stuff."

"Like what?" I asked, walking over. "I was just outside and didn't notice anything."

"It just started," said Ava. "Come see for yourself."

Thankful for a mostly overcast morning, I didn't have to shield my eyes much from the glare. Staring out of town, past hills, forest, and distant low mountains, the sky flickered like a wind-blown candle, shifting in and out of oranges, reds, and purples. Other than the speed of each flicker not much had changed from minutes before. Or so I thought.

As the last deep purple ended, an almost lavender color pulsed, a white flash reminiscent of lightning followed, expanding and contracting before the color sequence started over again.

"What in the name of Molak was that?" I asked, stepping away.

"I told you the artifact wasn't done. I assume it will keep on erupting until it does whatever it's supposed to do."

"I don't understand why anyone would want to build something that would destroy so much," Zadok said.

I put a hand on his shoulder. "Me either. Unfortunately, there are a lot of things in this world I don't understand and that number seems to grow by the day." Another white flash at the end of the color sequence occurred. "That one seemed brighter," I said to Ava. "What does that mean?"

"I'd guess that with each white flash, the artifact is that much closer to releasing the next wave of power. I can feel something in the air. It's not good."

"Define not good."

"I can't. The sorcery is just different. Twisted almost."

I tore my gaze from the foreboding sky to the street where many of the townsfolk congregated. They pointed and stared in the direction of Hol, exchanging worried and excited looks. Several looked back toward our room at the inn. I wondered how many thought we had the answers to the very questions I had running through my head.

I swore. "We might not be able to wait until tonight."

"What?" Ava asked.

"I was coming to tell you that we are going to leave tonight. Things are happening in town and I thought it best if we snuck away." I looked at the sky once again. "But now, I think that might not be soon enough."

I recalled my conversation with Balak about the artifact from months ago. We had yet to see fire and brimstone raining down on us or the earthquakes.

"How much time do we have before the next eruption?"

She shrugged. "I have no idea."

"We'll just have to leave now and take our chances. Zadok, go tell the others to come in here? I'll keep an eye on your Aunt Ava."

"Sure Pa, but she really doesn't need it anymore."

I looked down, realizing that though Ava and Zadok had been standing next to each other, they had not been touching. My mouth opened, ready to yell at them.

Ava placed a hand on my arm. "I'm fine," she said calmly. "It was my idea."

Of course it was. I couldn't see Zadok making that call on his own. "Are you crazy?"

"Calm down. I had to see how I would feel. You think I wanted to live the rest of my life with someone holding my hand like a child. Don't worry, we did it a little at a time."

"You still should have waited for me."

"But I didn't. And I'm still alive."

I sighed.

"You aren't upset with me, are you, Pa?"

"No, it's fine."

"All right. I'll go get the others."

"So, how are you feeling?" I asked Ava.

"A little dizzy if I move too fast, but otherwise good."

"That's a relief."

"There is some bad news though."

"I wouldn't expect there not to be at this point. What is it?"

"I can't perform sorcery."

"You mean because you're tired? That's not that big of a deal. Granted, your sorcery could come in handy while on the road, but we'll be fine until you get your strength back."

Ava shook her head. "That's not it. I wish it was. It's like I can't feel the power properly. Like I said, it's twisted. The artifact has done something to my connection."

I frowned. "Do you think being in contact with me, Zadok, and Myra had anything to do with that? Like we dulled your senses?"

"At first I thought that might be the case, but I've changed my mind. It's like the artifact is changing all the sorcery in the world to use for itself." She paused. "Ao be damned, I just hate feeling so helpless. So . . . normal."

I put my arm around her and gave her shoulder a quick squeeze.

I could tell she was hiding just how much this bothered her. Like many mages, sorcery and the ability to perform it had meant the world to Ava. In fact, I often wondered but never had the guts to ask where I ranked in comparison.

"Give it time," I said. "Unless Molak gets tired of his wife and kills Ao herself, I don't think you have anything to worry about. You'll figure out a way to use sorcery again."

She managed a nod.

"It's strange that my resistance still works though. You'd think that would have changed to some degree as well. I wonder why it hasn't."

"I don't know. I get a feeling it's going to be hard to explain a lot of things in the coming weeks."

In the silence I realized that Zadok had begun raising his voice at Ira in an attempt to bring him into the bedroom. Ira was telling him he needed to relieve himself first.

"With Ira, you know this will keep up until we go in there," Ava said.

I sighed. "You're right. Let's just go to them."

I took the first step when Ava's hand shot out and latched around my arm. "I think it's happening!"

I followed her gaze. The sky's color sequence had ended. It shone white in the distance and did not change except to brighten and expand.

"What's going on?" Ira asked as everyone finally clamored into the room, having heard Ava yell.

"The artifact," said Ava, voice low in wonder.

Ira swore.

"What do we do, Pa?" Zadok asked, voice edged with fear.

Myra put an arm on him for comfort. Her hand trembled as she caught a glimpse of the pulsing sky. It flashed quicker with each breath.

"I think all we can do is pick up the pieces when it's over. In the meantime, you and your sister stay near Ira and Dekar. They'll likely need your resistance. I'll stay near Ava." I finally said.

Outside, the townspeople ran around pointing and screaming while snatching up loved ones and making their way indoors. They looked over their shoulders in horror at the blinking light.

As a father, I've always wanted to be able to tell my children that I had everything under control. That everything will be all right. However, as a father, I never wanted to lie to my children either. But I had no idea what to do. This wasn't knocking out a communications outpost, or rushing the enemy from a poor position, or defending an undermanned ridge. This was prophecy of the worst kind coming to fruition and I didn't have the tools, people, or know how to do anything about it.

Ira swore again.

Dekar craned his neck around and caught his first glimpse of the horizon. "Should we even be looking at that? I mean it's getting brighter all the time."

Ava blinked. "He's right. Get away from the window." She pulled the curtains together and turned away, frantic.

"Everyone. Up against the back wall," I added, coming out of my stupor.

I couldn't stop this thing from happening, but I could at least try to keep us safe.

I had everyone sit on the floor against the wall while Ira and Dekar quickly flipped the bed over and threw it against the window. Then they came over and we all huddled together like a bunch of newborn puppies fighting for a spot at their mother's teat. I made sure everyone held hands. One of mine remained tightly around Ava's. The last thing I wanted was for her to be out for several days again.

Or worse.

Even with the curtains pulled, the room continually brightened as light pushed its way in through the cracks in the walls nobody ever sees. It could have been my imagination, but it felt as though thunder rumbled beneath the inn. The floorboards shook. We would not be able to pretend none of this was happening.

The artifact would get its due.

The air grew thick and it became harder to breath, like working in the fields on a sweltering summer day. Sweat poured off my skin. Ava's hand grew slick in mine.

The rising voices of panicked people sounded outside.

"I wish we could do something to help them," said Zadok.

"We can't even help ourselves," said Myra. Her voice edging on the hysterical.

I tried to remain calm. "We'll help when this is all over. Same as last time." I paused. "Only we won't wait as long as before."

He nodded, reassured.

A faint hum I wasn't sure if I was imagining tickled the inside of my ears.

"Xank be damned. All this waiting makes me feel like I'm back in the army," swore Ira.

I knew exactly what he meant.

My stomach rolled in that familiar way before leaving on a mission. The anticipation before any battle was often worse than the battle itself simply because that was when there was time to think and dwell on what may or may not happen.

I felt it pretty safe to say that no one wanted to think about what would happen next.

The dull hum grew, just as a howling wind blew. The inn shuddered. Things fell from shelves and chairs tumbled over. The dresser gyrated across the room like an uneven wagon wheel.

Ava yelled something, but I couldn't hear a thing because the blasted hum had grown so loud. The window of our room shattered, the force behind it knocking the mattress down. Glass showered inside like a spring rain, whipping the curtains away from the opening. The sound of other windows breaking followed. More light poured inside.

"We can't stay here! Everyone to the cellar," I yelled.

Dekar led the way out with me bringing up the rear half-blinded by light pouring inside. The wind gusted back and forth through our suite, following us into the hallway, howling like a banshee as it flung loose debris about.

We moved quickly. Our feet pounded the floorboards and stairs while thunder crashed and my children cried out in fear.

We ran into Boaz and his family on their way to the cellar. We followed them inside and then barricaded the door. I had him and his family huddle near us, grabbing onto either me or one of my kids.

Staring at each other with blank expressions, the whole inn rocked as the ground shifted and groaned. For a moment, I questioned whether I had made the right call in getting everyone to go below ground. The entire building could collapse on top of us.

Then thunder boomed, shaking my insides. The sound of a furious hailstorm followed, pelting the inn like a snare drum keeping time for the pace kept in hell. Outside, animals cried out in fear. I thought I heard a woman scream.

The end of the world had truly begun.

I wondered if even hell could be this bad.

Zadok squeezed my hand. "I'm scared, Pa."

I looked down. "Me too." I squeezed his hand back. "But I promise we'll be all right."

Somehow.

END

Thank you for reading my story. If you enjoyed it, please consider leaving a rating or review at the site of purchase as well as other places such as Goodreads and Librarything. Like many other indie authors, I do not have a marketing team working for me and a positive review (even if only a couple of sentences long) can go a long way in enticing others to give my works a try.

I hope you'll continue reading *The Chronicle of Tyrus* with *Wayward Soldiers* due to be released in early 2015. In the meantime, please consider checking out my other series listed below. If you'd like to know when new works will be made available, please consider signing up for my mailing list. It is used solely to announce new releases or other major announcements.

You can sign up at http://joshuapsimon.blogspot.com/.

Thanks again for your support.

Joshua P. Simon

ABOUT THE AUTHOR

Joshua P. Simon is a Christian, husband, father, CPA, fantasy author, and heavy metal junkie. He currently resides in Atlanta, Georgia, and hopes that one day he can leave the life of a CPA behind and devote that time to writing more of the ideas bouncing around his ADD-addled brain.

Made in the USA
Middletown, DE
06 December 2016